THE
DAY THE BOOKIES
TOOK A BATH

THE
DAY THE BOOKIES
TOOK A BATH

Arthur P. Hagan

SHERBOURNE PRESS, INC.   *Los Angeles*

c. 3

Library of Congress Catalog Card Number
70–151857

First Printing

Composed, printed, and bound in the United
States of America by Kingsport Press,
Kingsport, Tennessee

Typography by Shirley Shipley

Dedicated with Love to My Wife, **Eileen**

THE
DAY THE BOOKIES
TOOK A BATH

ONE

Gus Scott, the public relations director for the Treasure
City Race Track, shivered in the soft warmth of the pleasant morning. He stared at the big brown envelope. Here,
he thought, is a presentiment of doom.

He hadn't seen Dandy Dan Devon or Chalky Boyle in
almost ten years. Indeed, he hardly ever thought of them
any more except, sometimes, when he had a headache or
when he fell to musing about the terrible things that
could happen to a man in this cockeyed business. And
now the morning mail delivery had brought to his desk
this envelope from Chalky himself, with a postmark that
was hard to accept: Bloody Hatchet, Oklahoma.

Gus knew that this had to mean trouble. With Chalky,
the only questions were what kind and how much.

Yet he was glad to hear from the old faker. Why not?
So many years had fled since that night when Chalky and
Devon had skipped out and left him to face the howling
mob alone. Devon's behavior had been perfectly predict-

9

able. A man could trust him, always, to find a way to do you in.

Dear Buddy, Chalky wrote. *I'm doing great. I got a terrific aquatic carnival now. I need a little favor for two very dear friends, Calvin Oakley and Themastocles Christoforidis. They own the Flowering Tree Stable and they got two great horses, and some meathead named Randahl turned them down. Please straighten this jerk out. Wire tonight okay for two stalls and oblige your dear pal, Chalky Boyle. P. S. What do you hear from Dan Devon?*

Enclosed was a handwritten press release which gripped Gus with nostalgia. He hadn't seen such gaudy fiction since he had quit handling wrestling publicity. To hear Chalky tell it, this Rustling Breeze was the three-year-old of the century.

The Fabulous RUSTLING BREEZE, he wrote, *hereby challenges Kentucky Derby winner HORSEPOWER to a MATCH RACE for a SIDE BET of $10,000 OR UPWARD!*

Poor Chalky. First a sleazy sideshow and now this undistinguished little colt. Without Devon, he was a man who starved by his wits.

He was asking for enough. The track had turned down stall applications for more than 600 head. With the opening for the thoroughbred meeting only a few days away, it was getting worse by the hour. Yet Buzz Randahl, the track president, could always find room for two more if he wanted to.

Nancy Kingsley broke in on these ruminations. "You had three telephone calls while you were out," she announced in her most businesslike manner, handing him the list.

Nancy isn't big, maybe a shade over five foot. She is softly moulded, as graceful as flowing water, and everything she has, well, there's a reason for it. Yet she has her shortcomings. She is forthright, for one thing, and strong-willed, for another. Why does a woman like that need strength of character?

"Hi, Nancy. Any word on our new publicist?"

"*Your* new publicist, Mr. Scott," she responded icily. "He called. He's on the road. He should be here in perhaps an hour."

"Aw, you're still sore, aren't you? I had to find somebody. I was desperate. I know. I waited too long. All the good men had jobs. This fellow Mason has experience. He is apparently sober. He'll be all right."

"I'm sure," she sniffed.

She didn't like the letter from Les Killgallen, for whom Mason had worked at Wellington Park. Killgallen's letter wasn't exactly a recommendation. He had written: "Mr. Mason has considerable experience in thoroughbred racing. He is aggressive, energetic, and sober. And I must say he is sharp. If this is the kind of man you want, he will meet your needs admirably."

Nancy was annoyed that Gus Scott had hired this man despite her disapproval. She would have been even more annoyed if she had known Gus had telephoned Killgallen for further enlightenment.

"You want to know what I really think of that slob?" Killgallen had seethed. "He works, and he knows the name of the game, but he is an oily, back-stabbing hypocrite who will try to get your job any way he can. He will crucify you if he gets half a chance. He's pure poison."

Gus decided, nevertheless, to chance it. He sometimes

11

felt that if there was one thing the men he hired had in common, it was shortcomings. Some drank. Some womanized. Some wrote rubber checks. At least this Mason would work.

After Gus had disposed of the morning mail, he left for his daily briefing session with Randahl. He remembered the day, amost eight years ago, when Caius Montgomery Randahl III had purchased the Treasure City Race Track. Gus had been appalled. How could he publicize a man with a name like that?

The Caius commemorated an ancestor who had been the state's second governor. The Montgomery referred to a renowned great uncle, the late United States Senator and Secretary of Commerce. The Randahl meant nothing but money: real estate, grain, oil, stocks, chemicals, electronics. The Randahls could issue their own currency.

If only Buzz's mother had bought the track! A PR man could do something with her: Dolly LaBrecque, the redheaded night club chorine who had married Caius Montgomery Randahl Jr. and had bent the world of the Social Register to her own imperious will. When her husband died, she took charge of his vast business interests. She was an ideal executive, hard-headed, acquisitive, ruthless.

Her son, at the outset, had one thing in his favor. He had plunged into horse racing despite her kinetic opposition. He bought the track with the money he had received from his great-aunt's estate. The purchase took all he had, and Dolly had no intention of subsidizing his folly. He was on his own.

He had inherited ten million from his father, but Dolly had dictated the terms of that will. He couldn't touch a penny of his inheritance without her permission. She told him flatly that she would never give him a nickel for horse racing.

He frustrated her by turning the track into a wildfire success. He had a passion for the sport, and a fierce pride in the probity of his track. Yet he invested the operation with human warmth, too. He owned a respectable stable of his own, regularly got himself stiffed by the track hangers-on, and generally conducted himself like a proper turfman.

The door to his office was always open. He would drop everything to argue with the punters, or to commiserate with them. After the first week, everybody called him Buzz.

But how could a press agent convey this warm, human quality of the man to the millions who had never met him? This was the problem, and Buzz resolved it the first time he had lunch with Gus.

"I'll bet the waiter recommends corned beef hash," he offered.

"I'll bet a nickel he doesn't," the little publicity man replied. The waiter recommended the corned beef hash.

"You owe me a nickel," Buzz said firmly, holding out his hand.

"A nickel? Can't you make it to pay day without it?"

"With me, a bet's a bet," the track owner said solemnly, pocketing the coin. "Remember that, Gus. I always pay my bets, no matter what. When I win, I expect to be paid. A gentleman always honors his sporting commitments. I'm not a man who refuses many wagers, and I never welch."

That gave Gus an idea. He went to work, persuading Connie O'Toole, the sports editor of the *Clarion-Call* to

13

challenge Buzz to a bet. Buzz had boasted that he'd get the winner of the Kentucky Derby for the Colt Stake that first year. O'Toole took him up on it. Buzz lost, of course, and he paid off by selling the *Clarion-Call* in front of the city hall while the cameras clicked. O'Toole wrote half a dozen columns that summer about Buzz Randahl, his favorite patsy.

Buzz went along willingly enough with the suggestion that he bait Clarence Ridgeway, the owner of the Jewels, into betting that his major-league baseball team would show a greater percentage increase in attendance than the race track during the first month that they ran together.

Buzz won that one: Ridgeway had to announce the post time for the Treasure City races every day for a week over the public address system in his ball park. Since the baseball people had never before admitted the existence of the horse track, the publicity rocked the town.

By the end of the first year, everybody cherished Buzz. He rarely refused a bet, no matter what it was. The papers, over the years, had built his readiness to bet on anything into a part of modern sports folklore.

Buzz greeted his PR man pleasantly enough that morning.

"I need a favor," Gus began.

"Later," Buzz said. He walked around his desk and put his hands on his visitor's shoulders. "Gus, you won't have any trouble with publicity for the Stake this time. You're home free."

"I am?"

"Indeed you are. I'm going to get Horsepower for the

14

Colt Stake. That's right—Horsepower, winner of the Kentucky Derby and the Triple Crown, the greatest three-year-old of the year, maybe of the century. He's going to run right here in Treasure City. I'll show those wise guys who said I couldn't get the horse. I'm working on old J. C. Jensen now, and I'm going to get the colt. With a horse like that, I don't need a publicity man."

"You'll need one," Gus dissented. "I don't care if you get Man O' War, you can't sell a one-horse race. In fact, if Horsepower does come in, he'll scare everything else out. The race won't fill."

"The Colt Stake will fill," Buzz replied. "I'll see to that. And with Horsepower in, the race will publicize itself. Don't say I don't take care of you."

He sat down on the arm of an overstuffed chair, pulled out his pipe and tobacco and made a further announcement:

"We don't need publicity, but there is one thing I do want from you . . ."

"I know. Publicity."

Buzz ignored the interruption.

"Listen carefully, Gus. This means a great deal to me. I want you to get the eight-column banner in the *Herald-Chronicle* on the Colt Stake. The words Colt Stake *must* appear in the headline. Get it! I don't care how. If it costs some money, just let me know. But get it."

"What kind of nonsense is this?" Scott said.

"I want that banner, Gus. I've never wanted anything more in my life. I'm depending on you."

"You're kidding, Buzz. Idiocy I expect, but . . ."

The smile slid off his face. His jaw was set in a firm

15

line. "I've never been more serious. Get that banner, and you can call your own bonus. Now, do you still think I'm joking?"

"But I don't understand. Why?"

"You don't have to understand. Just get the job done. Okay?"

"You've made another crazy bet!"

"Don't push me, Gus. This is between me and you. Don't even think of mentioning it to anyone. But you better believe this is for real."

He walked over to the desk and sprawled in his big swivel chair. "We're up to our armpits in horses," he smiled. "We're boxed in. I accepted applications for 2,000 head, and you know we can't handle more than 1,700, even with the temporary stalls. I was counting on the usual shrinkage between the stalls that were requested and the stalls that were claimed. We've always had a shrinkage of about fifteen percent, but this year—no shrinkage. We're in a bind.

"I've turned down some rather fair stables already. All day long, all I've heard is how I've got to find room for just two more horses for somebody. It's making me ill. And now, what was this favor you mentioned?"

"Nothing much. I just want you to find room for two more horses. For a buddy of mine."

"You, too!" he yelped. "Impossible. Out of the question."

"For publicity," Gus Scott persisted. "I can get some ink on one of these horses—Rustling Breeze, a Colt Stake nominee by Trade Winds out of Silk 'N Lace."

"Trade Winds I know," pondered Buzz. "But did you say Silk 'N Lace?"

"Yessir. As us horsemen say, the mamma."

"The dam," he rebuked the impertinence. "Now I remember. Jake Hadley bred that one. I swore I'd never let another of his horses on the grounds. They're all pigs. And he let this one go. This must be the granddaddy of all bums, the worst colt ever nominated for the Colt Stake."

He regarded his press agent warily.

"What's the publicity stunt?"

"It's no stunt," Gus returned, with some dignity. "It's a feature idea, and you've named it. This is the horse least likely to succeed in the Stake. You see? Great idea, isn't it? You know, the temerity of this dreamer. The unconquerable optimism. This guy Cal Oakley has got to be the man who defies the odds. It's off-beat. We'll get some mileage out of it."

"Nothing doing!" snapped Buzz. "If I take that goat, I haven't got an excuse for turning down any other horse in the world."

"Only two stalls," Gus pursued.

"I'm not going to make a joke out of my track. If that bum had any class at all, I'd give you the two stalls, but I'm not going to take that billy goat."

"If you want publicity, you've got to cooperate."

"Nobody cooperates with his PR man more than I do. I've gone along with some pretty ridiculous gags, but this is where you lose me. Forget it! I don't want to hear any more about it."

"You've got to . . ."

"Like hell I do! I won't take those horses. Period."

Like hell you won't, Gus said to himself. As he walked out of Buzz's office, he made up his mind. No matter what, he was going to get those stalls for Chalky's friends. Chalky himself had become unimportant.,

Now Gus had to prove something to himself.

TWO

AFTER BUZZ's rebuff, Gus wanted time to cool off. He headed for the backstretch. A man can find sanity here in the stabling area, for this is an alien kingdom from a gentler time.

Gus surveyed the ragged procession of exercise boys on their proud mounts. Solemn youngsters and an enchanted owner or two were "walking hots." Several boys were drowsing in the spring sunshine. Grooms were rubbing down the handsome animals. A stablehand was making a pretense of cleaning a tack room.

What's so special about the *Herald-Chronicle*, Gus pondered. Yet the Randahls had always made a big thing out of the paper. The Senator had served on the board of directors for twenty years. The family had always felt a proprietary interest in the publication.

He remembered, too, the first time he had met Dolly Randahl. Her slim good looks surprised, and he told her so.

"Yes, I know," she said, unsmiling. "You're the fellow who writes those publicity stories about Montgomery. I've read them."

"That's nice, Mrs. Randahl."

"Nice, indeed!" she responded. "They're dreadful, quite dreadful. They make Montgomery seem like an oaf. He is, of course, but I dislike advertising his bizarre tastes. Monty and this poor little track have no prestige at all."

"I assure you, Mrs. Randahl, your son is extremely well regarded. And some of our finest citizens . . ."

"Call me Dolly," she advised. "And don't tell me about those old fools who race their horses here. They're senile." She removed a compact from her cavernous purse and began touching up her red lips. "Race tracks are simply not accepted," she went on. "Consult the *Herald-Chronicle*. That paper is a great civic institution. It reflects the thinking of our best people. You know, Gus, the track has never been able to get one of these big headlines on the top of the page. The reason is obvious. The *Herald-Chronicle* feels as I do: running a race track is very much like operating a bordello."

In their infrequent conversations over the years, Mrs. Randahl constantly reverted to the fact that the *Herald-Chronicle* never gave the Treasure City Race Track the accolade of an eight-column banner. This was the way she measured prestige. And now, apparently, she had Buzz doing it, too.

"Mr. Scott! Mr. Scott!"

"Wade, buddy! You look great!"

"I've been on the wagon for ten months," he said, in his

19

direct way. "I scraped bottom at the Fair Grounds. Things got so bad, they wouldn't let me on the track. I never want to get any lower, Mr. Scott.

"Then Jamie Lattner took me in. I was broke and sick and I hated myself, and Jamie took me in. He moved a cot into the tack room and that's where I slept. I didn't leave the track for weeks. I'm galloping horses now. I feel good."

"I'm glad to hear it," the stubby publicist said, and he was. If Wade could only stay away from the booze and the broads he could be a winner again.

"Mr. Scott, I want to ride again. I can do it. I'm down to 109 pounds. Jamie has gone to bat for me, and the stewards are going to reinstate my license. I sure would like to get a few mounts. If you can put in a good word for me with any of the owners, I'd take it most kindly."

"Just keep your nose clean, Wade, and you'll be back on top."

He had the tools. Before he went into his tailspin, the friendly little Virginian was one of the best jocks who sat a horse. He didn't bounce around on a horse's back, the way some do. He knew how to keep his horse quiet in the gate, he had a superb instinct for pace, and he was a magician with the whip. He could switch the stick from hand to hand three times in a sixteenth of a mile without ever altering the flowing rhythm of his ride.

I could use him in the advance publicity, perhaps in a film clip or two, Gus decided. That might help give him a hand up.

"You're walking, Gus! You'll kill yourself. Hop in!"

Pierre Gauthier pulled up in a gleaming white station wagon with the legend "The World's Greatest News Pho-

20

tographer" in chaste blue lettering on the side panels.

"Do you have any ideas for pictures, Pierre?" Gus inquired. Pierre's eyes lit up the way they always do when he is thinking of girls.

"I got a terrific idea," Pierre assured Gus. "This you'll love. We dress a girl in a jock's outfit, see, with real tight pants. I know just the broad. She's got . . ."

"Forget it," Gus said. "Get me some human-interest stuff on the backstretch. Kids and mascots . . ."

"And girls?"

"Okay, if they're trainers or outriders. And, please, don't give me another picture of a horse leaning over a groom's shoulder to study *The Daily Racing Form*. I've got eighty-two pictures like that in the files."

"It's a cute idea," Pierre said, defensively. "And listen, kindly cut out that jazz about all my girl friends when Nancy is around. I got plans for that broad, and you're lousing things up."

"Forget her, Romeo. She's not your type."

Pierre smirked. "Any time they're put together like that little babe, they're my type."

"You leave her alone, Pierre. I mean it."

"Aw, don't get sore, Gus," he was still smirking. "I'm just kidding around."

When Gus returned to his office, Jay Mason was waiting. A ruggedly handsome young man, he had a flashing smile, a very direct glance, and a firm handclasp. His lemon-and-white silk sports jacket looked outrageously expensive. If this is the way he usually dresses, Gus thought, people will think I'm working for him.

"I'm very happy to meet you, sir," Jay said.

"I hope you'll like it here," Gus countered. "Did you just get in?"

"I took a motel room and freshened up first." He spoke with buoyant enthusiasm. "I had a very pleasant drive this morning. I put the top down on my Caddy convertible and soaked up the sunshine. Now I'm ready to work."

"I'll show you where to start, and I want you to meet Nancy Kingsley, the girl who runs the office. Nancy, this is Jay Mason."

Mason turned on the charm. "I've heard some wonderful reports about you, Miss Kingsley, but they don't do you justice."

"How do you do, Mr. Mason," Nancy said, turning back to her typewriter.

Mason winked. "I know I'm going to like it here. Now, what can I do for starters, sir?"

"Call me Gus. If you're sure you're ready, I have a little job. I want to find out everything I can about two horses, Rustling Breeze and Bumbling Bertie.

"Rustling Breeze is a three-year-old that was bred by Jake Hadley at Windblown Farm, near here. The colt has never raced. Bumbling Bertie is a five-year-old and you may find something on him in the old Racing Manuals. That's all I have to go on."

Jay Mason was back within half an hour.

"I have it," he smiled. "Jake Hadley filled me in on the colt. I checked the Racing Manuals and made a couple of calls and got some information on the five-year-old."

"What did you find out?"

"Rustling Breeze is a state foal . . ."

"That I know," Gus interrupted. "The colt was born, or

foaled, in the state, on Hadley's farm. What else did you find out?"

"He broke a small bone in his foot as a two-year-old. Even Hadley gave up on him. You know Hadley. When he gives up on a horse, it must be pretty bad. I thought this had to be the worst bum I've seen until I looked up Bumbling Bertie. Now, there's a real pig.

"His breeding is good. He's a Nassau colt, but he must be a cull. He was lightly raced as a two-year-old and a three-year-old. He never broke his maiden, and his times were hideous. I understand he's done some racing in the bush since then, and he's won a few quarterhorse races, but he doesn't belong here. I could run in hip boots and beat that kind."

"I can get that from Randahl," Gus protested. "What I want is some reason for giving these two animals stall space here. Randahl says there isn't any reason."

"He's right," Mason shrugged. "They're both dogs."

Gus can be pig-headed, and this report only annoyed him. He had to get space for the Flowering Tree Stable, but how? The problem absorbed his attention so completely that he did not notice the entrance of Duke Jones, the long-time turf editor of the *Herald-Chronicle*.

"What do you do here?" he barked. "In all the years you've been the PR guy here, you have yet to give me story number one. Don't you ever come up with anything? Just once, give me a decent story."

"I have a great one, Duke. Exclusive. The management is spending $10,000 for artificial petunias for the infield."

Duke almost choked.

"Not quite what you had in mind, eh? What about the blacksmith? He's great copy when he's sober. No? The clubhouse restaurant expects to sell 40,000 cups of coffee . . ."

Each time the press agent spoke, the more derisive Duke became.

"What do you want, Duke? I've given you some great leads."

"They stink. Honest, what do you do in this office? How do you kill time?"

"You don't understand, Duke. I have a million things to do. Here, this is an example. Look at this. It came in the mail this morning."

Gus tossed him the picture of Rustling Breeze, and Boyle's blurb sheet. He studied them.

"The guy wants publicity, Duke. I've got to write him a polite little note to tell him I'm sorry, but I can't help him. These little things all take time."

"Hey, this colt is a state foal," Duke remarked. "Jake Hadley had him. We have some pretty sorry owners, but Jake has to be the sorriest. Even he gave up on this one."

"Sure, Duke. I thought there might be an off-beat story in it. You know, the tiny stable that defies the world. Another David going out to meet another Goliath. Imagine, anyone thinking a third-rater like that could beat Horsepower in a match race! I still think there's a very funny story here, but it's extremely difficult to do. You have to write with a light touch. Connie O'Toole could take this story and win a Pulitzer Prize with it, but I don't know anybody else who can make anything out of it. Nobody but Connie. That guy can write."

Duke's eyebrows arched. He fixed Gus with a steady stare.

"Mind if I take this?"

"No. I was going to throw it in the waste basket."

"I'll see you tomorrow," Duke said.

"Hey, don't go. I'll get you a story. Did you know that if we built a tank big enough to hold all the beer we'll sell during the meeting, we'd have to build a tank that would cover six city blocks . . ."

But Duke was gone, whistling as he went.

Gus called Chalky at once. Chalky sounded sleepy, of course. He is a man of regular habits. He never gets out of bed before one o'clock. "Now get this straight," Gus told him. You have to talk that way to Chalky, Gus reflected. Otherwise, he wouldn't know you wanted him to get it straight. "Ask the sports editor of the nearest daily newspaper to request special coverage from the Treasure City bureau of Worldwide Press on any comment in the papers here on Rustling Breeze. Any comment, you understand? Good or bad. Can you swing it?"

Chalky said he could, so Gus repeated the instructions three more times and hung up. Then he dialed Tacks Barnett in the Worldwide Press office. He told Tacks how things were.

"Still throwing curves, eh?" Barnett commented. "I'll go along, since I can use a couple more season passes, but what good is this going to do you?"

"The way things are going, Tacks, nothing will do any good."

THREE

Gus tossed the story to Jay.

"I'm getting out a little piece on your joining our publicity staff. Will you check it? I might as well get one story straight this week."

Mason held up his hands in protest. "I'm not interested in personal publicity."

"Neither am I, but the papers may use it. I've mentioned the name of the track and our opening date."

Jay scanned the paper. "First rate, Gus. Very good. The facts are all there, except for one or two little things that really don't amount to anything."

"So, what's wrong?"

"Nothing, really. Send it as it is."

"Jay, my friend, don't be cute."

"Well, if you think it will help—I was an associate director of publicity at the last track, not an assistant. And oh, yes, I made Phi Beta Kappa at Gladwin College. Do you think that should be in?"

"We've got so many jocks and trainers that made Phi Beta Kappa that it's hardly worth mentioning," Gus snorted, "but I'll include it.

"I'm going down to the papers," he continued. "Would

you like to come along and meet some of the sports writers?"

"I'd love to, but I should be on my way over to Buzz's office right now. He's expecting me. If you see Connie O'Toole at the *Clarion-Call,* tell him I said Hello. He's an old buddy of mine."

Gus told Nancy he wouldn't be back for the rest of the afternoon.

"Your publicity man doesn't waste any time," she said archly. "He hasn't been here a full day, and he's buttering up Mr. Randahl already."

"He's smart, Nance. Mr. Randahl is the boss."

George Hall pulled angrily on his corn cob pipe. This crusty little bald man was a legend in his craft. For forty years, he had been sports editor of the *Herald-Chronicle.* No other man had ever given so many ulcers to so many press agents over so many years. How could they know that beneath that frightening facade was a human being as warm and compassionate as a thicket of thorns?

"Damned impertinence!" he growled, shaking a stubby finger at Gus. "What do you mean, you want the banner on your Colt Stake this year? Do you think your sleazy race track can get the banner on my sports page any day you name? My sports page!"

He knocked his pipe out in his enormous ash tray, and ripped his visitor with an indignant glance.

"I thought you'd like to know," Gus smiled. "I'm counting on you, George."

"You're counting on nothing!" he thundered. "You know what I think of horse racing."

"I know. Everybody thinks the baseball team owns your sheet. I don't know why they think so, except it's true. No matter how they mess things up, they always get the *Herald-Chronicle* banner. It's automatic. I figure it's part of their ad contract."

Hall rose heavily, his fists clenched. "Some day I'm going to throw you out of this office on your fat head," he howled. "I'll be damned if I'll tolerate that."

"Oh, knock it off, George. You've overplayed that ridiculous baseball team for so long that you're beginning to believe what you write. That's the beginning of the end."

"Baseball is our national pastime," he snorted. "Every schoolboy knows that."

"When Babe Ruth played for the Baltimore Orioles, maybe, but no more. Horse racing is the new national pastime. We outdraw baseball by about two-to-one. Just look at the paid attendance figures."

Hall made an eloquently disdainful face. "Horse racing is no more a sport than Russian roulette. Your crummy track brings out all the tin-horn gamblers, the touts and con artists, the easy-money boys and camp followers."

"Yeah, like J. C. Jensen, who owns a colt named Horsepower."

Hall began refilling his pipe, giving the operation his undivided attention. As he applied the match to the tobacco, he spoke in the solemn tones appropriate to the appraisal of men of great wealth. "Mr. Jensen is a fine, public-spirited man. I respect him."

"I'd respect him, too, if he spent all that money advertising his cars in my paper," Gus concurred. "So what are you going to do if Jensen wins the Colt Stake? Do we get the banner?"

"I've never given your track the eight-column line on the Colt Stake yet," he agreed, not without pride, "but I'm always fair. You'll get the line if you rate it, and I'll use the words 'Colt Stake,' too. But you won't get the banner unless the Stake is the big sports story of the day."

"Fair enough, George. We'll make a sports page out of your sheet yet."

Hall's face clouded up again. "You always were a pop-off, Gus. That's why you never cut it as a newspaper-man."

"With the kind of reporters you've got today, I'd cut it. On my very first assignment, I had to try to out-scramble Davey Gordon. He was so nice. He introduced me to everybody, he paid for the drinks, and he even shared his notes with me. Then we went back to our offices and wrote our stories and it didn't look like we were talking about the same thing. How that man could write!"

"The best newspaperman ever hit this town," Hall said softly. "He was like a son to me. I brought him up from copy boy. He was only thirty-nine when he died. Thirty-nine. I'll never see another like him."

Hall seemed old and tired now. Gus liked him better when he was loud and unreasonable.

"By the way, Gus," the old editor said, "I need an-other dozen passes. My milk man, the gas station guy, my wife's hair dresser, my own kids—they're all bugging me for passes."

"You know too many sure-thing gamblers, touts, and con men, George."

Gus went from there to the *Clarion-Call* to see Connie O'Toole.

"Hey, what do you hear about Dan Devon," O'Toole greeted him. "Now, there's a sweet old man."

"There's Jesse James in high-button shoes," Gus corrected him. "I have no idea where he is. I haven't talked to him in years, and I haven't seen the latest Most Wanted List of the FBI."

"Jonesy was telling me you'd heard from Chalky Boyle. I thought, naturally, Devon could not be far behind."

"They've split up. Chalky was asking me if I knew where Dan is."

"I miss the old brigand," O'Toole mused. "Whatever he's selling, I hope the natives are buying. There was a champion, with class. You don't think he's gone to work, do you?"

"Never," Gus answered. "That man has principles."

"Is Boyle bringing horses here for your meeting?"

"Don't say that, Connie. He's trying to get places for a couple of hay burners that a friend of his owns. They're not his horses. If they were, I'd turn them down myself. The last people I want to see are Boyle and Devon."

"Why, Gus, I thought you liked them."

"I do, the way I like the Chicago Fire or the San Francisco Earthquake. Impersonally, and from a distance. Lewis Merriam still thinks they rigged that fight here almost ten years ago. Merriam doesn't forget. If they ever turn up, he'll rake over that whole scandalous mess again. And that moron Merriam thinks I was in on it, too."

"He can't prove anything, or can he?"

"He doesn't have to prove anything. At the first bleat from him, the track will dump me. They can't afford to have anybody on the payroll who is even suspected of playing footsie with the bookies."

O'Toole smiled dreamily. "I'll never forget when Devon brought his reluctant dragon, Lefty Hernstein, in for the fight with that tough little hood, Rocky Toledo. They say TV killed boxing, but my vote goes to that Toledo-Hernstein horror. Rocky stood there all night, waving for Hernstein to come in and get his head knocked off. Naturally, the suggestion terrified Lefty. The more Rocky waved, the faster he ran."

Gus winced. That was the night Dandy Dan Devon had scooped up his pay and scurried off with Hernstein and Boyle, leaving so many questions that had never been answered. Lewis Merriam, the boxing commissioner, still had nightmares when he reflected upon the fog of scandal that seeped through the corridors of the arena that night.

"The referee gave it to Toledo, eight rounds to two," Gus remembered, "but the two judges called it for Lefty—five, four, and one even."

"I can see the look of sheer bewilderment on Lefty's face when the referee raised his hand," O'Toole was roaring now. "He realized then that in this life you can't be sure of anything."

Gus rose to go. "By the way," he said, "your buddy, Jay Mason, says Hello."

"And who," O'Toole answered, "is Jay Mason?"

All the way back to his hotel, Gus kept recalling that fight. Toledo had been an overwhelming favorite. Nobody thought Hernstein could win. The odds on Toledo to win by a knockout were fifteen-to-one.

The decision for Hernstein touched off a violent demonstration. Gus hadn't sensed the temper of the crowd until the patrons began tearing seats out of the floor and throwing them from the balcony. After that, they began lighting bonfires in the upper reaches of the arena.

Devon, icy calm in the swirling storm, was ready for the reporters.

"This is highway robbery," yelled a fresh-faced kid. "You don't think you're going to get away with this, do you, Devon?"

As he faced the hostile writers, Devon's pale eyes were hard and cold.

"The natives are mutinous because you men misled them," he spoke so softly they had to strain to hear him. "Fight writers? You men should be covering women's fashions. If you had been assigned to the battle of the Little Big Horn, you would have made Custer the favorite.

"You all said it, all except Davey Gordon," Devon's voice was rising now. " 'Toledo will knock him out inside of five,' 'Toledo will murder him in three,' 'The mismatch of the century,' 'Hernstein has no possible chance.' I'm quoting, gentlemen. You were all so sure Hernstein couldn't last ten rounds.

"He lasted. Toledo didn't lay a glove on him. Lefty made the champ look like a clown. Don't tell me Lefty didn't deserve the decision. Who did—your boy, Toledo?"

After the reporters had left him, Gus remonstrated with Devon.

"You shouldn't have been so rough with them, Dan. You made it sound as though they weren't as bright as you."

"But, Gus," Devon said, "they aren't."

The police needed reinforcements to clear the building

of Toledo's enraged partisans. They patiently herded the bitter throng down the corridor and into the street. The disappointed crowd remained outside the exit, chanting defiantly: "You gotta come out some time, Devon, you burglar. You gotta come out."

Devon said casually: "This unseemly disturbance is making Lefty ill. My tiger abhors violence. Should we use the truck entrance again?"

Devon had gone that way before, and he never forgot an escape hatch. When the cabbie blew his horn the stadium attendants pulled up the door of the freight entrance and the taxi rolled in. As they lifted the door again to let the cab out, the mob around the corner was shouting: "We know you're in there, Devon. C'mon out, Devon, you thief. How many bets did you cash tonight, you burglar?"

Devon leaned out of the cab window and waved jauntily. "Persistent, aren't they?" he observed. "See you at the hotel, Gus. We'll have a going-away drink."

I'm still waiting for that drink, Gus recalled. By the time I got downtown that night, Devon was back in New York.

He had scarcely left the arena when an outraged boxing commissioner bore down upon the little press agent. Lewis Merriam had just stopped at the box office to tell the auditor that he was impounding Lefty's purse. He was too late, of course. Devon had been in to pick up his check and cash it while the judges were tallying up their score sheets.

"I'll have your head, Scott," Merriam bellowed. "You've sneaked Devon and those other thieves out of here, haven't you? You won't get away with this. I'll bar you from boxing. I'll sue you. I'll throw you in jail . . ."

Before Gus got out of that mess, he had had enough of Devon, too. That was long ago, however. Almost a full decade. Now he wondered whether Devon still lived. Did he have anything good going for him? What was he doing now? Gus prayed that his old friend had not been brought down to the cruel helplessness of an improvident old age. That would be enough to destroy his faith in the brave American dream that any man, if he is resolute and zealous enough, can prosper without honest toil.

After he had eaten a lonely dinner in the coffee shop of the hotel, Gus went into the lobby and waited for the *Herald-Chronicle*. When the papers arrived, he turned hurriedly to the sports page. Jones had his story in, right on page one:

WATCH OUT, HORSEPOWER!
HERE COMES RUSTLING BREEZE
By Duke Jones
Herald-Chronicle Turf Writer

Hope springs eternal in the racetraker's breast, but this year's prize for witless optimism surely belongs to Calvin Oakley and Themastocles Christoforidis, two bucolic innocents from the metropolis of Bloody Hatchet, Okla.

These dreamers have the temerity to ask—nay, demand!—a match race between the great Horsepower, winner of the Triple Crown, and their pride and joy, a completely unsung little animal with the lyrical name of Rustling Breeze (and not much else).

34

Rustling Breeze?

He hasn't had a race in his life, but apparently he wants to start at the top. Or rather, the Messers. Oakley and Christoforidis do. I'm inclined to think the little colt knows better.

The way I see it, this Rustling Breeze has one distinction: He has got to be the worst bum ever nominated for the Colt Stake. Yet here are Oakley and Christoforidis braying about challenging Horsepower to a match race for a side bet of $10,000 "or upward." And I think they mean it.

I really do.

Jones continued for another half column, and every line dripped acid. Gus was delighted.

He called Tacks Barnett at once, and told him what he wanted.

"I've sent it," Tacks said. "I put out about 350 words on Jonesey's story, but I don't think those farmers will like it. He sure took off on their little colt, didn't he? Don't forget, pal, I need two more passes."

Gus wasted no time in getting through to Chalky. "I want you to level with me," he began. "You don't own a piece of this horse, do you? If you do, forget the whole thing. You'll just get us both in a grease by coming here. Lewis Merriam is still looking for you. And for Dan Devon, too, wherever he is."

Chalky sounded hurt. "You know you can trust me," he protested. "I give you my word, Gus. On my sacred honor. I swear on my sainted mother's grave . . ."

Oh, well, it was a silly question. Boyle wasn't the man to deceive anybody. He might not be honest, Gus allowed, but he was so dumb it came to the same thing.

Gus spelled out in great detail what he wanted done,

35

rehearsing the moves with elaborate care. He was so pleased that Jones had taken the bait that he didn't remember, until he hung up, that he had meant to call collect.

At times like this, thought Gus, I miss Sue most. She would always listen with interest as I recounted my petty victories. Who else could understand my elation at the prospect of managing a favor that wouldn't be appreciated for a friend I didn't really like?"

FOUR

NANCY HAD STUCK the note in Gus's typewriter: Call Mr. Douglas D. Dye. IMPORTANT.

Here we go again, he thought. Round Nine coming up. Come out punching, and protect yourself at all times.

Dye, however, couldn't have been more friendly.

"Gus, how nice to hear from you," he boomed. "I'm glad we're coming up to another racing season. It's the only time I see you, old friend."

"You sure you heard right? This is Gus Scott."

"That's what I miss most, Gus—your wit. These fellows here are so solemn and pompous. Give me your wonderful sense of humor any time. I've got to run down to New York this afternoon. I'll be back Sunday night.

Why don't you have dinner with me at the club Monday? We'll have a little broiled steak and some good Scotch, and we'll hash over the advertising and publicity program for the track. I've got some ideas you're going to love. Right?"

"I'll pass the dinner, Doug. If it's convenient for you, I'll see you at your office the first thing Monday morning."

"You're too businesslike, Gus. I really do enjoy your company, but if you want to make it at the office, fine. About nine o'clock?"

Douglas Dye is no mean adversary, as Gus knew. He is the founder and president of the advertising firm of D. D. Dye, Heppleworth, Myron, and Bennington, whose billings last year were the third highest in the industry. Dye is fond of saying that he refuses more accounts than he accepts. Any agency that can satisfy Twentieth Century Motors, the biggest name in automobile manufacturing, must be good. And Dye's agency has had that account for the past quarter of a century.

He has also directed the advertising for the manifold Randahl business interests for years. When Buzz took over the Treasure City Race Track, he gave the account to Dye.

He is accustomed to offering his clients advertising and public relations services in a single package. Although it is a lesser part of his operation, he employs the biggest public relations staff in town. He sets up and coordinates publicity and advertising campaigns so that they complement each other.

He was appalled to discover that Gus had been hired by the track to do its PR work. For the little publicity man was independent of ad agencies, and he wanted to stay that way.

At the outset, however, Dye did not seem much concerned about Gus's independence. "We'll be happy to counsel and guide you, Scott," he said. "We'll make a great team, won't we?"

"If I can be the quarterback," Gus responded sweetly.

Dye took a closer look at the little man.

Since that day, Dye never quit trying to tell Gus how to handle publicity. Gus and Dye inevitably reached a point, every season, where they were yelling at each other.

Dye has never quite made the publicity man's position untenable, but he has been responsible for many annoyances. The Kiddie Tour, for instance. This was his idea, and he sold it to Buzz Randahl over Gus's strong objections.

The idea has appeal: Every Saturday morning the publicity department holds conducted tours of the racing plant for children from orphanages, community centers.

The track earned goodwill, and once in a while a paper would print a picture of the kids in the backstretch. Gus never liked the idea, however, for he had a horror of turning small children loose anywhere near anything as potentially dangerous as a thoroughbred race horse.

The thought of the Kiddie Tour was unsettling. Gus was still fretting about what might happen when Duke Jones, the *Herald-Chronicle* race writer, called. "Why didn't you tell me the track wouldn't give Rustling Breeze stall space?" he inquired.

"I'm no mind reader. Why didn't you ask me?"

Jones was silent for a moment. Then he resumed. "The

people in Bloody Hatchet—Oklahoma, you know, where the colt is—are very excited about their little horse. Their local paper requested coverage on any stories that appeared here on Rustling Breeze and the Colt Stake. You know, home town pride. I guess they were pretty upset when Worldwide Press sent out a few hundred words on my story."

"Very funny piece," Gus inserted. "You gave it to those farmers straight. You didn't pull any punches."

"Well, I think maybe I was a little too rough on them. The colt's a nothing, of course, but I don't like to hurt anybody's feelings. Anyway, I had a call this morning from one of the owners. He was almost bawling. He said he had wanted to bring his colt here so he could get used to the track and to the climate, but Randahl turned him down. When he read my story, he thought Randahl had ordered me to write it to discourage them. Imagine! Randahl ordering me around."

"What do you care what those farmers think? Forget 'em, Duke."

"Now, wait a minute, Gus. You know me. I give everybody a square deal. This poor fellow just begged me to get him two stalls. I told him I'd personally guarantee him the two stalls, because I always fight for the underdog. Take care of it, will you? Tell Buzz to write them today. Maybe I'll do a follow-up story on how this thing got straightened out. You know, the spirit of fair play."

"You shouldn't have said we'd accept the horses, Duke. There isn't a chance. We're full up."

"Don't hand me that. I said to get the horses in."

"And I said there isn't a chance. Don't worry. I'll drop them a note and tell them they were misinformed."

"Get Randahl!" Jones was furious now. "I'll see whether I have any influence around this lousy track. I want Randahl!"

"You can't bother Buzz, he's busy. Forget it. I'll take care of those farmers. I'll tell them what they can do with their horses."

Gus hung up, and waited for Randahl.

"What the devil is going on in your office?" he howled. "I just had Jones on the line, and I've never heard him so mad. Why didn't you say he was interested in those Oklahoma horses?"

"He shouldn't have bothered you, Buzz. I explained how you said we just couldn't find room for them. We haven't got an empty stall. Right?"

"Can't you get it through your head? I can always find room for two more horses if I have a good reason. I can't have Jones and the *Herald-Chronicle* on my back. Drop those guys in Oklahoma a note. No, don't write. Call."

"Call? For what?"

Buzz sounded like a man struggling for self-control. "Tell them," he said slowly, "that we will be glad to have their horses. They can bring them in any time they want, any time at all. Tell them we're sorry. It was all a misunderstanding."

FIVE

"COME IN, GUS, old boy. Come in, and welcome! You've been away too long, friend."

Doug Dye had never been more engaging. He waved Gus to a big leather chair which was drawn up beside his enormous, shining desk. "A cup of coffee? I always keep some perking early in the morning. Keeps me awake, eh?"

He filled the cups with hot, black coffee. After a moment, he began to talk. He spoke slowly, his forehead wrinkled in thought. "Gus, do you have any idea what the parts division of Twentieth Century Motors spends with our agency each year? Over two million dollars, and that is only one part of the corporation." He gave his visitor a moment to think that one over before he continued. "The Twentieth Century account is our heart's blood, Gus. We'd be dead without it, with the overhead we've got. That account is big, big money. That's why we have one cardinal rule: What Twentieth Century wants, Twentieth Century gets. We deliver, by God, and nobody stops us."

His voice had risen, but now he paused. He soon resumed in a pleasant, conversational tone. "I'm going to lay it out for you, Gus. By a curious chance—a freak, really—your little race track has suddenly become crucially important to us. The whole Twentieth Century account—the very life of my agency—depends upon the way you do your job this time. What do you think of that?"

"Don't lay it on too thick, Doug. I know you."

"But do you know old J. C. Jensen, founder, president, and chief stockholder of Twentieth Century Motors? He *is* Twentieth Century, and horse racing is the great passion of his life. He's always dreamed of owning a great champion. He's spent millions on it, and now he has the horse—Horsepower, the Triple Crown winner. That man loves Horsepower more than anything else in the world."

"More than anything else?"

"Even more than Twentieth Century Motors," Dye affirmed, his eyes misty. "This will touch you, Gus. He flew down to the farm last New Year's Eve and gave a party for the stablehands right in Horsepower's barn. He wanted to be with his colt as they welcomed in their year of destiny. I almost cried when I heard it.

"Old J. C. will race Horsepower in the Colt Stake here if the horse is fit. I kid you not! Your track has never had a horse like that, I know, but J. C.'s roots are deep here. This is his home. Call it civic pride, but he wants to let his friends and neighbors see his great colt race.

"He may not announce it for a few weeks, but Horsepower will go in that Colt Stake."

Dye leaned back in his huge swivel chair, and winked. "You've got it made, boy. With Horsepower coming in, the Colt Stake will sell itself."

Gus started to reply, but Dye kept talking. "I've formulated a coordinated advertising and publicity campaign for the track, Gus, and I must insist that there be no deviation from it. We must all work unceasingly, as a team, to create the image of horse racing at Treasure City as the sport of kings. Dignity, class, rich old traditions—old J. C. won't take anything less. And since he is bringing his magnificent colt here, surely the least we can do is to show our appreciation."

He leaned across the desk toward me. "That means—" his voice was hard now "—that we will have no more cute little stories about the cheap gambling element at the track. Forget them. I don't want one word about the kooks, the oddballs, the shabby hangers-on, all those with larceny in their hearts."

"That leaves me the horses," Gus said.

Dye began a retort, but he checked himself. "I understand you, Gus. You enjoy a little joke, but some people think you're a troublemaker." He seemed saddened by this calumny, but he soon brightened. "Your job is simple, Gus. Just write nice things about Horsepower, and you can't go wrong. Lay it on good and thick. Old J. C. will love it, and we'll all keep our jobs. That's the way we're going to do it. Right?"

"No," Gus said. Dye was on his feet in an instant. Gus rose, too.

"You want a dignified publicity campaign, Doug, but dignity is something you get with paid advertising, not with race track publicity. You want me to take this whole cockeyed, wild wonderful world of horse racing and treat it with lofty solemnity. When you do that, you lose it.

"As for Horsepower, that animal doesn't need publicity. If he keeps winning, he'll get a ton of it, and there's no way to stop it. My job will be to sell the idea that Horsepower can be beaten in the Colt Stake. I have to build up the horses that will go against Horsepower. And that is the way I'm going to go."

Dye sat in silence for a long moment. When he answered, he spoke quietly. "Do you know Ed Hamilton, Gus? He's retiring this fall. Ed's got a very big job in our agency, and I think you might be the replacement we're looking for. The job needs ideas and imagination, and you've got them. What you're making now is peanuts compared to what we'd pay. I like you, and I think you could go far here, yet I've hesitated to mention this to you. Do you know why?"

Gus couldn't imagine.

"You've never grown up. Hell, when I was a college boy, I thought it was smart to thumb my nose at authority. It's a phase with most men, but with you it's a career. Grow up! Just cooperate. That's all I'm asking. Play ball, and I've got a big job waiting for you."

"Will I get a nice, fat expense account, too?"

"Our people always go first class," he said expansively. "We never question . . ." The smile froze on his lips. "You think I'm conning you, don't you? Dammit, Scott, when will you ever get some sense? This is your chance. Don't you see, you hold that whole Twentieth Century account in your hands?"

"But, Doug, you're exaggerating. Surely Jensen wouldn't take the account away from you just because he didn't like something I wrote. He can't hold you responsible for what I do."

"He can, and he does," Dye grated. "And he's right. Are you aware that I handle all the public relations for

Twentieth Century? And for half a dozen other clients almost as big? Do you think I'm going to tell Jensen that we're good enough to his PR work, but not good enough to do race track publicity. He knows that you aren't on my payroll, but I've explained that this is merely a matter of bookkeeping. I told him I would guarantee the Treasure City publicity campaign to have dignity and taste. And I'm going to deliver, by God, no matter what."

"I'm sorry, Doug," Gus replied. "Please try to understand. Our interests simply do not run together. I wish they did. I really do."

"Don't patronize me, you squalid little flack!" he roared. "Do you think I'm going to let a punk like you put me out of business? We'll see how much power I have. We've had differences in the past, but they were so petty, I let you have your way. But this is no trifling matter. You do what I tell you or, by God, I'll put such heat on Buzz Randahl that he'll have to fire you. And the next press agent the track hires will work directly under me."

"I've got a contract," Gus said.

"Oh, you've got a contract, have you?" Dye mocked. "I've broken dozens of contracts, and I dare say they were drawn up better than your precious contract. I do not propose to waste time with you. The first time you defy me, I'll have your head. I am not going to warn you again. Good day!"

"All right, all right, hold everything," Pierre barked. "You, with that horse, stay right where you are. And listen good!"

The big blond youngster at the top of the ramp stared. So did the scattering of grooms and exercise boys who had paused to note the disembarkment of the Flowering Tree Stable.

The benign rustic chatting with the stable superintendent must be Cal Oakley or Themastocles Christoforidis, Gus decided. The stable superintendent always greeted new arrivals, welcoming them and collecting the first month's stable rental in advance.

"Before you take that horse down from the van, stand there for a second and point to something," Pierre was telling the blond boy. "You're showing the horse his new home, see? He's glad to be at the Treasure City track. Get it?"

The boy reacted with a blank, unbelieving stare to the revelation that the horse was happy to be here. This spurred Pierre to new histrionics.

"Look at the horse! Don't look at me!" he thundered. His indignation was marvelous in view of the fact that nobody had given him a glance until he began yelling.

Then the kid led the horse down the ramp. Gus shuddered. This animal was a travesty on the whole thoroughbred breeding industry. He was bony and awkward, with a neck that seemed too slender for his great head, and he walked as though his feet hurt.

"Is that Rustling Breeze?" the press agent burst out. "That ridiculous animal?"

"My five-year-old," the rustic said softly. "An honest kind. I'm Cal Oakley, mister."

"I'm Gus Scott, the PR man. I didn't mean to offend you."

"No harm meant, none taken," he said, "but when will people learn, this is a race horse, not a show horse."

A groom appeared at the top of the ramp with the second horse. This one was more like it. A little on the small side but compact and muscular, with a shining coat and the lordly air that can make a man fall in love with a thoroughbred. Rustling Breeze! *This* animal had a suggestion of power, like coiled steel springs. Maybe he could run.

Oakley posed patiently until Pierre grew tired of shooting. Then Duke Jones moved in and began asking questions.

Afterward, Gus walked with Oakley to his new barn. The old horseman told his story readily enough: He had been a racetracker himself as a boy. He had begun by mucking out stalls. Then he had graduated to walking hots and exercising horses. At sixteen, he had the bug—he was an apprentice jockey.

"I lasted two-three years before I got too heavy," he related. "I won a few, but never anything to amount to much. I had the mount on Pioneer's Pride in the Stake here in '29, but they took me off because I couldn't make the weight. Pioneer's Pride won it, you know. I always felt bad, coming so close and all."

"Have you been out of horse racing a long time?"

"A normal lifetime, mister. Racetracking is no life for a family man. Always pulling up stakes, always traveling. Chicken one day, and feathers the next. Not for me. After I married, I went to farming and raised me a family, but I've always loved the races. I've raced some mighty quick quarterhorses.

"Then last year I picked up Rustling Breeze. Biggest bargain I ever saw. He had a damaged sesamoid bone in his foot, but he's sound as a dollar now. Sound as a dollar.

"I began training the little colt. When I saw how he could go, I got a yen to try the Stake one more time. I always kind of figured somebody owed me a Colt Stake win. At my age, however, a man isn't as fast out of the starting gate as he once was. I talked about going back to the races, but that's all I ever would have done—just talked—if it wasn't for Mr. Christoforidis. He got me moving."

"Did Mr. Christoforidis come with you?"

"Him? In a horse van? Nossir! He's flying in one of them jetliners."

"How about your five-year-old? Is he as bad as he looks?"

"Maybe so. Maybe not. He beat some awful good quarterhorses for me, but I don't know how he might do over a distance of ground. I brought him along for the colt. He's company. Horses are like people, you know. In strange parts, they like to see a familiar face. The colt is a mite jumpy. The five-year-old gentles him down."

"You'll need a rider, Mr. Oakley. I'd like to recommend a good one. Maybe you've heard of him. He's won some big ones—Wade Parkinson."

"Wade Parkinson? He still drinking?"

"He's been on the wagon for ten months," Gus assured.

"If he tends to business, I might use him. I'll talk to him."

"Do you train the horses by yourself, or does Mr. Christoforidis help out?"

"Him?" Oakley's eyes lit with mirth. "He can't abide

48

horses. You'll never catch him near the barn unless he needs money."

"Then where does he fit in?"

"That man can evermore play poker," Oakley said, with a touch of awe. "He bluffed me, sitting there with nothing but a jack high. And I thought I could judge a man. That's how he happens to be part owner of my two horses, but I can't say I'm sorry. He brought me back to the races. That man is older than me, a good bit older, but he's full of get up and go. And he talks so grand. He convinced my missus that I should get this horse racing out of my system. Then he convinced me."

"How long have you known him? What does he do?"

"He blew into town with some kind of a traveling show. Diving and swimming and like that. The show went broke, but he landed on his feet. He's like a cat."

Wheels were beginning to turn in Gus' head, and lights were flashing. No, he told himself, nobody could have that kind of luck, but a dreadful foreboding made him keep talking.

"What did he do for a living? Before the swimming show?"

"He's done a lot of things, but mostly he was in the prize fighting business. What grand stories he can tell about the prize fighting. He's a talker."

"Let me guess," Gus murmured. "Boyle is his errand boy, and Christoforidis isn't his straight name, is it?"

"That's his legal name, if that's what you mean. That's the name he signed on the ownership papers for the horses, but he doesn't use it much. He says nobody could spell it. For a fellow with a name like Christoforidis, he uses a might peculiar monicker."

"Never mind," Gus said. "I know."

What he knew was that he had been taken again, and this time by an expert.

SIX

THE TELEGRAM did not surprise Gus. Dan Devon always liked to make an entrance.

ARRIVE CITY AIRPORT NOON. PLEASE SET UP PRESS PARTY AT FLEUR DE LIS HOTEL TO ANNOUNCE MY ASSOCIATION WITH FLOWERING TREE STABLE. OPEN BAR AT ELEVEN. LUNCH AT ONE. DO IT FIRST CLASS. IMPORTANT MAYOR AND CITY OFFICIALS ATTEND. ARRANGE HELICOPTER TRANSPORT FOR ME FROM AIRPORT TO HOTEL. NO PRESS AT AIRPORT PLEASE. JUST COME YOURSELF PAL. BEST REGARDS. DAN.

"He uses a lot of words," Nancy noted.

"Dan is a master at not saving money."

"The telegram came collect."

"He spends money. Yours or his."

"But how can we ever arrange a press party on such short notice, Gus?"

"Don't bother about it. Mike Stern is still the catering manager at the Fleur de Lis, and he's still dreaming about collecting for the last press party Dan threw there."

Gus tossed the telegram into the waste basket.

"Press party? What Devon faces is more like a lynching party. I'm going to meet him at the airport and head him off. If anybody calls, tell them nothing."

Dan was in trouble, partly because the state racing and boxing commissioners issue licenses to all participants in their sports. They can get rid of anyone they consider unsuitable simply by revoking their licenses. There is no recourse from the commissioners' judgment; their power is absolute.

Now Dan was trapped between the two commissioners. The Flowering Tree Stable, of which he was part owner, had been granted a license to race so he came under the authority of the racing commissioner. On the other hand, Boxing Commissioner Lewis Merriam was still out to nail him for his behavior as a fight manager years ago.

Dan was caught in a political crossfire. Since the Liberal party's sweep of the state elections last fall, Boxing Commissioner Lewis Merriam was the last Conservative appointee still in office. The Liberals had tried to pressure him into resigning but Lewis would have preferred to resign from the human race. His term had four months to go and then, he knew, he was through.

As a parting shot, he would dearly love to embarrass the new administration. Now he just might do it. There would be a frightful dust-up when it was discovered that a man with Devon's complicated background had been approved as an owner by the racing commissioner.

This is one Dan can't win, Gus told himself. He will have to go. There is no other way.

While he waited at the airport, Gus thought of the days that were gone, when Devon had a big fighter in town and the advance sale was good and the publicity was popping and the world was a prize to be easily taken. How many times he'd sat up until dawn in the bar rooms and the blind pigs, listening to Devon. Why did it have to end like this?

Gus recognized the jaunty little gamecock when he appeared at the top of the exit ramp, but he was shocked at what ten years had done. For all his buoyant step and erect carriage, Devon was old, old. His hair was perfectly white now, and he had the curious waxy fragility of great age.

Gus went out to meet him at a trot.

"Gus, how wonderful of you!" he said with warmth. "It's good to see the best PR man in the business."

"Best PR man in the business, eh? You finally perceive the truth."

"I know it's a line," Devon twinkled, "but you know it's the truth. And it *is* good to see you. I hear you have a delightful little track."

"Full of old world charm," Gus responded, "like a thieves' bazaar. I hate to tell you this, Dan, but you can't stay. Believe me, there's no way they'll let you race here. Cut and run. It's your only chance."

"You worry too much," he grinned. "These days I'm so respectable I can't sleep with myself."

"Dan, you know I'd swing with you if I thought you had a possible chance, but you haven't. Remember Lewis Merriam? The boxing commissioner?"

"Lewis Merriam? Of course. An authentic oaf. We're well rid of him."

"But we aren't rid of him. He's still boxing commissioner, and he's still out to get you. And Charlie Smith is *still* the commission secretary."

52

"Charlie Smith?"

"Sure, you remember. Fat, oily, witless, and self-important."

Dan pondered the description for a moment. "Hmm. I see. My enemies survive, eh? Well, I never believed I could outlive them all." For just a moment, his insouciance fell away and he was a little old man in a tailored suit he couldn't afford, but he bounded back. "The perils of a democracy," he shrugged. "This is the kind of thing that could bring back the czars."

"Dan, Lewis will blast you and Patrick O'Sullivan, the racing commissioner, will suspend your license, and you'll be dead. You can't lick this one."

"Patrick O'Sullivan, eh? How much will it cost?"

"This O'Sullivan is no good, Dan. He's dumb, lazy and, worst of all, honest."

"Not only weak but eccentric," Devon mused. "The pure in heart defy reasonable organization."

"We're wasting time, Dan. Take the next flight out. You'll find some place to race, but not here."

"I'm weary of running, Gus. I'll see this thing through here, and I'll beat it. Merriam hasn't got a thing on me."

"He doesn't need to, Dan. This is horse racing, which is conducted on such a high level that you can't possibly get a fair shake. You're facing public opinion, which is just as blind as private opinion and somewhat more widespread.

"Lewis will accuse you of fixing that Hernstein-Toledo fiasco. O'Sullivan will suspend you while he conducts an investigation. Then he will kick it around until everybody forgets the whole thing. The Colt Stake will come and go, and you'll still be suspended, not only here but at every other parimutuel track. You're licked."

Devon offered a faint smile. "Nothing is more vulnerable than innocence," he said. "If I had rigged that fight, by this time I would have found ten ways to prove that I couldn't possibly have done it."

"Nobody knows who Themastocles Christoforidis is. Not yet. Please, old friend, blow. I forgive you for conning me on that Flowering Tree Stable. I forgive you for running out after that Hernstein disaster. I wish you could stay, but you can't. Take off while you have a chance."

Devon's smile was fixed now. "Oakley won't race his horses anywhere but here," he replied quietly. "I'm staying."

Gus shrugged. Under Devon's probing questions, he explained the enmity between the racing commissioner and the boxing commissioner.

"And O'Sullivan? What does he know about horse racing?"

"Nothing," Gus offered. "But he ushers for four masses at St. Patrick's every Sunday, talks with a thick brogue, and the Micks in the Fourteenth Ward vote the way he tells them. What does horse racing have to do with it?"

"No sense in cluttering your mind with irrelevant detail," Devon agreed. "This political situation may be just what we need. Listen."

With the detachment of a five-star general laying down a plan of battle, Devon explained what he wanted done.

"In view of your obdurateness, I haven't an alternative," Gus answered. "And maybe you can bring it off. I'll call Charlie Smith, the boxing commission secretary. He's just about bright enough."

Charlie was happy to hear from Gus.

"Have you ever heard of Themastocles Christoforidis,

54

Charlie? You haven't? Then let me suggest that you search your files for a copy of the manager's license which Dan Devon used when he was here ten years ago. Although it is not generally known, Dan Devon and Themastocles Christoforidis are the same person. What do you think of that?

"No kidding, Scott? That's a good one."

"This is a better one. Devon is part owner of a stable that has been accepted by the Treasure City Race Track. It is the Flowering Tree Stable and Themastocles Christoforidis, also known as Dan Devon, owns a substantial interest in these horses. What is the commissioner going to do about it?"

"Race horses? Mr. Merriam isn't the racing commissioner. Call the windbag O'Sullivan."

"O'Sullivan's too stupid to count his toes. I thought Mr. Merriam would be interested. Or are you worried about protocol? Lewis doesn't want to do anything that would make O'Sullivan look bad. Is that it? You fellows sure stick together."

"Oh, gosh no," Charlie blurted out. "I mean, yes. I mean, that isn't it."

"I think it is Mr. Merriam's duty to expose men like Devon. Somebody has to be man enough to act, and you know O'Sullivan isn't up to it."

"You're right," Charlie spoke with spirit now. "Don't worry. I'll look into this myself personally. Just keep your mouth shut, Scott. I'm a public servant, and it's my duty to protect the citizens and taxpayers."

Gus shared the telephone receiver with Devon for that last remark. Dan nodded. "I think we have the right man," he said as Gus cradled the receiver. "That boy

can take a tired line and make it sound like a tired line."
Dan was feeling chipper now. "We could be on the right
track, Gus. Never underestimate the vindictiveness of
your fellow man. Now, I'll need someone to run a little
errand for me at the public library."

Gus volunteered, after Devon had explained what he
wanted. "But, tell me, why are you fooling around with a
nothing horse like Rustling Breeze?"

"My colt will win your Colt Stake, that's why."

"You'll have to make better sense than that, Dan."

"If I make too much sense," he beamed, "I may lose
you."

No matter what developed, Gus knew he would have
to hold a press conference. So he called Nancy and told
her to make the arrangements for an assembly in the conference hall at four o'clock. "Don't tell anybody what it's
about. Just say I have an announcement. Reserve a room
at the Hot Time Motel in my name. We'll tuck Dan in
there until it's time for the conference."

Gus prayed Hall wouldn't come. He is a hatchet man,
and he sets the pattern. Both the wire service editors,
plus Jones and half the other sports writers in town,
learned newspapering under him. Once you have worked
for such a gifted tyrant, you never really escape from him.

The shifting throng in the air terminal didn't give
them a second glance, which was comforting. Gus
wanted Devon's presence an absolute secret until at the
press conference.

As he drove out of the airport parking lot, Gus just had
time to tune in Marty Kensington's twelve-thirty broadcast.

"Listen to this. Marty Kensington, the guy I told you

56

about, Dan. He sends up the trial balloons for our esteemed boxing commissioner, Lewis Merriam."

Kensington came on, his voice filled with the wonder of his message. "This is Marty Kensington, your ten-star reporter with the twelve-thirty sports news! Sports Flash! Ten-Star Flash! Here is the story that will shock every lover of fair play and decency in sports! Boxing Commissioner Lewis Merriam, today accused Racing Commissioner Patrick O'Sullivan of quote criminal laxity or worse unquote in issuing a horse owner's license for a known professional gambler and one of the most notorious gangsters ever spawned in the jungles of professional boxing—that scandalous fight fixer, Dandy Dan Devon.

"Mr. Merriam, with the help of some fine detective work by the dedicated boxing commission secretary, Charles T. Smith, has learned that Devon has been granted a license to race horses at the Treasure City Race Track under the name of Themastocles Christoforidis. In a strongly worded statement, to be released to the press within the hour, Commissioner Merriam will point out that Devon is still sought for questioning in connection with a fight which he allegedly fixed here ten years ago. Commissioner Merriam will demand that O'Sullivan revoke Devon's license and explain, if he can, how he ever thought he could get away with this highly questionable course of action . . ."

Devon was preoccupied during the ride to the motel.

"Cheer up," Gus said. "Kensington was great. If I had written it myself, I couldn't have laid it on any thicker."

"He might be so good he's disastrous," Devon replied. "Do you think O'Sullivan might panic?"

"He might."

When they were in the motel room, Devon opened his overnight bag and removed his electric razor. Gus gazed at the books he had brought—Shakespeare, Toynbee, Churchill, and the newest edition of *The American Racing Manual*.

"You haven't kicked the habit, I see."

"What are you nosing around for?" Devon flared.

"Don't worry. I won't tell anyone you're a solitary reader. I wouldn't dare. If word got out that reading was your secret vice, the mothers of America would be on the march tomorrow, burning down libraries."

"I think I'll give O'Sullivan a ring," he broke in.

Devon wanted to change the subject, Gus reflected, for he never liked to be accused of respectable preoccupations.

But Devon meant it. Before Gus could stop him, he was making the call. Gus tried to retrieve the phone, but he was too slow. Devon had O'Sullivan on the line.

The old man began talking in a rich brogue.

Gus saw no humor in this present whim.

"Mr. O'Sullivan? This is Mr. O'Brien of the Fourteenth Ward. My son tells me he heard that that terrible man, Dan Devon, has brought race horses here. As a citizen, I'm calling upon you to throw that scoundrel Devon out. Nits and lice, that's what his kind are, I'm thinking. You'll never see his carousing, whiskey-swilling breed marching on the glorious anniversary of the Battle of the Boyne. You follow me, O'Sullivan?"

There was a rumble over the phone, and Devon spoke again.

"No, this isn't the Cornelius O'Brien who ushers at

seven-thirty at St. Patrick's. This is Oliver Cromwell O'Brien."

The noise over the phone rose to a wail. Devon hung up.

"At a time like this," he remarked, "I like to have a little something extra going for me."

SEVEN

JAY MASON grabbed Gus before Gus could hang up his hat. "Mr. Dye is furious," he announced. "He is really terribly displeased."

Gus snorted.

"You are to call him just as soon as you have ordered this Devon off the track." Jay followed Gus to his desk. "He is going to dictate a publicity release for you."

Gus busied himself with the day's mail. He didn't look up.

"Mr. Dye called four times," Jay offered. "Gus, I've never seen a madder man."

"Mr. Dye can go to hell," Gus said slowly.

Mason's head jerked up in disbelief, and the sweet smile fled from his fresh young face.

"I don't need you or Dye to tell me how to handle this, Jay. I'm giving Devon every bit of support I can.

59

I'm not asking your opinion. I am telling you the policy of the Treasure City publicity department. If they want to throw Dan Devon out, they'll have to throw me out first." He gave his assistant a long, cold glance. Mason blinked under it.

"You're the boss," he yielded. He put his hand on Scott's shoulder. "You understand, Gus, I'm in your corner all the way."

"With Dye trying to tear me down, young man, I don't need you trying to build me up."

Jay hesitated. "Would you tell me," he began, "why you're sticking your neck out this way for Dan Devon?"

"Years ago, Mason, before I was married, I knew I never had to drink alone if Devon was in town. I never went to him for a story that he didn't dream up something. Once he gave my wife a magnificent pair of bronze candlesticks, simply because she collected them. Dan Devon is my friend."

"Yes," said Jay. "Yes, of course."

"The press conference begins in less than half an hour, Jay. Would you greet the guests? I'm hiding out for the moment. Tell them you don't know what the conference is all about."

"I don't," Jay pointed out.

"Good. You're perfect."

Gus told Nancy to hold the phone calls, unless they were urgent. Then he closed his office door. Waiting was the hardest of all. Any minute the racing commissioner might call—or he might send his chief aide, Billy Riley —to announce that Devon was suspended. Then Dan would be done before he had a chance to defend himself.

Would Devon get a brief reprieve? The press conference was less than ten minutes away when Nancy buzzed.

"Mr. William Riley, from the racing commission office, is here to see you," she said, regretfully. Gus told her to send him in.

"What are you trying to pull off this time," Riley inquired. When Gus made no reply, Riley lowered his bulk into the most comfortable chair in the room.

"That Dan Devon of yours has given the commissioner fits," he growled. "The old man heard that radio broadcast, and I thought he would go straight up. He hates the suggestion of a race track scandal, but he hates Lewis Merriam worse. If it had been anybody else, the old man would have suspended Devon on the spot, but this was too much.

"He didn't know what to do. He hated to give in to Lewis, and he was afraid not to. Then he got another call from some Mick in the Fourteenth Ward. Whatever the guy said, he sure ticked Pat off. He was so mad he couldn't see. He told me to say I didn't know where he was, and he took off. I thought I'd mosey out here to see what the hell is going on."

"We're going to discuss the matter at the press conference in about five minutes, Riley. Be my guest."

Before Gus left, however, Nancy wanted a word with him. "Jay Mason said you might be fired," she said quietly. "He's hateful. I just wanted to say that if you go, I go. I'll quit, Gus."

He didn't remonstrate. Trying to get that girl to change her mind is like trying to get Niagara Falls to run back up.

When Hall saw Gus from across the room, he started

for him. The crusty old editor's jaw was thrust out, his mouth a grim line, his eyes flashing. At his heels trotted a covey of reporters, eager to be near the great man at the confrontation.

"I swear, I knew you'd get too cute to live," Hall began. "Now they've got you red-handed, you and that burglar Devon. I'm going to tear you apart."

"That's what I like about you, George—your open mind. You've already gotten your story, haven't you, and the press conference hasn't even begun. Why did you bother to come?"

The old lion paused, surveying Gus with angry concentration.

"I see Marty Kensington, the great radio announcer, is here," Gus added. "When you're so righteously indignant, George, you sound just like him."

Hall jabbed a stubby finger against Gus's chest. "This thing smells," he growled. "There's something very fishy about the way Devon's horses just happened to pop up here."

The attendance was better—or worse—than Gus had anticipated, with several police and crime reporters in the assembly.

"Why not?" asked Connie O'Toole. "If somebody stole the Pieta, would you send the art critic? Oh, this will be fun. There's Bloody Mary, the sweet girl reporter."

"That's Bloody Mary?"

"Yeah. Throws you, doesn't it? She looks so harmless, but she can slice you up pretty good."

"She wouldn't be bad to look at," Gus decided, "if she would dress like a girl."

At precisely four o'clock, Dan Devon walked in. He was

carrying a thick manila envelope and he waved jauntily to the concert of hangmen. Dan always relished a well-attended press conference, especially when the writers had their switch blades out.

A low murmur ran across the room. Even Hall's eyes popped. They didn't expect Devon. They didn't expect him at all. For the moment, he had them off balance.

"Is that Dan Devon?" asked a fresh-faced youth. "That inoffensive little man. What can he do?"

"If you shake hands with him," a crime reporter advised, "count your fingers."

Gus raced through his part in the conference, sketching in the background of the boxing commissioner's accusations. Then he turned the microphone over to Devon.

Dan stood quietly for a moment, smiling at the crowd and waiting for the babble to subside. A benign and diminutive old party, he stood against the world with nothing but his elan, his wit, and his brass knuckles.

"I'm happy to see the sports editor of the *Herald-Chronicle* here," he began. "You're looking fit, George. I'm glad. So often, when I return to scenes of happy memories, I see the empty chairs. I was in Miami when I heard of Davey Gordon's death. I still can't believe it. He was so filled with a hunger for living. I miss him. Men like that you never stop missing."

He talked on, in a voice not much above a whisper, acknowledging old friends and ancient enemies with equal aplomb. He hadn't been back in ten years, but he never missed a name. As his fluent phrases fell upon the crowd, some of the younger reporters began to stir restlessly. Hall glared at them.

63

"Quit stalling, and get on with it," Kensington called out.

"Shut up, you punk," Hall rasped. "Take your time, Dan."

"Please, couldn't we have the social hour later?" spoke up Bloody Mary. "I'm a working girl, you know. I want to ask a few preliminary questions."

"Yes, of course, sweet child," Devon bowed to her. "My pleasure."

"You have been accused of arranging a fraudulent boxing contest in order to make a betting coup," Bloody Mary began in a matter-of-fact way. "I'm concerned with the cynical underlying assumption that illegal gambling exists. Does it?"

"If a man wants to get himself separated from his money, my swan, he can always find someone to oblige him," Devon smiled. "The custom is ancient and universal. Recluses, I suppose, book their own bets."

Bloody Mary surveyed him coolly. "The president of the Anti-Gambling Assembly has just issued a statement denouncing you as a treacherous, deceitful, dissembling old man. Any comment?"

Devon's countenance darkened. "Reformers do not enchant me," he said sourly, "because they always want to reform somebody else. You can't play any game if it isn't their game. Treacherous, deceitful, dissembling, indeed! Nothing affronts me more than the inept insult."

"Just a minute!" a little man in the back called out. "Gambling is a cancer that can destroy our society. This is a matter of morality."

"I dissent," Devon's voice was harsh. "When our vices become profitable, we don't abandon them. We give them more pleasant names. Greed becomes ambition, obscenity becomes realism, niggardliness becomes thrift. And so it is with gambling.

"If a man loses two dollars at his bookmaker's, he is a criminal and a worthless bum. Yet, if he makes a million dollars gambling on the stock market, he is a prominent business leader and a wizard of finance. That's not morality. It's snobbery."

Devon peered over the lectern, his frank gaze probing his listeners.

"Are you presuming to discredit the dedication of the Anti-Gambling Assembly?" Bloody Mary sniped at him.

"Pooh!" Devon spat it out. "I know the breed. I remember the days of Prohibition, when a man's social status was judged by the quality of the bootleg whiskey he served. The reformers did it. They raised hypocrisy to the dignity of a status symbol. They are still at it, with their refusal to acknowledge the national conscience, flaying away at gambling."

Gus nudged Connie O'Toole. "Devon makes a great devil's advocate," he whispered, "because he admires his client."

Devon was addressing his remarks directly to Bloody Mary now.

"Heavens, child, man is born to gamble," he declared. "He takes his chances every day of his life. What a curious civilization we have, where they outlaw charity bingo games and sanctify the biggest gamble of all, which is holy wedlock. You can bet your life, but not your small change."

Devon stopped, and relaxed his grip on the lectern.

"I cherish my right to throw my money away," he said.

65

"It's one of the things I do best. It helps a man keep things in perspective. Your reformers do not frighten me. They will never whip gambling by hypocrisy alone."

"Spare me your little homilies," Bloody Mary came right back. "I do not condemn a little innocent wagering, but race tracks bring in professional gamblers."

"My cherished one, that is akin to saying that you may find women in a maternity ward. Horse racing is a gambling game. What do you expect to attract—abstract painters? Were I running a track, I'd send cabs for the pros. The tracks control and police their game. There's no way you can rig a horse race. Believe me, I've given the matter some thought. But rigged football games, the shaved points in a basketball contest—these are the curse of the gambling man.

"The safeguards at a race track are fantastic. Cheat the races? You'd have an easier time raiding Fort Knox. Horse racing is clean, because it is under constant scrutiny from without and within. The sports that are *above* suspicion make me suspicious."

Connie O'Toole leaned over to Gus.

"Isn't that wonderful," he said happily. "Devon is preaching to Bloody Mary."

"The fight!" called out Hall. "Let's get to the fight."

"Right," said Devon. He winked, and Bloody Mary bit her lip.

He poured himself half a glass of water, and sipped it slowly.

"Now, ladies and gentlemen, let me tell you how it was," he said as he put the glass down. "I am going to prove to you that no man in possession of his sense would have tried to cook the bout in question. I'm on the record, of course."

66

The reporters leaned forward, pencils at the ready.

"Lefty Hernstein, my tiger, was fast and frightened. He wished to avoid violence and bloodshed. Rocky Toledo, the lightweight champion, could take a man out with either hand but he was a counterpuncher. And smart? If Toledo ever went fishing, the fish would catch him. If your boxing commissioner, Lewis Merriam were not an Olympian buffoon, he would never have sanctioned such a mismatch."

"Why do you say that?" Bloody Mary was on her feet again, ignoring the wails of her male colleagues. Devon seemed delighted to resume the dialogue.

"Their styles were wrong, my dearest. A counterpuncher will not throw the first punch, he waits for the other fellow to strike. Then *he* strikes back. It's a highly specialized technique. My tiger's only wish was to avoid getting hit. The idea of initiating any unpleasantness distressed him, for these things can spread. He ran like a thief, while Toledo stood flat-footed in the middle of the ring and urged him to come in and get hit. Rocky waved at Lefty a few times as he whizzed past but, except for that, there was little action. This displeased the patrons."

"Didn't you tell your boxer to fight?" Mary protested. "He was paid to fight, wasn't he?"

"I told him to get on his bicycle and stay on it. If Toledo ever hit him, he would never be the same again, my little swan."

"Then why did you agree to the contest," Mary retorted.

"Lefty was a spar boy. A nice kid, but no talent. He was making fifty a week. Toledo had flattened his last nine opponents, which caused some reluctance among prospective victims. When the promoter asked for Lefty,

67

I pushed the price to $3,500. Lefty was ecstatic, fair lady."

"Will you please stop that 'fair lady' crap?" Mary spoke with annoyance. "I'm a newspaperman."

"My dear, yield to an old man the privilege of chivalry," Devon spoke with paternal solicitude. "And don't repudiate your natural advantages. In boxing, we had an axiom: Go to your strength. If you're a puncher, punch. Don't seek to deny your evident beauty, my child. Would Shakespeare or Shaw have written their plays about Cleopatra, Ace Reporter?"

The writers, who had heard Bloody Mary's outbursts before, braced themselves. She said nothing. She stood for a moment, bemused. Then she sat down. The shadow of a smile softened her unrouged lips.

"Cut it, Dan," Hall intervened. "The odds on Toledo could have been a thousand-to-one. Lewis Merriam says you rigged the fight and cashed bets with both hands. How about it?"

Devon reached into the manila envelope and removed a handful of thick sheets.

"You accuse me of something worse than dishonesty," Devon said. "This is stupidity. Let me show you. A friend went to the library for me this afternoon and made me photo copies of the pre-fight stories of all the major writers who covered that match."

He handed out all the sheets, except one.

"All these writers picked Toledo by a knockout. The consensus was that Lefty wouldn't last four. You will note that the odds were twenty-to-one that Lefty wouldn't go the distance.

"There was so much money offered on Toledo by a

kayo that nobody would book it. If you wanted to bet my tiger would go the full route, you could get sixteen-to-one. At those odds, who would pick Lefty to win? Your bookie wouldn't give you better than sixteen-to-one if you wanted to bet the sun would rise in the West." Devon handed the last sheet to Hall. "I didn't think Toledo would ever catch my tiger, and he didn't. The odds on Toledo by a knockout were a tempting overlay. This was like finding money."

"The writers didn't think so," somebody yelled. "Donnigan, Hirt, Tomkins—they all called it Rocky by a kayo inside of four."

"Not everyone," Devon demurred. "One man called the turn exactly. He said Rocky should never have taken the match, because there was no way he could catch my tiger. Right, George?"

"Right," Hall agreed, staring at the sheet Devon had given him.

"One writer," came another voice. "Who? Some second stringer, I'll bet."

Hall wheeled in a cold rage.

"Who?" Hall growled. "Davey Gordon, the greatest fight writer I ever saw. That's who. Dan is right. That was an overlay. A sucker bet. If Dan saw it, more power to him."

Dan knew he had them.

Hall stared at the page for another moment before he muttered, "Thank you, Dan," but reporters were already hurrying to the phones.

Then Devon went before the TV cameras and recited his story of injured innocence. After that, he was ready for the radio boys.

Hal Smith got to Devon first, but Kensington broke in, grabbing his arm.

"Over here, old timer," Kensington yapped. "You don't mind, do you, Hal? I can't waste any more time out here."

Devon stiffened and tried to pull his arm away but Hal shook his head.

"I'll wait, Dan, as long as the bar is open."

Kensington hustled the old man to the other side of the room where he had set up his tape recorder on a card table. He half-pushed Devon into a chair, and sat down beside him.

Kensington grinned at Devon's bewilderment. As he turned on his recorder, the thrusting young man advised Devon: "I don't go for this party-line garbage, pop. I've got a few questions, and you better have the straight answers."

Devon looked confused and helpless. Gus felt a momentary twinge of compassion for Kensington.

"All right, old timer, we're on," Kensington said. Then he began: "I have here at the Ten-Star microphone Dan Devon, the storm center of the raging controversy at the Treasure City Race Track. Now, Danny boy, I want the truth. Commissioner Lewis Merriam has stated flatly that you fixed a fight here ten years ago. This is a serious charge. I know Mr. Merriam—he doesn't say such things without reason. You've denied it, of course, but I want hard proof. What about it?"

"I made a formal statement," Devon stumbled. "At the press conference, I mean . . ."

"Don't stall," barked Kensington. "Give. Can you prove that you didn't fix that fight?"

70

"I made a statement at the press conference. I don't see why I must pursue it further."

"You don't huh? Well, I'll tell you. Because I'm Marty Kensington and I am famous for digging up the story behind the story. I never settle for press conference poop. Last year when the Wolves hired their new manager, I got the story twenty-four hours before they made it official. You know why? I threw away the press release with that garbage that they had no intention of firing their old manager. I did the kind of detective work for which I'm famous. I worked, and how! I worked without stopping for six days and six nights . . ."

"I remember you now," Devon broke in. "On the seventh day, you rested."

Dan had discarded the camouflage. The contempt in his voice cut like a lash.

"You old creep," Kensington yelped, "I'm taping this . . ."

"You talk a lot, son," Devon replied softly, "But nobody listens."

"Listen, you old crock, you're not going to make me sound like a damn fool!"

"The way you bray, buster, you don't need me. In an earlier broadcast today, you stated that I fixed a fight. In your next broadcast, you will retract that slander and make a suitable apology, or I will begin legal action at once against you and your station. I'll sue, although I recognize the risk—I may end up owning your scabrous little station and your pitiful little contract."

Devon rose and, without a backward glance, sought out Hal Smith.

"That ties it!" bellowed Kensington, slamming his fist

down so hard Gus feared the shaky card table would collapse. "That old fool can't treat Marty Kensington this way."

"Devon likes you," offered Gus. "Just keep yapping about fixed fights. You'll make him rich."

Kensington studied the jaunty old man in disbelief. "He wouldn't dare," he muttered.

"He'd dare," Gus said. "Nothing awakens his lust for combat like the smell of easy money."

EIGHT

WHEN A PRESS AGENT has a client like Dan Devon, he prays he can get to the papers with the first indignant denials before they print the first outraged accusations. And that is the way it was this time.

Lewis Merriam, the politicking boxing commissioner who wanted to finish Devon off, committed a public relations gaffe. His timing was bad. He set off his blast in the early afternoon when the afternoon papers had put the last edition on the presses, sports broadcasts were at a minimum, and the evening papers wouldn't be on the streets for another six hours. He shouted into a vacuum.

Gus held his press conference at 4 P.M., in ample time to make the evening papers and the rush of early evening sports shows. He liked to think of the folks who would learn that Dan Devon was innocent before they knew that anybody had thought he was guilty.

Devon swept the boards in his confrontation with the press. The whole newspaper, radio, and TV corps, led by crusty George Hall, rose up in his defense, perhaps delivering a fatal blow to the notion that honesty is the best policy.

Even Marty Kensington, whose earlier broadcast had started the furor, spoke peevishly of the boxing commissioner. Did Lewis have any proof of his charges against Devon? In all fairness, Kensington felt impelled to say that he had not seen any. Therefore he must exonerate Devon and apologize for Lewis Merriam's conduct. If the commissioner had any proof, Kensington orated, now was the time to come forward with it. Otherwise, his irresponsible behavior served only to embarrass those who, like your Ten-Star reporter, fought constantly for honesty in sports.

Patrick O'Sullivan, the reluctant dragon who held the racing commissionership, ventured out of hiding some time after midnight with a pious announcement that dismissed Lewis Merriam's attack as a cowardly attempt to discredit the high standards of horse racing under the enlightened Liberal regime. He was sorry, O'Sullivan said, that he had not learned of Merriam's contemptible trickery earlier.

Of course, not everyone was pleased. Doug Dye called. He spoke more in sorrow than anger.

"This Devon affair has been most unfortunate," he began. "The Treasure City Race Track has been smeared, and Mr. Jensen is outraged. I won't have any more of it.

73

Can't you understand, Gus? We simply cannot tolerate a notorious Devon at the track, even if we can't prove anything against him. He's no good. Throw him out."

"A man has a right to a fair chance, Doug. Where is your sense of justice?"

Dye boiled. "We've got a multi-million dollar account at stake, and you talk about justice."

He stopped. When he resumed, he was back to the soothing, well-mannered approach. "You can't have any conception of the damage you've done, Gus. Old J. C. abhors any association, however remote, with Devon's sleazy kind. You know how touchy these big executives are. And rightly so. What can I tell old J. C. when he asks me what the hell's going on at the confounded track?"

"Tell him it's out of your hands."

"Like hell it's out of my hands!" Dye roared. "My agency is spending almost a quarter of a million dollars to advertise that track. We're creating the image of the Treasure City Race Track as a showplace for the sport of kings, a classy place that appeals to the most distinguished and aristocratic sportsmen. I'm damned if I'll let a small-time press agent like you sabotage our campaign by publicizing that scabrous old bandit, Devon. You hear me! You cross me up one more time, and I'll put so much pressure on Buzz Randahl that he won't have any choice. He'll have to fire you."

A moment of silence, and then Dye resumed with more moderation.

"What's done is done, but we must have no more of this bumbling. Perhaps we shouldn't make a martyr out of Devon. Just ignore the bastard. You understand? He doesn't exist. I don't want you ever to put his name in print again. That is a direct order."

"You got to be kidding," Gus replied. "I can't drop Devon now. He's terrific copy. You should see the ink we're getting."

Dye was almost incoherent. "Your irresponsible behavior could alienate old J. C. and cost me the wole Twentieth Century account. Do you have any idea what this means?"

"Not really, but I'm going to keep the Dan Devon story hot."

"Don't challenge me!" Dye screamed. "You miserable little flack. You straighten out or you'll be out of a job and you'll never get another one in this town. I'll see to that."

He crashed his receiver down with such a bang that Gus's ears rang. He was still trying to shake the sound out of his head when Jay Mason walked in.

"You did it," he said, with calculated zest. "You saved Devon. Congratulations."

Gus studied his smiling, candid countenance. This boy, he thought, never quits.

"I didn't do it, Jay. Devon did. He called the signals."

Mason winked broadly. "If you say so," he grinned. "Now that Devon is out of the way, I suppose we can all get back to work preparing for our opening."

"I'm not through with Devon and Rustling Breeze, chum. Devon is a gold mine of publicity. With a little luck, I can keep the story alive for weeks."

Mason shook his head. "Devon means nothing in horse racing. He's just a nickel-and-dime operator."

75

"Devon is many things, Jay, but a nickel-and-dime operator he isn't. He doesn't believe they mint such coins." Gus took off his glasses and tapped them against his teeth. "I see it now, Jay. Rustling Breeze, the mystery horse. Has he really got a chance in the Colt Stake? Can old Dan Devon bring off the comeback of the decade? Can this obscure little horse, which has never been to the post, beat the incomparable Horsepower? Tune in tomorrow for the next thrilling chapter in the Dream of Everyman. That will do it, Jay."

The young man looked so baffled it had to be genuine.

"We're going to hide the colt at Dean Hewitt's farm near here, Jay. Hewitt's place has first-rate training facilities, including a mile track. We'll bar all newspapermen. Devon can hint at new training methods which will revolutionize racing. Dan's the best at that sort of thing. We'll whip up a frenzy of speculation. We'll have everyone talking about the colt, and the Colt Stake."

"It's too far out," Mason balked. "And Oakley will never go for it. Do you know why he picked this track?"

"Sure. He was taken off Pioneer Pride, the winner of the Stake in '29. All his life, he's wanted another chance to take the Stake. And now . . ."

"Moonshine," Mason cut in. "Oakley knows better. Rustling Breeze hasn't got a prayer in the Colt Stake, but Oakley doesn't care. This track has an exceptionally attractive stakes program for state foals. He thinks he can win some money in the statebred races. That's what brought Oakley here."

"I'll talk to Devon, Jay. He'll understand. This is publicity—creative stuff."

"Oakley won't go along."

"What does Oakley know about publicity? He's fallen in love with that colt. He brought that silly Bumbling Bertie along just so Rustling Breeze would have somebody to talk to, didn't he? A man like that is too sentimental for this business."

"I've watched them work out, Gus. Listen, Oakley brought the five-year-old because he's a work horse. Rustling Breeze is lazy. The other horse sets the tempo. Oakley's giving you a snow job. Devon is, too."

"Devon I know," Gus assured Mason. "He's found an angel—a money-man. The longer he can keep Oakley thinking this colt can win, the longer Oakley will keep picking up his tabs. Dan doesn't want to get that colt beat any more than I do."

Mason threw up his hands helplessly.

"I think you're mistaken," he said, a little stiffly. As he turned to go, he almost bumped into Pierre, who was staggering under a load of lights, reflectors, and stands, plus his camera case. Mason made no move to help him.

"Hi, Gauthier," his voice was frosty. Pierre made no acknowledgment as Mason walked out.

"Some day," Pierre said, "I'm going to hit that big phoney right in the mouth."

"Do it some night," Gus suggested, "On *your* time. You're a big guy, Pierre. Six-foot-four, I'd guess. You must have six inches on Mason. That gives you a very unfair advantage."

"Yeah," said Pierre, "and that's the best kind."

"What have you got all that paraphernalia for?"

"I'm going to set up in the Paddock Room. Good background. I'm going to take some portrait studies of Devon.

77

Real arty stuff. Do you think Doug Dye would like a six-foot blow-up for the lobby of his place?"

"Dye would rather have a dead elephant in the lobby. Who ordered these shots?"

"Dan's been having a tough time trying to get a decent portrait. All the big New York guys have tried, and no dice. He asked me, as a special favor, to take the picture. He says I'm the best he's ever seen."

"That guy is a real con artist,"

"Who is?" Pierre responded absently.

When he showed up in mid-afternoon, Dan Devon was a model of conservative good taste. The rich tweed coat, the well-cut dark trousers, the custom-made shoes, the chaste white shirt, and simple silk tie—all bespoke the man who would be embarrassed beyond endurance if anyone guessed how much his wardrobe had cost.

"You did the impossible, Dan," Gus greeted him. "You made those reporters think you were innocent."

"The gentlemen of the press," he replied gravely, "are men of discernment."

"They were impressed. One of the radio guys said he thought you were a little bit precious, but Hall said you were magnificent and most of the boys agreed."

"A little bit precious?" Devon answered. "Who said that?"

When Devon met Nancy, he responded with a courtly bow.

"The pleasure is mine, my dear. You light up this office with your radiance. Nothing is more beautiful than a beautiful girl."

She flushed.

Then Gus introduced him to Mason.

They surveyed each other wordlessly. Dan's cold blue

eyes bored into Jay. The young man stared back without wavering.

"How do you do, sir?" Jay said finally, in a flat, noncommital way. "I'm happy you're going to race here."

"I'm sure you are," Devon returned dryly. That ended the conversation.

"Where did you find that one?" Devon asked when they were back in Gus' office.

"Jay? He's a worker, and he knows the name of the game."

"Perhaps, but let me give you some advice. If you're ever walking up a dark alley with him, don't let him get behind you."

"Sit down, Dan. Remember how we built up Lefty Hernstein for the Toledo fight? The secret workouts? We wouldn't let the reporters in, and it drove them crazy. Remember?"

"If anybody had seen Lefty train," Devon mused, "we wouldn't have filled a phone booth for the fight."

"Exactly. Let's give Rustling Breeze the same treatment. People are wondering if he can run. Let them wonder. We'll hide him out at a farm near here, a place with excellent facilities . . ."

Devon held up his hand.

"Hold it, Gus. I've got news for you. Can we still catch the *Herald-Chronicle?*"

"What news?"

"Rustling Breeze will go to the post for the first time in his career in the $10,000 State Inaugural Sprint on opening day."

"Oh, no! You're lousing up the publicity story of the year."

Dan never looked cockier. "In this business, Gus, how

79

much you make depends on how much nerve you have," he said. "Don't worry. When they hit the wire in the Inaugural, Rustling Breeze will be there, or thereabouts."

"But, Dan, if he loses, we're dead."

Dan beamed. "Don't worry, everything is going to be all right," he gave Gus his baby stare. "You know, Gus, you can trust Dan Devon."

He rose to go. Then he turned back to the press agent. "One more thing, Gus. Which radio guy said I was a little bit precious?"

NINE

Gus SHOWED UP early at the party which the Treasure City Race Track throws for the radio, TV, and newspaper colony on the eve of its opening day. Dan Devon, however, was there before him, the gracious host, bidding the guests partake of his humble hospitality. By ten o'clock, a visitor had actually mistaken Devon for the president of the track. By midnight, a dozen guests had thanked him for a wonderful party.

This was a considerable achievement, since Dan hadn't even been invited. Dye had insisted upon removing his name from the guest list over Gus's strong protests.

"You're coming to the party, aren't you, Dan?" the

press agent had asked him earlier in the day, knowing Buzz wouldn't throw Dan out once he got there. "I didn't bother with an invitation," Gus told Dan, "because you know I want you to come."

"Of course, I'll come." Dan answered. "Nothing could keep me from your little bash."

Nancy was serving as the publicity department hostess, handling the protocol of seating so many people who were so sensitive to affronts. They never found it easy to become angry with such a beguiling girl. Gus tablehopped for a while, greeting the assembled writers, editors, horsemen, and track officials.

Gus had reserved a table for himself, George Hall, Connie O'Toole, and their wives. As they started on their second cup of after-dinner coffee, Hall remarked:

"Look at Devon. An amazing man, and nothing is more amazing than the fact that he has lasted so long, the way he used to abuse himself. He's closed his share of blind pigs. My share, too, and yours. When he was thirty years younger, Gus, I never saw the man who could stay with him. He never slept.

"Some people know how to make it, and some know how to spend it, but Devon is my all-time champion, going both ways. He could make it, and he could spend it, better than anybody I ever knew."

Hall lighted his pipe, leaned back comfortably and continued. "I remember the time just after Hurricane Harrison had defended his title for the sixth time. Those were Devon's big days. I was in New York for the World Series and he asked me to come over to his hotel. He thought he had a story for me.

"He had the sixth floor of the Washington Arms, and

you know what a posh place that was. I found Devon and Hurricane, giggling like a couple of school girls. They had gathered together a million dollars in canceled checks and dumped them in the bath tub. They were going to burn the paper, and they thought I might make a column out of it. A million dollars! How many girls, how many gifts, how many all-night parties is a million dollars? We'll never see days like that again."

Hall gazed broodingly into the muddy residue of his coffee. "Now he's trying to hustle for a couple of fourth-rate horses. Two goats that have never won anything, and never will. It's pitiful."

"It is sad," offered Yvonne, Connie O'Toole's wife. "He's outlived his generation, and his productive years. Can you imagine a man with his pride in a home for the aged and indigent? When I was a little girl, my very favorite uncle spent his last years in a poor house. That's what we called it then. He was a handsome man, always careful about his appearance. He had gorgeous white hair, thick and beautiful. When he went to the poor house, they shaved his head. They robbed him of his dignity as a man. I cry even now when I think of it." Her voice trailed off. The others sat in uncomfortable silence.

"When he had it, Dan would have picked up the tab for this party," Gus observed. "He would have been insulted if we didn't let him. Now he's a free loader. He wasn't even on the guest list tonight."

"What is he really up to?" Connie O'Toole mused. "What's his angle?"

"This is just the best he can do," Gus explained. "It beats shilling for a ratty water carnival, even if that's all it beats."

82

"I think you underestimate your man," Connie returned. "The obituaries may be premature. And now, I could use a drink."

Gus went to get the drinks, which wasn't easy since the thirsty were packed five deep around the counter. Getting back through the throng was even more difficult. He might have lost the whole tray of drinks but for Dan Devon's nimble intervention.

"I'll give you a hand, Gus," he said as he steadied the tray. "You can't manage this tray and the crowd, too."

They were almost back to the table, with Dan carrying a couple of glasses, when Randahl and Dye overtook them.

"Hey, Scott, I've got a dandy item for you," Dye's face was flushed, and he was almost friendly.

"We got Ol' Ham Caulk at our table, Ol' Ham himself. Vice president of Twentieth, you know. Sales. He's a keen student of racing, and he says Horsepower is the best ever. Ol' Ham says Horesepower will win the Colt Stake all alone. No sweat. Great item for some columnist, huh? You want to take notes?"

"Sure. You hold the tray."

"You'll remember," Dye decided, backing away. "Give it to one of those chatter columnists. They'll eat it up."

"I don't believe you've met my friend." Gus said politely. "Doug Dye, this is Dan Devon. You remember Buzz, Dan?"

Randahl waved amiably, but Dye stared past Devon with stony alcoholic dignity.

Without acknowledging Gus or Devon, Dye began to recite: " 'It is a tale told by an idiot, full of sound and tumult, signifying nothing.' By my favorite copy writer,

Buzz, a fellow named Will Shakespeare in a little something he tossed off called *Hamlet*."

" 'Sound and fury,' " Devon amended negligently. "*Macbeth*."

Dye wheeled on the old man.

"I won't stand for any more of your meddling, you old pirate!" he grated. "I'm going to create a new image for the Treasure City Race Track, and I'm going to do it in spite of you and Scott. I'm going to make this little track the jewel of the turf."

"How can you manage it," Devon mocked, "with nothing but brass?"

"I'll show you: I'm laying out an advertising campaign that will present Treasure City as the new showplace of the true, authentic sport of kings."

"The true sport of kings? Then you'll rename the track, of course," Devon responded icily. "Call it The Madame Pompadour. Or call it the other sport of kings."

Dye appealed to Randahl. "Buzz, this person is intolerable. He's a dirty-minded, sleazy fraud. How can you hang this albatross around my neck and still expect me to maximize your advertising and public relations program? I've had enough, Buzz. I say this Devon goes."

"And I say he stays," Gus countered. "He stirs things up. If we did things your way, Dye, we'd kill the Colt Stake build-up stone cold dead in twenty-four hours."

"Devon can take this sorry hack with him, Buzz," Dye bellowed. "As a press agent, Scott is a walking disaster. He has no class, no taste. He's a low carney pitchman in a tab-collar shirt. He's a buffoon, and his public relations department is a joke."

"Now, that's quite enough, Doug," Buzz doesn't lose

84

his temper often, but when he does you know it. "You are my guest tonight, and so is Mr. Devon. We can pretend we're civilized. Let's get back to the table, Doug. Come, please."

"Rustling Breeze is a nice looking colt, Dan," Buzz flung over his shoulder. "He may win a race or two for you. I hope he does."

Devon watched his departure through half-hooded eyes.

"So that's Doug Dye," he remarked, with obvious satisfaction. "I should have given him strokes."

"Sure, you're the wit of the week," Gus seethed. "I stick my neck out for you when he says you have to go, but you clammed up when he got the idea that I should go, too."

"It isn't the same thing," Devon said, reflectively. He looked at me as though he were seeing me for the first time.

"We both said too much, you and I," he went on. "I shouldn't have baited him. If I have a weakness, it's that I sometimes talk too much."

"Aaaah, you were afraid to open your mouth when he started swinging at me."

"No. I'm going to settle with that man. He'll wonder how his throat got slit."

"Yeah, yeah. Tell me what you're going to do."

"Gus, did you ever think what a wonderfully lethal creature the rattlesnake would be if he had any brains? He could control the world if he would forget that idiotic rattle and get on with his work."

By midnight, half of the crowd had melted away but the remaining merrymakers had doubled the din. One fellow was nearly decapitated by a flying glass and a few inept fist fights broke out but these were only incidents in the mounting revelry.

Nancy, freed from her earlier duties as publicity department hostess, was having a high old time. She is beautiful, Gus realized, just beautiful, and such a wonderfully graceful dancer. He liked to see her having fun.

Jay Mason was doing all right, too. He must have paid three hundred bucks for his Edwardian dinner jacket and his silk ruffled shirt. Whatever he paid, it was worth the price. He never looked more dashing. He danced every dance with a different girl, and every one was a stunner. He and Nancy were picture-perfect together.

Gus was through working. Hall, O'Toole, and most of the press had left. The little press agent realized he was tired. He saw Dan Devon at the bar, and moved beside him.

"Congratulations, Gus. This has been a perfect party. Perfect."

They leaned against the bar, and Gus ordered a double Scotch. The orchestra leader was at the microphone, saying how much he and the boys had enjoyed playing for such nice people. And now, he said, get your favorite partner. This is the last dance.

Gus saw Mason approach the table where Nancy was sitting. He got there first. She seemed to be trying to turn him away, but he wouldn't be refused. He took her hand and gently pulled her, half-protesting, to her feet. He led her to the dance floor.

"That Mason is a hustler," Devon nodded approvingly. "Just like me when I was young. Always on the make."

Gus frowned. "Nancy didn't want to dance with him. She just did it to avoid a scene."

86

Devon smiled dreamily. "She wants," he said. "Can't you see, Gus, he excites her. He's got what every young man needs: animal magnetism. He can take her any time he wants her."

Gus slammed his glass down angrily on the bar. "Like hell!" he exploded. "She'd never marry him."

Devon's glance was a weary rebuke. "Perhaps not," he said, "but in two weeks he'll be laying her."

TEN

THE PADDOCK ROOM was crowded with the usual opening-day throng of society names, track officials, horse owners, and politicians. Buzz was standing at the bar, alone for the moment. Gus went to him.

"Buzz, keep Dye off my back," he demanded. "He doesn't have a damn thing to do with the publicity, and neither does anyone else except me."

"That isn't quite the case," Buzz said mildly. "Read your contract. Everything is spelled out very clearly. I make the final decisions on publicity policy, and you carry them out. That's what the contract says."

The little press agent started to protest, but Buzz checked him. "Don't get excited, Gus. I'm not hard to get along with. I don't see any big conflict between you and Dye. He can advertise the sport of kings and you write about the two-dollar bettors, and we'll get 'em going and coming."

Buzz finished his drink before he continued.

"I will be damned . . ."

"Simmer down, Gus. Dan Devon has caused the fuss between you and Dye, and Devon is through. This is the day his bubble bursts. By nightfall, he will be finished as far as publicity goes. You and Dye will have to find something else to fight about. I know at least three colts in today's Inaugural that will measure Devon's bay. He's gone as far as he can go."

"Suppose Devon's colt wins?"

"He won't," Buzz replied. "He won't be in the money."

Gus felt stirred, as always, when the bugle sounded for the post parade for the first race. The start of another season! The handsome animals walked proudly down the racing strip in front of the grandstand, disdainful of the eager handicappers who lined the rail to search for some occult sign that defined a winner.

The coats of the sleek thoroughbreds shone in the golden sunlight, a gentle breeze ruffled the gaudy silks of the solemn little men they call boys as they swayed in easy balance on their hazardous perches. The newly painted plant, even the artificial petunias in the infield, were enchantment under the warm sun. For just a moment, a man might wonder if the two-dollar window was all there is to horse racing.

The mood was broken, however, when Gus noticed the number eight horse shuffling along in the post parade, stepping as though his shoes were too tight. Bumbling Bertie was going in this one.

"Cal Oakley insisted upon entering him," Devon had explained. "He doesn't want any underprivileged horses. He says Bumbling Bertie likes people, and he wouldn't think of keeping him in the barn on opening day."

Gus was pondering this when track announcer Gary Mills called: "They're off!" Nine horses charged out of the gate and another season was under way. This was only a six-furlong sprint, but Bumbling Bertie seemed intent upon lapping the field. As the field fled down the backstretch to the far turn, Bumbling Bertie began to lose air speed coming out of the far turn. His pursuers overtook him as they straightened out for the run to the wire. He was done. He stumbled in ninth in a nine-horse field, a dozen lengths off the pace.

Bumbling Bertie was in the wrong business. How could any animal dissipate a six-length lead and come in last by a dozen lengths against these platers, and all in six furlongs? Yet Devon was undisturbed when Gus found him sunning himself on the bench across from the paddock area.

"Bumbling Bertie doesn't understand the game," Devon allowed. "Don't tell him. He might brood."

"He wouldn't believe me," Gus answered. "There is a horse that a man can trust. He looks ridiculous, and he is ridiculous. I hope Rustling Breeze will know what he came for."

"You'll see, Gus. Say, isn't that Manny Goldblatt over there? I haven't seen him since he worked in Toledo's corner for the Hernstein fight."

"That's Manny, all right. I'm going to say hello to him, and I'll tell him you're here. Good luck."

Manny was in a huddle with a punter Gus had never seen before. And he wasn't a man you'd be likely to forget, not with that enormous head, the thick glasses, the stooped shoulders, and those unbelievable high-laced shoes.

"Hey, Bubblehead, here's the track PR guy!" Manny whooped as he joined them. "He wants to interview you, Bubblehead."

"Me? An interview? For the papers? Oh, heavens, I couldn't. I'd die." He was gone like a frightened fawn. Manny chuckled.

"That's Bubblehead," Manny explained. "Publicity scares him to death. This is the first time I've seen him, and he don't make sense."

"He don't, uh, doesn't?"

"Nah! He's some kind of a nut. He comes up, and he's asking a million questions about the ponies, but he says he never buys a ticket. He just makes mind bets, I guess."

"That sounds reasonable, Manny. If he never bets, he always ends up even. I've heard of worse systems."

"Agh, what fun is that? A guy is going to be that chintzy, he might as well stay home."

Bubblehead was soon lost in the crowd, but Gus hadn't seen the last of him. Indeed, nobody in the tumultuous meeting caused him more grief before it was all over than Bubblehead did, but the little press agent had no way of foreseeing that. He couldn't read the future, which is the next best thing to not being able to remember the past.

Gus returned to the press box for the State Inaugural Sprint. Rustling Breeze was going to the post for the first time. This he had to see.

The betting was crowding the all-time high for an opening day. The crowd was pouring it in for the Inaugural Sprint, too, but the speculators were leaving Rustling Breeze alone. And no wonder. The colt had never been to the races.

As Gary Mills announced "The horses are nearing the starting gate for the eighth race," Rustling Breeze was thirty-five-to-one. In the last minute, just before they shut off the betting line, he fell to eighteen-to-one. Devon, Gus imagined, getting in with all he had.

He has made worse bets. Rustling Breeze never gave him an uneasy moment. Wade Hampton Parkinson just sat there, as though he were in a rocking chair. He waved his whip a couple of times and it was all over. Rustling Breeze won by four open lengths, and he hardly seemed to be trying.

A couple more like that," said O'Toole, "and that Rustling Breeze could make a believer out of me."

Half a dozen papers had requested special coverage on the opener, so Gus pitched in and split the job with Jay Mason. He had to admire his new assistant's cool efficiency under deadline pressure. He could bat out the copy.

Gus waited after the last race for the final attendance and mutuel figures to add to the stories. Then he finished sending the copy. That is how he happened to be there when the attendant brought up the unexpected libation for the press.

"Champagne, compliments of Mr. Devon," he bawled as he put the two cases on the floor.

"I been working here for fourteen years, and I never seen anything like this before," said Johnny, the bet runner. "The other owners, they don't even send up beer."

"Devon is different," Gus explained. "He has this trick he does with money. He spends it before he gets it."

ELEVEN

DAN DEVON closed the book, stretched luxuriously, and leaned back in the great overstuffed chair. Reading was the one thing for which Dan Devon would have given thanks, if he had known whom to thank.

The old man rose stiffly, tugged his attache case out from under the bed, and pulled out a thick manila folder. He put on his bifocals, an indignity which he could endure in the privacy of his own room. Then he sat at his desk, in the muted opulence of his hotel suite, scanning the closely typewritten sheets.

These fishing expeditions cost money, and most of the time they didn't turn up a useful thing. The occasional discovery, however, was worth it all. These gave a man leverage when he would perish without it.

Nothing on Buzz Randahl. The man had an incredible fondness for wild bets, and it was more than a publicity device, but who didn't know it? The racing commissioner was an oaf, but incorruptible. The public doesn't mind if its officials are weak-minded, mused Devon, as long as they are honest.

Chalky had found nothing on Cal Oakley. The trail is too cold for Chalky, Devon reflected. I could find something, but Oakley wouldn't like it if he knew I was probing his past. And right now I need Oakley.

The telephone's ringing interrupted his meditation. Marty Kensington, the Ten-Star-Flash radio reporter, was on the line. "I got your little, uh, communication, Dan," Kensington said. "Don't worry. I'll give you a great build-up. Indirect and subtle, the way you explained. And if that cheap slob Lewis Merriam gives me any more of his exclusives, just see what I do with it. But, Dan, I just don't like the check. I don't think I should cash it. This is, well, unethical."

"I do all my business by checks," Dan said firmly. "Cash the check, and spend it in good health. I won't talk. Hell, I wouldn't dare." He'll cash it, Devon thought as he hung up. And then I'll have him in my hip pocket.

The report on Jay Mason was interesting, and perhaps useful. If the kid is on the make, Dan reflected, that's his business. But if he tries to cut Gus Scott up, I'm making it my business. Gus is too soft for that young Turk, but I'm not.

As he stepped from the elevator into the lobby, Devon was debating where to eat. The Knockout Bar and Grill would be crowded with the newspaper boys, the horse players, and the remnants of the old fight crowd, all useful citizens, Dan acknowledged, but not tonight. I can endure their banalities four nights in a week, but five nights is just too much.

"I'd like a nice, quiet place to eat," Devon told the cab driver. "Something with a touch of class. Refinement, my man, and dignity."

The cabbie recommended the dining room in the Wilton Plaza, and Devon found it acceptable. The paneled walls, the subdued lighting, the flickering candles, the aristocratic disdain of the maitre d'—these suited his mood.

The dinner crowd was gone, and the after-theater throng had not yet come. There was a scattering of late diners, and a big party in the far corner, but the room was more than half empty.

The maitre d' bowed him to a table on the side of the room with the big party, but they were too far away for Devon's failing eyesight to distinguish anyone. He waited with growing impatience for someone to take his order. He sat there for almost half an hour before he caught the attention of the maitre d' and suggested mildly that he had come to dine. Devon saw the maitre d' in earnest conversation with one of the waiters. He observed the latter's jerky, angry gestures. A waiter finally came from the other side of the room to take his order.

After he had finished the poached egg on toast and had drunk the warm milk, he had to summon the matire d' again to get a waiter to take his order for a cup of custard and a pot of tea.

"We're short of help tonight, sir," the waiter apologized when he brought the custard. "This isn't my station. Sorry, sir, that it took so long."

Devon ate the custard without appetite. The poor service had robbed the evening of its savor. They don't know who I am, he thought. They don't know who I am!

"Dan Devon, what a pleasant surprise! You're in the pink, sir!"

94

The old man looked up and surveyed Jay Mason, self-assured, handsome, the beautiful smile in place.

"I'm over at that dinner party," he waved toward the group in the corner. "We've got some important owners with us tonight. Big men, all of them, but when I saw you sitting here by yourself, I just had to say hello. I hope I'm not intruding."

"You're not," said Devon. "Can I buy you a drink?"

"Thanks, but I can only stay a second. This is rare luck. I've been wanting to have a little private talk with you."

"Talk, son."

"I can't tell you how pleased I am at the way things have worked out. It would have been a rotten shame if you couldn't race here. Mr. Dye says he's glad you're here. You know, Doug is a very generous man. He never carries a grudge. He's too big for that. He's just a sweet, lovable guy."

"Yes, Jay," Devon agreed, "as lovable as leprosy."

"Oh, he ruffled your feelings, Dan. Forget it. That's just his way. He has spirit."

"Ah, yes," nodded Devon. "The fiery spirit that can turn a defeat into a disaster."

Mason reddened. "Vaudeville is dead, Devon. Let's not try to revive it. I just want to tell you that Mr. Dye hopes you do well. And you will, if you stick to those statebred races, where you belong."

"I didn't come here to beat those statebreds, Jay. Rustling Breeze is going to win the Colt Stake."

Mason threw him a conspiratorial wink. "You don't have to feed me that line, Dan. I'm your friend. Let me give you a little advice. Forget the Colt Stake, and stop popping off about how Rustling Breeze will beat Horsepower. That will just get you into trouble."

Mason was still smiling, but his voice was cold and harsh. Devon listened with icy dignity.

"No dice, kid. I'm pointing Rustling Breeze for the Colt Stake. Nothing will change my mind."

"No? I think something might. Those rubber checks you wrote when that swimming show of yours was folding in Oklahoma, for instance. Tssk. Tssk. Most imprudent. I know, Oakley bailed you out, but it was a close thing, wasn't it?"

As Devon listened in inscrutable silence, Mason pushed on. "And the Business Standards Association was on your neck for wilfully misleading advertising. You didn't think you could get away with advertising those bums as Olympic champions, did you? Careless, my friend, careless."

Mason's smile broadened. He put his hand lightly on Devon's shoulder. "You're still out of jail, Dan, but in horse racing that isn't enough. We like to feel our owners are above suspicion. You're living on borrowed time, here, Danny boy. If somebody rehashed those old scandals, I do believe the racing commissioner would take another look at your papers. I'm your friend, Dan. That's why I'm telling you this. I don't want you to get hurt. I'm giving you a break. Just stay out of the Colt Stake and quit shooting off your mouth, and you'll be all right. You better think I mean it, Danny boy."

Devon studied the empty custard cup. Then he pushed it away, folded his napkin and deposited it on the table. "May I congratulate you, Jay? You are more thorough than I had realized. I like to see a man who does his homework, although it must have been simple enough. What did you do, call the newspaper in Bloody Hatchet? Isn't it curious, Jay, how few men would have had that much initiative?"

The two men measured each other. Their eyes met and held.

"I like you, son, but let me give you some advice: Never underestimate the other man. I could be fatal." Dan waved to the maitre d' and motioned for his check. Then he resumed. "I read the story Gus got out when he hired you. Worked in the racing secretary's office, patrol judge, clerk of the scales, and, finally, publicity. Minor inaccuracies, of course, but we'll waive them. But how did you ever forget your glorious military career?"

Mason, taut and alert, flexed his hands. The smile died. He said nothing.

"Your military career is news, Jay. Three months and two days in the infantry, wasn't it, including the time you spent in the brig? And then they found you guilty and drummed you out. You got off easy, at that. You could have done time at hard labor."

Mason was pale under his tan.

"Don't hustle me, kid," Devon spoke negligently. "You're not ready for the big times. Not yet."

Jay hesitated. Then he pushed back his chair and stood up. As he walked away, Devon swung around in his chair and called after him: "It's been nice talking to you. Enjoy your dinner."

When he turned around, Devon saw that the absent waiter had come to the table for the first time that night.

"Do you wish anything else, sir?" the waiter asked.

Under Devon's unspoken reproof, he wavered. "I'm sorry I got tied up. Has the service been satisfactory, sir?"

"Service?" inquired Devon.

"Like I said, I'm sorry I couldn't take your order," the waiter spoke with angry defiance. "I had all I could do to take care of that party over there. They're special customers. They come first. Sorry, but that's the way it is. Your check, sir."

Devon dropped a hundred-dollar bill on the tray. When the waiter brought his change, Devon picked up the two twenties, the five and the change, leaving the fifty-dollar bill. Then, with a flourish, Devon removed the fifty and held it in his hand.

"I'm Dan Devon," the old man explained. "If I ever blunder into this upholstered morgue again, I want you to remember my name."

He held the end of the crisp fifty-dollar bill between his thumb and forefinger, and cooly shoved the edge into the candle's flame.

The waiter grabbed for the blazing bill.

"Watch out, sir! The money! It's burning! Here, let me . . ."

Devon pulled the half-consumed bill out of the waiter's reach and watched as the flame approached his fingers. Then he tossed the last burning scrap into the air. With a flick of his napkin, he dispersed the fiery ember into a myriad of gossamer wisps.

"Are you nuts!" the waiter yelled. "Fifty bucks! You burned it! Are you out of your mind?"

Dan arose and prepared to leave.

"If I had put that back in my wallet, my good fellow,"

he replied, "you might never understand how much I appreciate a little civilized attention when I come to dine."

The guests at the big party were calling to the waiter now, but he ignored them. He watched in gap-mouthed wonder until the dapper little man had disappeared into the outer lobby.

Dan Devon stood outside the hotel for a moment, breathing deeply of the warm night air. He tilted his hat at a jaunty angle, straightened his shoulders, and began to hum tunelessly.

He hadn't felt so good all day.

TWELVE

RUSTLING BREEZE was starting to make Gus read his own press handouts.

The little colt went to the post for the second time in the $12,000 added Simeon Butteridge Memorial on Saturay, June 20, twelve days after his victory in the Inaugural Sprint.

And he did it again. He broke on top, ran on the lead all the way, and won by three good lengths in 1:39. The time wasn't bad, since none of the other colts had mounted a challenge. The Butteridge Memorial is a mile test, but the added distance bothered Rustling Breeze not at all.

Duke Jones, the *Herald-Chronicle* turf writer, is not a man to give praise lightly. Yet he called Rustling Breeze the finest statebred he had seen in a dozen years.

A publicity campaign, of course, is many things, and they must all fall together. Now they were falling.

For on Sunday J. C. Jensen announced that he was sending Horsepower back to the races. The big colt had been taking it easy after sweeping the Triple Crown. Now, Jensen said, his brilliant three-year-old was rested and ready to go. Jensen revealed that he would enter Horsepower in the $100,000 added Continental Stakes in New Jersey on Saturday, July 4, two weeks away.

If he was satisfied with Horsepower's effort in the Continental, Jensen said, he would send his magnificent colt out again in the Colt Stake at the Treasure City Race Track two weeks later. No reservations, no qualifications, just the flat statement: if Horsepower was ready to run, he would go in the Colt Stake.

If we could sustain the fiction that Rustling Breeze might upset Horsepower, Gus thought, the publicity would come in a landslide. The prospect of an obscure little colt beating perhaps the greatest three-year-old of the quarter century could be the publicity story of the year.

And, so far, Rustling Breeze was doing his part.

Gus hadn't expected this, but he had dreamed about it. What he had never anticipated was what a publicity windfall Bumbling Bertie would be. This foolish-looking animal, which couldn't finish anywhere but last, was get-

THE DAY THE BOOKIES TOOK A BATH

ting almost as much newspaper space as Rustling Breeze.

This creature looked so little like a race horse, and he ran so little like one, that the wags in the press box claimed him for their own. They were enchanted by what he had done in the second race on the day of the Simeon Butteridge Memorial. The race was a $2,000 claimer for nonwinners in the past two years. Of course, nobody claimed him.

He came busting out of the gate like a fire-wagon horse and streaked to a five-length lead. After perhaps four furlongs, he ran out of speed again. He came stumbling in tenth in the ten-horse field, beaten by a horrendous nine lengths.

"The suspicion is growing that Bumbling Bertie could run backwards and win," wrote Duke Jones. "That's the way he runs—backwards. He's first at the start, when it doesn't count, and last at the finish, when it does. This equine perversity gives the railbirds reasons to think that The Bumbler is in the wrong line of work.

"To consider this odd animal seriously, we should note that he has raced in the bush for years, mostly in quarterhorse races. He has just one short burst of burning speed. We've heard that he is unbeatable at any distance up to three hundred yards, and we can believe it. But even a master saddlesmith such as Wade Hampton Parkinson can't keep Bumbling Bertie from running as though he were still in the bush."

Connie O' Toole devoted his entire Monday column to "Bumbling Bertie, dear to the legions of losers everywhere." Wrote Connie: "If you've ever walked into an open manhole, or tripped on your own shoelaces, or spilled Scotch on your wife's new gown, you must feel a rapport with Bumbling Bertie. He has a mission: to show that horses can be just as confused as people. I'm falling in love with him. We have something that ties us together —our feet hurt."

Things were going so well that Gus was sure it wouldn't last. He knew he was right when Buzz Randahl showed up, grim and subdued.

"I have shocking news for you, Gus. Just terrible news. I'm going to give it to you straight."

"What's wrong? Now, I mean?"

"Gus, you remember Tilden Fenby, the clerk in the racing commission office? Poor Tilden is dead. We have lost a loyal and cherished member of our little official family. He was killed a little after four o'clock this morning. He missed a turn on Highway 29, and he must have been doing a hundred. They had to use a blowtorch to get him out of the wreckage. Tragic. Just tragic."

Gus mumbled sympathetically.

"Well, don't sit there and grieve, Gus. I know how you feel, but we must carry on. Send telegrams to the radio and TV. Get out a release for the dailies and the wires. Let's hear it for Tilden."

"The city side has the whole story by now, Buzz. They don't need anything from us."

"This is a sports story, too," Randahl insisted. "Haven't you got a picture of me and poor old Tilden, such a nice quiet man. I think we had one taken four, maybe five years ago. I'm wearing a white sports coat. Write a nice piece, Gus. Quote me any way you want. You know what to do. Fix it up."

Then he put his hand on Gus' shoulder and gravely in-

formed him, "This is the way Tilden would have wanted
it."

Gus was deep in this unwelcome chore when Devon
came in, stepping jauntily. "I'm taking up a collection for
Tilden Fenby, the clerk in the racing commission office,"
Gus said. That seemed inadequate, so he added: "He's
dead."

Devon stopped short, perhaps nettled at this unfair
competition for newspaper space. "Fenby, eh? They'll
have to hire pall bearers."

"Did you know him, Dan?"

"Of course. I never saw a meaner, surlier man." Devon's
face was a tight, inscrutable mask. He had seen so many
old companions cut down, and so many hated enemies.
Each time the blade swung closer to him, but he showed
no emotion. Just a cold, fixed smile.

"I think we should do something for him," Gus fumbled.

"Bury him in the infield, between the sixteenth pole
and the tote board."

Gus recoiled. "Aren't you going to contribute for
flowers?"

"For Fenby?"

"He wasn't a bad fellow, Dan. He must have had his
good qualities."

"He hid them well."

"Give me ten bucks. You can charge it to your everlast-
ing self-promotion."

Devon's dark eyes were cold and taunting. Then he
pulled out his wallet and began counting.

"This is a small, anonymous tribute to someone who

has come to a better life—his widow," he said. "I know Fenby. He didn't leave her a cent—and you can make book on that." He tossed the money to Gus. Five twenties. "Now, you can do something for me, Gus. I need two season passes." He could make such a request sound as though he were conferring a favor.

"Okay, Dan, but who wants them?"

"One of our bright young statesmen."

"I know you, Dan. A politician becomes a statesman when he goes on your payroll."

"Wrong, pal. A statesman is a politician who stays bought. Makes the passes out to Charlton Dressage. You know him. He's the deputy road commissioner. He runs the department."

An hour after the first race went off that afternoon, Gus went into the clubhouse for a sandwich. Connie O'Toole motioned to him.

"Sit down, Gus, and have a drink. You may need it."

Gus sat down, and ordered the drink. He needed it already.

"Have you heard the latest?" O'Toole asked. "Oakley and Devon have taken Parkinson off Rustling Breeze. He's burning, and he refuses to discuss it. You know how well I know Wade? Well, all I could get out of him was 'No comment.' How do you like that?"

"Wade needn't worry, Connie. He can get all the mounts he wants."

"Sure," nodded Connie, "but why did they take him off? He rides Rustling Breeze twice and wins big both times. No sweat. So they drop him. Why?"

"I don't know. I suppose they wanted to make a switch."

"Wade is an honest jock, Gus. He won't do business with just anybody. He keeps his nose clean."

"So what? Who's making any deals?"

"If I knew that, I just might have the story of the year," Connie spoke slowly. "I have this feeling that Devon is up to something, and getting rid of a jock like Wade is part of it. You know how Devon loves to wheel and deal."

"What are you putting in the knock on Devon for?" Gus asked irritably. "What have you got against him?"

Connie looked hurt. "I like Devon, Gus. He's the biggest patsy I ever saw. The hustlers don't even bother to give him a story when they hit him for money. They demand it. He can't refuse anybody."

Connie drinks his Scotch straight, and he savors the refreshment. Gus waited for him.

"He does favors for people who need help, and for those who don't," O'Toole resumed. "Did you know that he conned Randahl into hiring a bum named Robert Sens as a ticket seller? Why? Sens didn't need Devon. Not really. He's married to the only daughter of Charlton Dressage, the deputy road commissioner. Dan's trouble is that he has such difficulty with a simple word like 'No.'"

"He likes people, Connie, because that's what audiences are made of. I remember one night, just before the Hernstein-Toledo thing. I'm driving Dan to the Knockout Bar and Grill in a terrible snowstorm. All of a sudden, he tells me to stop.

"'Why, there's old Rod Stokley,' Dan says, and he's out of the car in a flash. I see this shabby little man walking slowly down the street, bending into the wind and snow. Then Devon is on him, clapping him on the back and shaking hands like this guy is his dearest friend.

"I see Dan stick a bill into the guy's coat pocket, talking the way he always does, with those delicate gestures. In three minutes, Dan is back in the car.

"I ask him who in hell Rod Stokley is and he says 'Don't you remember? He worked in the corner in the old arena in Philly. Your boy gets a little cut, and old Rod jumps into the ring between rounds and starts patching him up, and it's even money your boy will bleed to death.' I know what you mean about Dan."

"Yeah, it's pathetic, this compulsion he has to make people like him, Gus. But if he thinks he's going to throw a curve past me, it better be a good one. I tell you, Gus, something's cooking. I can't put my finger on it, but I know Devon is up to no good. You better take care, Gus, or you could be in a real mess. When it comes to money, Devon doesn't care who he hurts."

"I could be in a mess? What have I got to do with whatever Dan's cooking, if he's cooking anything."

"He's your man, Gus. You've defended him and you've built him up. If Devon comes up with a really audacious piece of thievery, the kind that has his trademark, nobody will believe you aren't in on it. You should pardon the expression, Gus, but you two have been thicker than thieves."

THIRTEEN

JAY MASON wanted to slip unnoticed from the track that morning, and he almost made it. He was within twenty feet of the parking lot entrance when he heard Dan Devon's mocking voice. "You're never going to cut it, son."

Mason suppressed a profane comment, turned, and smiled.

"Why did you let them do it, my boy?" Devon asked, motioning disdainfully toward the younger man's tan silk jacket.

"Do what?" Mason answered, not quite able to keep the irritation out of his voice.

Dan appeared lost in a study of Jay's coat. He lifted the sleeve with the controlled loathing of a housewife removing a dead mouse. "Your sleeves are creased, lad. Have you no sense of decency? Tell the cleaning establishment to roll your sleeves, son."

Devon dismissed the subject abruptly, with the air of a man who has managed an unpleasant duty. "I've been looking for you, Jay. I hoped we could talk."

"I'm, well, afraid I've been avoiding you, Dan. I'm just ashamed of myself, the way I talked to you that night at the Wilton Plaza. I'm not like that, really. I'm truly sorry."

"Young fellow, don't waltz me around," Devon spoke softly.

"Waltz you around Honestly, Dan. . ."

Dan shook his head sadly. "You think you can make it alone, Jay, but you can't. You need a friend or two. If Gus hadn't thrown me a lifeline here, I would have been sunk without a trace. Do you understand? If you get caught robbing the bank, a friend doesn't ask why you did it. He wants to know if you need bail money. You must have a friend, young man, and I'm always available for any disreputable purpose. I do not offer my friendship lightly."

Mason shuffled his feet and stared at the ground. "I don't know what to say, Dan. I don't deserve your friendship."

Devon permitted himself a slight shudder. "A friend," he said, "is an enemy who can do you a favor. Think it over, Jay. I'll see you around."

If I thought that old con artist would throw in with me, Jay reflected, I'd skip my luncheon date. He must have an angle, but what? Jay remembered the occasional fierce loyalties that the mention of Devon's name could bring to the surface. Not many, and not always the ones you'd expect, but those who were in Devon's corner were with him all the way. Gus Scott is simple-minded, Jay realized, but he'd go to hell for Devon.

Thinking this way, Jay knew, was dangerous nonsense. A man travels fastest when he travels alone. Jay drifted back to the dark day in the stockade when the little captain, with the tired lines under his eyes, had met him in the visitor's room.

"I've been assigned to defend you before the court-martial," the captain said, with distaste. "Why in hell did you do it? It wasn't any skin off your nose, you know. You do-gooders cause nothing but trouble, for yourself and everyone else."

This wasn't Jay's day. Devon's truce offer had caught him off balance, but the one who had really shaken him up was Nancy Kingsley. And just when I thought I was starting to make some headway with that broad, he reflected.

He saw her again, her face flaming with indignation. Why had she come in just in the few seconds he needed to riffle through Scott's mail?

Mason had known beautiful women before. Maybe not as beautiful as this one, but beautiful enough. They had all come around, but he wasn't getting to first base with this doll. And what a lay she would be.

"Are you looking for something?" she challenged, her voice edged with scorn.

"I'm expecting a letter," he said. "I thought it might be in Gus's mail, by mistake."

"Gus won't read it," she bit off. "He isn't interested in other people's mail."

"Oh, really, Nancy," he gave her his most incandescent smile, the one that is all sincerity. "Surely you don't seriously believe that I'd . . ."

She stamped out of the office. Even in her anger, she moved with a liquid grace that could make a man forget what the fight was all about.

When it came to that stupid Gus Scott, she was like a tigress defending her young. For a brief moment, Jay had wondered whether he had stumbled into an office affair, but he soon abandoned the idea. She was woman enough for it but Scott belongs to that curious breed that is completely absorbed in his own little job.

That's all he ever wants to be—Treasure City publicity director. I'd like that fine next year, Jay told himself, but when I'm his age I'll own the track, or something just as good. It's simply a matter of building up the right contacts and knowing when to move.

Jay knew he was right, but he was not happy in the knowledge. A girl like Nancy would never understand how things are in the jungle of free enterprise.

He tried to shake his uneasy mood as he wheeled into the parking lot of the Hidden Vista Golf and Country Club. This was the summons for which he had angled so carefully. Now he was almost sorry the call had come.

He had scarcely stepped inside the front door when the anonymous gray uniform was at his side.

"Good afternoon, sir. A very pleasant afternoon."

Jay realized that it was a question.

"I have a luncheon appointment with Mr. Dye. I'm Mr. Mason.

"Yes, Mr. Mason, Mr. Dye is expecting you. The dining room, on the second floor. The elevator is straight ahead. Your hat, please, Mr. Mason."

Another anonymous gray uniform guided him noiselessly across the almost deserted room. Dye rose at once and gripped his hand.

"You're punctual, young man. Good. I'm happy to see that the old-fashioned virtues survive. Jay, isn't it? Please be seated, Jay."

A waiter appeared at Mason's side with the biggest menu folder he'd ever seen.

"Reading that would take a week," Dye remarked. "I

recommend the Navy bean soup, and the steak sandwich is excellent. First, Jay, what are you drinking?"

"I'll pass, sir. Too early in the day."

"I'll have Scotch and water, Charles. Sure you won't join me? I dislike to drink alone. It's uncivilized."

"In that case, Scotch and water will do nicely, Mr. Dye."

"My doctor tells me I drink too much, Jay. And smoke too much, too. The damn quack! He smokes more than I do. Drinks more, too. Those medicine men want to take all the fun out of life."

He folded his hands and studied Jay for a moment.

"Can you tell me what in the bloody hell is going on at the track?" he growled.

Jay's smile tightened, but he said nothing.

"The situation is intolerable, Jay. I spend a quarter of a million dollars of the track's money to advertise Treasure City as a charming track with the highest standards and the most distinguished patronage. And your man Scott sabotages the whole campaign by publicizing the fact that one of the world's most notorious swindlers has horses there."

Dye offered Mason a cigar, but he declined. Dye lit his own before he resumed.

"There isn't room at Treasure City for me and Scott. One of us will have to go, and I promise you it won't be me. I'm going to take over that department. Publicity belongs under advertising anyway. Treasure City is the only client that separates the services, and I'm going to end that."

The drinks arrived, and Dye finished his quickly. "Do you know how much money I had when I started this agency?" he inquired. "Less than $10,000. Our billings today are the third highest in the industry. I refuse more clients than I accept. I've got the blue chip accounts. I've had Twentieth Century Motors for twenty-five years. Every other agency would cut our throats for the account, but we keep it because we produce.

"This means we keep J. C. Jensen happy, because he *is* Twentieth Century. Right now Scott is driving old J. C. right off his rocker with his yapping about that bastard Devon. Scott isn't a team man. He won't play ball."

"Give him enough rope, Mr. Dye, and he'll hang . . ."

"Enough rope! I won't give him *any* rope. I am going to destroy his attempt to build up Devon's sorry little colt. I'll put him out of business. Scott is going to find out that nobody kicks Douglas D. Dye around."

He had half-risen from his chair in his excitement, hammering the air with short, violent gestures. As the waiter brought another Scotch, he sat down and ordered luncheon. When the waiter left, he resumed his monologue.

"Do you know how I built this business? I brought in young men with brains and nerve. Tough, hungry young pros. We had a fire in our guts. After all these years, we still have it. That is why we grow in a business that is strewn with the wreckage of all those agencies that allowed dry rot to set in.

"I am not a much-loved man Jay. I don't need love. That you can buy. I want results. I hire men because they produce. And when they quit producing, I don't need them. I like the way you're gaited, Jay. You've got sand. I think there may be a place for you on my team."

He stopped, and Jay waited. Dye looked him over, like a poker player debating whether to raise or pass.

"I think you may be useful, Jay, but I'm not sure. One thing troubles me. You assured me that you could persuade Dan Devon to take his colt out of the Colt Stake. 'That harmless little old man.' I believe that was the way you described him. Well, you didn't produce. Why?"

"I tried, sir, but you see, his partner wants to win the Colt Stake more than . . ."

"Bah! Rubbish! Never give me excuses. I want facts. Why didn't you handle Devon?"

"Why didn't *you?*" Mason flared. "That harmless little old man is the coldest, shrewdest, toughest operator I've ever seen, and you know it. Nobody is going to talk him into anything without a gun at his head. And maybe not even then."

"That's better, Jay," Dye made grudging approval. "I don't want men who yes me all the time. You've got guts. Good, but have you got anything else? You asked to see me. Why?"

Dye spoke in a tone which indicated that the preliminaries were ended.

"Do you know an old-time fight character named Manny Goldblatt, Mr. Dye?"

Dye gestured for Jay to continue.

"Goldblatt may be just the man you need to give Gus Scott his comeuppance. Scott welcomes this Goldblatt into his office and consorts with him in public. Yesterday I saw them at the soft drink stand, laughing and kidding."

"Magnificent detective work, son," Dye's voice was acid. "He likes soft drinks. Great, but can you prove it?"

Now Mason's smile was touched with defiance. "But, sir, Manny Goldblatt is a professional gambler, a bookmaker. He makes his living betting on horse races."

Dye subsided at once into thoughtful silence. Mason continued. "In order for you to understand who Goldblatt is, I'll have to sketch in a background. He works for Honest Alfie Simpson, a loner and one of the biggest bookies in the country. Alfie always pays off in cash, and local legend has it that he can put his hands on two million dollars in an hour. He books some rather large bets.

"Manny runs bets to the track for him. You see, when bets are put down at a race track, fifteen percent of the amount wagered is siphoned off in taxes. The remainder goes into the betting pool. Track odds are computed by dividing the amount of money bet on a horse into the total pool. Do you follow me?"

"If the pool is $100,000 and $100,000 is bet on Twinkle Toes, the animal will return ten dollars for every dollar bet on him. The odds on Twinkle Toes are nine-to-one, and nine and one is ten. Okay?"

"A bookmaker, however, does not have the protection of the totalisator machine, which adjusts constantly so that the payoff will never exceed the amount of money in the betting pool, except in very unusual circumstances which do not concern us here.

"A bookmaker can take a beating if the wagers he accepts are not in reasonable alignment with the spread of bets at the track, remember—then he stands to lose $45,000 if Twinkle Toes wins.

"The bookie's only recourse is to send somebody out to the track to lay off enough money to drive the odds on Twinkle Toes down. He may not have to bet very much. Sometimes a relatively small wager at the right time can start a flood of bets on the horse."

Dye was leaning forward, listening intently. "And

that's what this Goldblatt does, eh, son? He carries the bets to the track for the bookmaker, and Gus Scott is his buddy? I think you have something, son."

"That's what Manny does, Doug. He will leave the track at intervals, go to phone somewhere near the track and call Honest Alfie for instructions. You see the possibilities?"

"For a betting scandal, Jay? Devon and Scott and Goldblatt? Beautiful, Jay, beautiful. I'm afraid I've underestimated you, my lad. But why does the track tolerate men like Goldblatt? I should think the track police would throw him out."

"They tell me that Buzz Randahl would never let a bookie inside the grounds, Doug, until two years ago. Then the Supreme Court handed down its ruling that it is a violation of a man's civil rights to refuse him admittance to any public place if he is behaving in, I believe the phrase was 'a proper and decorous manner.' So now Goldblatt can come and go as he pleases, and the track has no legal way of stopping him."

Dye rubbed his hands together. "I see, I see. If Devon and Scott are planning a betting coup, Goldblatt would be a very useful ally."

"He might doublecross his boss, or they might try to give him the shaft. In any case, if Devon is going to make a killing, he'll have to hit the bookies. They will accept bets at track odds, up to fifteen-to-one. You can make book on it, Devon wants those odds. He would be foolish to lay off his money at the track, for that could drive the odds down to one to five, the minimum the law allows, and that has to be a bad bet any way you look at it."

"Jay, my boy, your, uh, specialized knowledge is just

what we need. Keep digging. This sounds wonderful. Wonderful. We're going to hang that old pirate, Devon, and that smart-aleck Scott. We'll hang them, and dance on the corpses, and you'll be the new publicity director of the Treasure City Race Track. You have my solemn word."

"Of course, Doug, these things are very tricky. Solid proof is almost impossible . . ."

"I don't need a case that will stand up in court." Dye was exultant now. "Circumstantial evidence is enough. Buzz Randahl will be appalled at the slightest hint of scandal. He'll throw them both the hell out of here. All I want is a little imagination, a little creative ability, from you. Yes, indeed, that Scott is a very imprudent man."

The waiter served the soup, but neither seemed to notice.

"I must warn you, Doug, that this will take time. If we set a trap, we may have to wait until the Colt Stake before we can spring it. In the meantime, the publicity on Rustling Breeze could be hard to stop. What can I do there, Doug?"

Dye smiled, a hard, ugly smile. "I'm not worried about the publicity on Rustling Breeze," he said. "I've already attended to that. You can forget it. Just take care of Scott and Devon. They-ve challenged me for the last time. I want you to put them away. That's your assignment. Get rid of them."

"You can count on me, Doug, but I'm telling you Rustling Breeze will get a lot of ink if he comes up to the Colt Stake undefeated."

"Rustling Breeze is finished, Jay. No matter what that little horse does, everybody will see that the Colt Stake is just a one-horse race. Just a workout for Horsepower. I've got that locked up."

"How?"

"I'm going to hit Scott with one of the really magnificent public relations concepts of the century. He thinks he has ideas. Douglas D. Dye is the man who has ideas. I'll show that small time comedian."

"What are you going to do?"

"I hate to squander such brilliance on finishing off the Rustling Breeze publicity, but there's no help for that," said Dye. "Did you ever hear of Dr. Elliott Nichols?"

"A veterinarian?"

"A mathematical genius, a whiz kid of the brave new world. He is a scholar, a doctor of philosophy, and a teaching fellow at Lovecot College. He is also, in the great tradition of Greek tragedy, the nemesis of your smart-aleck boss."

"I don't follow you."

"You don't, but you will."

Dye chuckled. "Jay Mason and Dr. Elliott Nichols!" he said. "Gus Scott is going to curse the day he first heard those names. You, Jay, are going to take Scott down. And Dr. Nichols is going to make hay out of the Rustling Breeze publicity campaign."

FOURTEEN

THE GIRL WHO stood in the doorway was an encyclopedia of the distracting possibilities of the female architecture.

"Here I am," she revealed, batting her big blue eyes. "I'm the girl from the model agency. My friends call me Lem."

"Of course," Gus answered.

"Did you bring your bikini?" Pierre leered.

"Bikini?" The older man put in. "The next thing it will be topless bathing suits."

"What's wrong with that?" Pierre winked.

"In Bali, the girls go bare-chested, and it's very healthy," Lem said gravely. "They never have a cough."

"We aren't trying to cure the common cold," The PR man replied. "Did they tell you at the agency what we want?"

"We know what we want, don't we, Scottie?" Pierre laughed.

Lem giggled.

He started over.

"We hold a make-believe beauty contest each year to choose the girl who will reign as Miss Treasure City Colt Stake Queen," Gus explained. "You are the first candidate for this great distinction, and you have come out here to meet our track's president and learn something about horse racing."

Lem bubbled. "I just love beauty contests. Will I be the queen? Pretty please?"

"I'll take care of it," Pierre offered. "Just leave it to me."

"The first thing," Gus broke in, "I want to get pictures of you and Mr. Randahl, Lem. He is the president of the track and a very dignified gentleman."

She pouted. "He sounds stuffy."

"He is stuffy, and he owns this race track."

"I'll bet he's cute," said Lem.

He didn't sound cute when he called, just as Lem and Pierre were departing.

"Did you see that hippopotamus' head we just installed in the clubhouse lobby," he began. "I've had a lot of comments on it."

"From your interior decorator, perhaps?"

"Gus, this is a terrific trophy," Buzz declared. "An old friend of mother's took the hippo in Kenya last year. His white hunter said he'd never seen a specimen with more beautiful buttocks."

"Fine, thanks for the call," Gus said, grateful for the restraint that had impelled mother's friend to retain the head for a trophy.

"What do you mean, thanks for the call?" Buzz growled. "The generous donor doesn't want any money for the gift, so I told him we'd get him some publicity. Take care of it, will you?"

"Publicity? On that dumb hippo's head? How am I going to get any publicity on that?"

"You tell me, Gus. You're the publicity man. Just get this guy off my back, that's all."

So Gus asked Buzz to have Pierre call when he checked in with Lem. "Pierre, I want one more picture." he said. "You can use the model, but I don't want her to be recognizable. Just shoot a picture of her reaching up to touch the nose of that hippopotamus in the clubhouse lobby. I suggest you shoot from the rear."

"Will do," said Pierre. "That's her other good side."

Gus was so pleased with his inspiration that he had to tell somebody. Jay Mason was the only one around, so he told him. Jay was studying *The Daily Racing Form,* and he seemed to resent the intrusion.

"What did you say?" he asked. He seemed to be daring Gus to repeat it.

"Randahl is always saying that what this track needs are traditions; I'm giving it one. Know what we have in the clubhouse lobby? Harry the Happy Hippopotamus, the good luck charm of the Treasure City handicappers. The first thing a punter does when he arrives at the track, he rubs the hippo's nose and then he's walking around lucky. Great idea, eh?"

Mason muttered. "That thing has only been up one day, and it's so ugly nobody will go near it."

"They'll love Harry, as soon as they hear he's a lucky hippo. I'm getting out a general release on the new craze, with pictures."

"You don't think anybody is going to swallow that one, do you?" Mason sounded peevish.

"Of course, they will. So will the newspapers. They will know it has to be true, because nobody would invent such a fantastic story. That is a basic precept of the art of public relations. Never invent a story that is close to the truth. Editors will balk because, somehow, it doesn't hold water. If you're going to fake a story, make it an out-rageous fake. They will think it's the truth, because it's stranger than fiction."

Gus knew it was trouble when Nancy came in. Her mouth was a severe line, and she called him "Mr. Scott."

"You simply must do something about the Kiddie Tour, Mr. Scott," she remonstrated. "I won't let the children go out on Saturday unless we have a responsible, adult driver. I just won't. Two boys were lost near Barn 32 last Saturday; they could have been killed. The driver wasn't paying any attention, and they scooted off. You must get a responsible man to drive, Mr. Scott."

She was right. A thoroughbred race horse could be frightfully dangerous.

"I've tried everyone I can think of, Nancy," Gus answered, "but I'll find someone." He was wondering whom he could get when Lem and Pierre came bouncing in.

"Oh, that Petey is just terrible, Gus," Lem greeted him. Gus wondered how she had found out so fast.

"There was this poor man with the funny shoes, and Petey scared him to death. He is just awful."

"Old Bubblehead," Pierre explained. "You know, that oddball with the funny head and the high-laced shoes? He was talking to Manny Goldblatt, and I got this great idea. I told him we wanted a picture of Lem hugging him. She had just cashed a ticket, and she was so happy, see?"

Pierre was laughing so he had to pause for breath before he could continue.

"I thought the guy would die right there. He turned

eight different colors and then he just ran away. I mean, he was running for his life."

"Imagine, anybody being afraid of a little old girl." Lem babbled. "Lands, I wouldn't hurt anybody."

"We had such fun," she went on. "That Mr. Randahl was just a little old darling, and so young acting. And Petey had this divine idea. I put on one of those silk blouses the jockeys wear. I changed in the racing secretary's office, and all the boys were so nice. They didn't peek. Then Pierre took just oodles of pictures. I think you are the nicest people."

"We got some great art," Pierre admitted. "Lem's legs."

They started out together.

"Where are you going, Pierre?"

"Petey's going to take some yummy color shots of me, Gussie. For some old movie talent contest. Aren't you, honey?"

"I haven't got the lights for it here," Pierre put in hurriedly. "We're going to the studio."

Gus seized his elbow and escorted him to the other side of the room. "What studio?" Gus demanded. "We're paying that girl thirty dollars an hour."

"She's worth more," Pierre replied. Gus had this feeling he wasn't getting through. As they walked out, Pierre whispered to Lem.

"Oh, you're just awful, Petey, darling," she giggled.

Gus returned to the problem of the Kiddie Tour driver. He needed a dependable, aggressive, and capable man. Where could he find him?

Gus heard an apologetic cough. He looked up. Standing there was Jay Mason—dependable, aggressive, and capable.

"Jay, I have a little job for you."

"Certainly, Gus."

"You know the Kiddie Tour the publicity department conducts on Saturday mornings? The drivers we've had just haven't worked out. I can't find anybody else who can handle the job, so I wish you would do it, Jay."

"You want me to drive that shuttlebus?" he was aghast.

"I wish you would."

"That isn't part of my job," he answered cooly. "You can hire a kid for an errand like that."

"We've tried that, and it hasn't been satisfactory. I'd like you to do it."

"I'll find you a driver, Gus, if that's what you want."

Gus shook his head.

"We're coming up to the Fourth of July which, unfortunately, is a Saturday. We've had kids who smuggled in firecrackers before. They try it every year about this time. Nothing has happened, but it could. Imagine what a terrified thoroughbred could do. I don't consider this a trivial assignment. I want you to do it."

"What if I refuse?" he asked evenly.

"I really hope you won't."

"I'm not a bus driver, Gus."

"This could be more important than anything either of us will write during the entire meeting. What about it?"

"No," Jay said. "I won't do it."

Curious, Gus reflected, that our showdown should come over a relatively unimportant matter, but here it was.

"I don't blame you for disliking the job," Gus answered after a moment. "I think I can understand your reasons for refusing, but we've gotten down to a matter of who's

123

running the store. They need an assistant in the racing secretary's office. If you prefer that job, I can get it for you. The pay will be the same, but if you don't drive that bus, you're through here."

Mason stood for an interminable period in silence. Only his tightly clenched fists revealed an inner turmoil. Then the iron smile came back on. Slowly, but it came. His fists, however, stayed clenched.

"You're really on the spot, aren't you, Gus? I didn't understand how desperate you are, but I see it now. I won't let you down. I'll take the job, as a personal favor to you. When you're in a tight corner, Gus, you know you can always count on me."

FIFTEEN

"You're going with Rustling Breeze in the Chancellor here Saturday? You must be out of your mind!"

The outburst evoked only a glance of tolerant amusement from Dan Devon, who was relaxing in Gus's swivel chair with the air of a beneficent monarch accepting petitions from the peasants.

"Don't try it, Dan," Gus pleaded. "Your colt has already raced twice in two weeks. Be reasonable. We can't get your colt beat now, just when I'm building him up for the Stake."

124

"Rustling Breeze can do it," Devon responded airily. "If he can't beat every horse in the Chancellor, how can he beat Horsepower?"

"He can't, but that could be our little secret."

"Are you going to get out a story on Rustling Breeze entering the Chancellor, Gus, or aren't you?" Devon challenged Gus.

"Parkinson riding?"

"We're going with Scotty MacTavish. He's hot right now, and I like the race track.

"Connie O'Toole has been nosing around, Dan. He's asking why you dropped Parkinson. He's digging. I hope he doesn't find anything."

"I share your hope, Gus."

"Don't try any tricks, Dan. You're shaky enough as it is. You must be honest and forthright in everything you do."

"The prospect appalls me, Gus. I'm a normal human being. I'd cook any race, if I knew how."

"Don't say that," Gus protested. "It sounds awful."

"Exactly, Gus. You don't want honesty. You want the appearance of honesty. Who can afford to be honest these days? What would bring on World War III faster than candor among international diplomats?"

"Sure, Dan, nobody expects them to tell the truth, but we can be honest. We're not that important. Personally, I pride myself on my honesty."

"I'm sure you do. And how's Harry the Happy Hippopotamus?"

Gus waved him off. "Harmless fiction. Perfectly innocent."

"Your harmless fiction is the other fellow's foul deceit. And the way you publicity men rhapsodize about horse racing strengthening the economy and improving the breed. Shame, Gus shame."

"Look at the tax money . . ." Gus began. Devon wasn't waiting.

"Horse racing may never wipe out all our pockets of prosperity," he intervened, "but it is making poverty fashionable. And your game improves the breed the way boozing improves whiskey."

"Horse racing is a sport that gives the fans a sense of participation, Dan. They handicap the races. They take an active part in the races."

"Participator sport is right," Devon spoke loftily. "You run one race, and you get 10,000 losers."

Gus stopped, too angry to reply. Dan leaned back, linked his hands behind his head, and stared at the ceiling. He felt like talking.

"You know, Gus, work has killed more men than women or whiskey, and given them less in return," he meandered. "I've made it big more than once, and I'll tell you what drove me to it—sloth. All my life, I've gone for the easy way. It's less tiring and more profitable.

"Man's instinct to avoid work is the greatest safety valve he can have. Only a strong-willed person can stifle this impulse and ruin himself. I'm not talking about doing things. When you have all the money you can use, everything you do is a hobby. I'm talking about work—doing the mean, monotonous, unrewarding things you come to hate. Like my old man did.

"A harder-working man never lived, and he was miserable all his life. We lived in one of those little company-owned coal-mine towns. My old man worked the mines and he hated it. He'd come home, night after night, too tired to eat, yet there was never enough money. Even as a kid, I knew there must be a better way.

"Every Saturday night my old man would get crocked at the corner saloon. Then he'd come home and kick my mother around. That was his only recreation, but it never seemed like much fun. When mother was gone, I lit out on my own. I was maybe ten at the time, and I haven't been back since."

"Your mother passed away?"

"She ran off with a buggywhip salesman. That was the way my mother unwound: She ran off with traveling salesmen. That always upset my old man, because he knew she would be back! Work ruined my parents. Too much work for too little money. That led to the great discovery of my youth: success is ninety percent somebody else's hard work."

He had a distant look in those cold eyes, as though he were oblivious of Gus's presence.

"An abhorrence of honest toil isn't enough," he resumed. "A man who makes it big has to have something the ordinary man lacks—luck. All my life, I've courted Lady Luck. If you're lazy enough and lucky enough, you can hire somebody else to do the work, but if you want to be lucky, you must be there when it happens. You must have a horse in the race. Like Rustling Breeze. I could get lucky with Rustling Breeze in the Colt Stake."

"You're kidding yourself, Dan. The only way Rustling Breeze can get home ahead of Horsepower is to rig the race, and that can't be done."

"You're sure?" Dan twinkled.

"It's impossible," Gus said flatly.

"A man likes to do the impossible. It's a challenge."

"Don't talk that way, Dan. It sounds terrible, even if you don't mean it. And you don't, do you?"

"I tell you the truth, and you resent it. You are not accustomed to simple candor."

"Sure, sure," Gus barked. "Everybody else is faking and you're the world's only honest man."

"No, Gus. I'm a realist. It isn't the same thing."

Gus had difficulty concentrating on his work that afternoon. He was beginning to suspect he'd made a catastrophic mistake in finding a haven for Dan Devon at the track. Nothing that happened the rest of the day did anything to lessen this concern.

Buzz Randahl checked in soon afterward, and he added to Gus's uneasiness.

"Doug Dye has been after me to throw Dan Devon off the track," Buzz told him. "And this morning J. C. Jensen himself called me. He says Devon cheapens horse racing, but what has really teed him off is the way Devon keeps saying his colt can beat Horsepower. Jensen considers that a personal affront. So tell me, what do we gain by keeping Devon?"

Gus mustered the old arguments. He tried to sound convincing.

"Rustling Breeze could double the publicity on the Colt Stakes, if he continues to win, Buzz. He could make this look like a horse race. He would be a big sentimental favorite. Even the fans who didn't think he had a chance would be pulling for him."

Randahl chewed on the stem of his pipe.

"Buzz, that little extra publicity could be the difference between getting the *Herald-Chronicle* banner and not getting it."

"Jensen thinks Horsepower should get the banner just for appearing here, Gus. Twentieth Century buys a lot of newspaper advertising space."

"That won't make any difference to George Hall, the *Herald-Chronicle* sports editor. But why is that banner so important to you, Buzz?"

"Never mind. It's a personal matter."

"You've made another bet."

"That isn't your worry, Gus. Just don't give me a bad steer in order to protect your pal, Devon. I wouldn't like that. I wouldn't like it at all." He reached into his inside coat pocket and extracted a folded sheet. "Take care of this, will you?" he said.

"And Devon stays?"

"I can't promise that, but I will tell you this: I won't do anything without talking it over with you first."

After he had gone, Gus examined the memo:

From: Douglas D. Dye
To: Montgomery Randahl, president, Treasure City
        Race Track
1. This writer deems it a privilege to represent such distinguished clients as Twentieth Century Motors and International Computer Systems.
2. This writer has searched tirelessly to find a single, high-level public relations project that would bring well merited recognition to Twentieth Century Motors' president, Mr. J. C. Jensen, and to International Computer Systems.
3. To this end, this writer has secured the assistance of Dr. Elliott Nichols, teaching fellow at Lovecot College and one of the world's acknowledged authorities on the most advanced uses of electronic computers.
4. With Dr. Nichols' assistance, this writer has developed a public relations concept that promises rich benefits to

the above mentioned. Dr. Nichols requests an appointment with the Treasure City public relations director at 2 p.m. Monday, June 29, to discuss his plans. This writer will be grateful for your good offices in enjoining the public relations director to complete cooperation.

5. This writer wishes to emphasize most strongly that this project was originated and is being undertaken entirely independent of the Treasure City publicity department, which has been less than cooperative in the past. The Treasure City publicity director is asked only to assure Dr. Nichols free access to sources of information which he will need, and to make arrangements for a series of press conferences which Dr. Nichols will require. Please instruct the public relations director to attend to these matters.

What was Dye up to now? He must think he had something. Gus didn't underestimate Dye. The man had ideas, and sometimes they were blockbusters.

"Raven's Wing and Rat-A-Tat-Tat are shipping in from Kentucky for the Chancellor," Mason told Gus. "They'll be in Thursday. Slam Bang is coming, too. Raven's Wing beat Grandma's Grandma in the Tranquility Stake, you know.

"We'll probably have Kentucky Babe and Bamboo Rose. Matt Smith will have an entry of Late Late Show and Horror Movie. Oh, yes, Oakley is entering Rustling Breeze. We'll have maybe a ten-horse field, with plenty of dynamite."

"What do you think, Jay? Has Rustling Breeze got a chance?"

"I'll tell you how it is, Gus," he sounded just the least

bit superior. "Raven's Wing and Kentucky Babe might get stuck in the starting gate and the Kentucky horses might dump their riders, and then Rustling Breeze would have an outside chance for show money."

"As bad as that?"

"Rustling Breeze is in over his head," Mason spoke with obvious patience. "He can't go against good older horses." Since the difference of opinion about the Kiddie Tours, Mason had treated Gus with cold and condescending reserve.

"I suppose he's still sore about the Kiddie Tour," Gus remarked to Nancy.

"He's mentioned it," she conceded. "I don't know why he acts this way. He can be so nice, when he wants to be."

She started away, and then she turned back.

"I almost feel sorry for him, Gus. He's afraid to trust anyone. He's a mixed-up, frustrated man."

"Just what I need," Gus replied. "A mixed-up frustrated publicity man."

"This may be the end of the road for Rustling Breeze," Gus told Connie O'Toole as they chatted in the press box, sipping coffee and listening to Gary Mills's chant: "To avoid the long lines at closing time and the possibility of being shut out, it is advisable to purchase your daily double and tote tickets early."

There was about an hour before the first race would start that Saturday afternoon.

"Rustling Breeze isn't in with those statebreds today," O'Toole remarked. "But I've got to get a ticket on him. I owe that horse something. Besides, Devon may have something up his sleeve. I don't mind a little chicanery, as long as I'm cut in on it."

"Oh, Connie, forget it. There's no way he can rig a race."

"I know it's impossible," agreed O'Toole, "but I'm not sure it's very impossible."

Bumbling Bertie complicated the publicity department's plans for the afternoon. Pierre usually shot the first and second races. He developed the prints during the third race and Gus sent them off to the papers and wires for the early Saturday night editions. This afternoon, however, Pierre had to shoot the third race for Worldwide Press, which wanted shots of Bumbling Bertie at the start and at the finish.

Bumbling Bertie proved perfectly predictable: He left the field far behind in the first two furlongs, and they left him just as far back in the stretch. That animal was dependable. He never improved.

"That act is getting to be old hat," piped up Duke Jones, *the Herald-Chronicle* writer. "We need a new angle. Can't you teach that freak to run sideways?"

"I'm getting sick of Bumbling Bertie myself," Gus admitted. "He's responsible for too many bad jokes."

He didn't have much faith in Rustling Breeze's staying power, but Gus went for a ten spot on the colt anyway. As Connie O'Toole had remarked, they owed the little horse something for past enrichment, but such bets represented a minority opinion. Raven's Wing went off at nine-to-five, and Kentucky Babe at two-to-one. The odds of twelve-to-one on Rustling Breeze amounted to a vote of confidence. Worse luck, Rustling Breeze had drawn the outside post position in a ten-horse field.

Rustling Breeze had gone to the front early in his other

races, but he couldn't start on the outside with these horses and take over at the outset. MacTavish didn't try to break him in front. As they came out of the club-house turn, Rustling Breeze was laying fifth on the outside, three lengths off the pace.

Rat-A-Tat-Tat and Horror Movie were neck and neck for the lead in the far turn but Kentucky Babe was starting her move under Wade Hampton Parkinson and Rafael Diego was bringing Raven's Wing up fast on the rail. Rustling Breeze, incredibly, was going right with them on the outside, just two lengths behind the two leaders.

The Babe overtook Rat-A-Tat-Tat in the turn. Horror Movie was fading while Raven's Wing was streaking through on the rail. Rustling Breeze was still within striking distance, and he seemed full of run.

At the top of the stretch, Diego brought Raven's Wing up inside Kentucky Babe. The Babe seemed to falter for a split second, drawing abruptly and unevenly to the outside and forcing MacTavish to pull Rustling Breeze out slightly.

Raven's Wing was on the pace now, but Rustling Breeze was almost even at the sixteenth pole. It was a two-horse race, their heads bobbing almost in concert until the last few strides.

Rafael Diego somehow got Raven's Wing up in the final yard to nip Rustling Breeze by a long nose at the wire. It wasn't much, but it was enough to lay a publicity campaign in ruins.

"Now Rustling Breeze is just another horse that got beat the last time out," Gus moaned.

"Hold on to your tote ticket," O'Toole advised. "That number's coming down."

"What?"

"See Parkinson down on the track? He's lodging an objection against Raven's Wing."

"He is? What for?"

"What for?" Connie was exultant. "Diego tried to bull his way through on the rail, and he interfered with Kentucky Babe. The stewards won't let this one stand."

The stewards studied the films of the race for twenty minutes before they announced their decision, but it was worth the wait. Raven's Wing was disqualified and placed third for interference in the stretch and Gus Scott cashed a ten-dollar win ticket on Rustling Breeze, at odds of twelve-to-one.

SIXTEEN

"How DID THE Kiddie Tour go Saturday?" Gus inquired. "The new driver didn't cuff any of the kids, did he?"

"Gus, you wouldn't have believed it," Nancy replied. "When he's with children, he's a different person. He isn't always trying to prove something. I don't know what it is, but he's relaxed and friendly. Nice, really. He probably wouldn't admit it, but I think he enjoyed himself."

Gus hated to see the morning slip away. This was Monday, June 29, two days after Rustling Breeze's victory in the Chancellor. The little PR man had a feeling that this might be the summit of his publicity campaign for the Stake. At two o'clock, he would meet with Dr. Elliott Nichols. By nightfall, Gus fretted, the publicity campaign for Rustling Breeze might be ruined.

He was glad to see Manny Goldblatt, despite the fact that Buzz Randahl never likes his employees even to be civil to Manny, who works for Honest Alfie, the biggest bookmaker in town.

Manny flipped a silver dollar, the way he's seen it done in the old gangster movies. Except that Manny took his eye off the coin, missed it, and had to crawl under Gus's desk to retrieve it.

"Tie a string on it," Gus suggested. Manny scowled.

"Gus, you're an old fight guy. You think maybe Dan Devon would buy a piece of Carlos Chavez? Carlos is the next champeen, if we can ever get us an angel. For ten grand, I'd give Dan forty percent of the contract. A steal!"

Manny and Gus went back a little way. Manny was a good, tough club fighter in his youth. Later he was a first-rate trainer and corner man. Manny and Gus worked together on many a story in the heyday of boxing. Gus liked Manny.

"Will Devon buy a piece of Chavez?" Gus repeated. "He just might, although I don't think he'd go for ten grand. He might stake you for a fight or two, but I'd wait, if I were you. Right now he has other things on his mind."

Manny drew closer to him, and spoke in a guarded undertone.

"Hey, what do you think of that hippo in the lobby?" he asked. "It's a lucky hippo. You rub his nose, and you're walking around lucky."

135

"Oh, Manny, you don't really believe that, do you?"

"Sure, I believe it. Where you been hiding? It's in all the papers, with pictures. I tried it Saturday."

"Does it work?"

"Sure it works. After I rub Harry's nose, I got photoed out in two races. I win one, but he's disqualified. I win two others, both favorites, and I get three horses scratched. Best day I've had all meeting."

"You were betting your personal money? Not Alfie's?"

"My personal money, Gus. The kind I lose with."

Gus was hurrying through lunch when Dan Devon stopped by his table.

"I haven't much time, Dan. I have a two o'clock appointment, and it's almost five to, now."

"I wanted you to be the first to know," he smiled. "We're shipping Rustling Breeze to the Roseler Race Track for the Courtenay Memorial Saturday."

Gus almost choked. "Roesler? That's a half-mile track. Rustling Breeze won't be able to handle the turns. He's never raced on anything but this mile track here. Don't ruin the build-up now. Keep him in the barn."

"If I took your advice, Gus, I would never have let him out of the barn," Devon pointed out. "We can't stay here. You know Sam Albright? Texan? Oil money? He tried to claim Bumbling Bertie here last Saturday. The claim was rejected because he hadn't raced at this meeting. Well, he's raced now. He'll grab Bumbling Bertie if I put him in a claimer here Saturday, and that's all there is for Bertie . . ."

"Why would anyone want that horse?"

"For quarterhorse racing. Bumbling Bertie can beat anything on legs at three furlongs. Albright offered me $5,000 for Bertie. I refused, of course."

"You must have a conscience, after all."

"I need Bumbling Bertie, friend. Believe me, I need him."

"So, just on account of your sentimental attachment for that misfit, you're going to send Rustling Breeze off to get shellacked at Roesler. You'll wipe out my publicity campaign."

"Don't think about it," Devon advised. "Enjoy your lunch."

Gus was annoyed to find a track character sitting in his office on his return. Dr. Elliott Nichols was due in about one minute.

"You're the publicity director?" the visitor asked, talking to his shoes.

Where had I seen this fellow before, Gus wondered? At the track? He thought so. And then it came to him: Those high-laced shoes, and that incongruously big head. Bubblehead, the man who had been talking to Manny Goldblatt on opening day. Manny had said: "He makes mind bets, I guess. He's an oddball."

"I'm the publicity director," Gus said, "but you've come at an awkward time. I have a two o'clock appointment, and it's that now. What can I do for you? In about two minutes?"

"An appointment? With whom?"

"A college professor who thinks he can beat the races. A genius with a lot to learn."

"Try me," he suggested, studying the backs of his hands.

"Huh?"

"I teach, although my primary interest is research. I am a teaching fellow at Lovecot College."

"You? You're the professor? You've been here before."

"I have come to the track with some frequency this summer. For scientific investigation."

"Some sciences, doctor, are more scientific than others."

"The time I have spent here has been most rewarding. I have explored many facets of these, us, extraordinary exhibitions. Do you know that some owners of race horses do not always undertake to win?"

"They don't?"

"No, indeed not. They lose in order to gain more favorable betting odds in a future contest. They are called betting stables by the aficionados. Very interesting, but predictable. Their behavior follows a definite pattern."

"What is the purpose of your visit here today, doctor?"

Then he said it—the flat, simple statement that losers have been making since the chariots rolled in the Coliseum in ancient Rome. "I am prepared to introduce a measure of certitude to the appraisal of the outcome of these contests. In other words, I have a system for beating the races."

"Welcome to the club. You're the tenth today."

Dr. Nichols flushed, but he went on: "I want to conduct a series of tests to demonstrate the validity of a theory which I have developed concerning a new use for electronic computers. I am told that I could require your assistance; in some areas I'm quite lost."

"You seek a guide through the wasteland?"

"I think my need might be defined in those terms."

Gus suppressed his glee. This was perfect. He'd fix

Dye's mathematical boy wonder so he couldn't pick the place horse in a two-horse race, Gus told himself.

"I know just the men who can help you, doctor. They are rather unconventional, and they have flamboyant nicknames, but they have devoted their lives to the study of horse racing. In fact, they have never done much of anything else. I guess you could call it their life's work. You will like them. They have hearts of gold—Hawf-Fed Ed, Hustling Herbie, T-shirt Thompson."

He lifted a limp, attenuated hand in a gesture of self-defense. "Not those jokers," he said. "They'd stiff their own grandmother."

"What kind of way is that to talk?" Gus rebuked him. He went back to staring at his shoes.

"I was assured you would arrange the necessary public relations procedures. Such matters baffle me."

"It's guesswork, doctor, like choosing a wife or raising a child."

He sat up straight at that, and quit ogling his shoes. "Guesswork! Humanity has always been harassed and frustrated by the wastefulness of guesswork. We don't know what is going to happen, and we can't explain afterward why it happened so we gain no profit from our losses. We attribute our deficiencies to such rubbish as accident or chance or free will. Nonsense! All effects flow inexorably from a ganglia of related casual factors. If we fully understood all these factors, we could weigh with precision the importance of each element in the relationship to all other pertinent elements. We could then foresee the future. Could? Indeed, we can!"

His shyness had dropped away. He hurried on, a man gripped by his own singular passion:

"The future is the unknown in a mathematical equation. If we knew the value of every element in one half of the equation, we could find the unknown quantity—the future. And now we have found the way. This is the most significant development in thrusting back the frontiers of knowledge since the invention of the printing press.

"From the dawn of history, men have sought to tear away the veils of the future with incantations and talismen, with theistic experiences and mysticism, with scholarly deductions. The infinite proliferation of detail in any mundane equation has always defeated even the most enlightened. They have never had enough time to resolve the problem, but now we have leaped over the dimension of time.

"We are ready for the breakthrough. We have the tool —the incredibly sophisticated electronic computer. Did you know that the speed of the International Computer Systems' most refined instrument is measured in picoseconds?"

"Come again, doctor?"

"In picoseconds, in trillionths of a second. It's fantastic, the characters that this computer can store in its memory bank, ready for instant recall. Now the task of finding the unknown quantity, the future, is . . ." He waved his hand, ". . . a piece of cake. The computer can unlock the future. If this concept is difficult to grasp, consider how the primitive computers foretold the approximate result of national elections hours in advance, or how we can foresee meteorological disturbances. These are rudimentary examples, as though we were comparing the first rude wheel to the most modern spacecraft, but the basic principle is the same. Astounding. Utterly astounding."

"If you can tout the two-dollar bettor, doctor, I'll be astounded, but why horse racing? We have troubles in Asia, there are still a few bugs in our space program, and not every disease has yielded to research. Why start with horse racing? That's more disreputable than statesmanship, I think."

"I wondered, too, but Mr. Dye feels that such a demonstration will have an optimum dramatic effect. He says people are more interested in horse racing than they are in foreign policy. He used the phrase publicity gimmick. In any case, if this unlikely medium can be used to demonstrate the soundness of my theory, Mr. Dye has promised a really lavish gift for research."

So there it was. Far-out enough to be in.

"We made rather extensive preliminary tests. I undertook to predict the order of finish in a number of races. I had been supplied, I thought, with all the pertinent factual data but it didn't go at all well in the beginning. I achieved seventy-one percent accuracy, but that wasn't good enough. My investigations had led me to conclude that I would approach total accuracy.

"Mr. Dye was quite displeased. He said I had duped him. I thought he would become violent. He ordered the whole undertaking abandoned.

"Then I found the flaw in my basic assumptions. I discovered that I needed to research the backgrounds and personalities of the owners, trainers, and jockeys as thoroughly as I researched the horses. After that, I managed a high level of certitude in my forecasts."

"Can you really do it, doc?"

"As surely as I can add two and two. Just as surely." He believed it, all right.

"Mr. Dye apologized for his earlier temper. He was quite excited. He asked for a final experiment. Curious, really. He assembled a list of horses that had been nominated for your Colt Stake. He told me to align them in all possible combinations of ten and to assume all possible conditions. Then he asked me to forecast which horses would win if the race were held forthwith."

"And what happened, Dr. Nichols? Horsepower won a few?"

"He won every time. Mr. Dye was delighted. He seems confident we can gain considerable attention from the newspapers if I conduct a series of public tests to demonstrate the validity of my theory.

"Here is what he proposes: I will begin on Monday, July 6, twelve days before the Colt Stake. Mr. Dye suggests daily press conferences with, I must say, some rather theatrical trappings. I will write down the names and order of finish for the first three places in Tuesday's feature race. I will not show my selections to anyone. I will put them in an envelope, seal it, and hand it to Mr. Dye. In full view of the newspapermen, he will put the envelope in a safe with a double lock. Mr. Dye will secure one lock. Then he will give the key to a newspaperman who will secure the second lock and retain the key.

"On Tuesday, I will make my selections for Wednesday. We will repeat the ritual. Then Mr. Dye will remove the first envelope and read aloud my choices for the previous afternoon. We will continue this procedure through Saturday, July 11. On Monday, July 13, my selections for the previous Saturday will be opened and read. On Tuesday, five days before the event, I will hold another press conference to announce my choices for the first three positions in the Colt Stake."

"But suppose your earlier predictions fail?"

"They won't fail. That's the whole point. I'm not guessing. I know."

He stopped in embarrassment. "I shouldn't say this, because Mr. Dye has been most generous, but this does seem like a sophomoric charade. It's really silly, isn't it?"

"It is," Gus replied. "It's the silliest thing I've heard since somebody thought he had a workable idea for an atom bomb."

"Can I see you for a minute, Gus?"

Manny Goldblatt was speaking in a conspiratorial whisper again. He carefully closed the door to Gus Scott's office.

"Sure, Manny. You can see me any time, as long as you don't start bugging me about the phone."

"You're blowing a chance, Gus. You got a direct outside line. If I made a call in an emergency, maybe once a month, nobody would know and you could get yourself a *C* note a week."

"Forget it, Manny. If I let a bookie call out from here just once, I'd be through here."

Manny sank wearily into the chair. For a man whose feet hurt, he has a job that requires a great deal of walking.

"What's Devon trying to pull off?" Manny inquired.

143

"I've heard rumbles that he is out to trim the poor books. Everybody is trying to cut the poor books up. Alfie is worried sick."

"Alfie is the worrying type. All rich men are, but what can Dan do?"

"Alfie still remembers the bath he took on that Toledo fight. He was one of the books that got clipped. Nobody but Devon could have done it. The timing! The night of the fight, this Hernstein money starts showing up from all over. Before they shut it off, there must have been a hundred grand down at different books for Hernstein to go the distance. A hundred grand at fifteen-to-one! No wonder Alfie's worried."

"Now, don't start telling me Dan's trying to steal the Stake! How could he?"

"Devon is going to try," Manny said firmly. "Alfie gets pretty good information. All the signs are there. Devon's got something up his sleeve."

"Manny, you know there's no way he can win with that colt. Forget it."

"Devon," mumbled Manny. "He's the damndest operator you ever saw, Gus."

"Sure, Manny, he's such a big operator that he has been starving for the last ten years. You know that. He hasn't made a score in ten years. I'm afraid he's over the hill, living in the past. He's had it."

"For a guy who has the shorts, like you say, he dresses very fancy and he's as cocky as anybody I ever see."

"Ah, yes, the viceregal manner," Gus said. "But don't you see, Manny, that's all he's got now—a big front."

"Maybe, Gus, but he has forgotten more cute tricks than we ever heard of. I admit he's got class. He talks so nice. He walks into a saloon and everybody gives him a big hello. They know his name. The big shots he knows! I mean, he really knows them, Gus.

"I went along as his corner man the time he took Hurricane Harrison to Europe, Gus. What days those were! We sold out the joint when Hurricane met Jacques Barceleau, the French champion, in Paris. The odds were three-to-one for the Frog, believe it or not. We bet everything we had, and Hurricane put him away in two.

"We stayed in Europe seven, maybe eight months. We lived. Hurricane belted out the German champion, the Italian champion. He had a fight every two-three weeks —and he won 'em all. All them European bums got glass jaws. We cashed bets with both hands.

"What a gang Devon had: Three sparring partners, three trainers, two secretaries, three publicity men, a masseur, and a photographer, all on his payroll. They loved that over on the Continent—Europe, that is. We bought them high hats and them morning coats and them striped pants. We used to get dressed up every morning just to walk down the street. Those society broads were crazy for us. Some days, I swear, Devon never got out of bed."

Manny's eyes grew misty as he dreamed of vanished glory.

"You know the best part? When Devon got ready to come home, he was flat broke. He must have made a million, and he didn't have a cent left. He had to wire Lou Epstein, the New York promoter, for money to get out of town. What class that Devon has!"

"You see," Gus said, "he's a nice guy. Don't knock him."

"He's not a nice guy when it comes to getting money.

145

He's only nice about spending it. When he's got the shorts, he's like a big cat. He'll go for the jugular every time. Remember the Hammerhead Kid?"

"Vaguely."

"Well, if you're ever over in Jersey, stop in at the state hospital and say hello to the Hammerhead Kid. He was a big, tough clown. Strong, with a baby face. Dumb, and no left hand, but a nice kid. Always smiling. Go visit him now. It'll turn your stomach. He's in his fifties, bald and fat, and he looks at you with that empty stare. He's training for a fight that he lost thirty years ago.

"Hammerhead was a crowd-pleasing club fighter, a fair preliminary boy with some following. Devon gave him the old build-up. He fed Hammerhead a dozen setups. Dives? Anybody within four rows of the ring got splashed. Then Devon threw the kid in with the champ, and they sold out the ball park. The fight done a hundred grand, very big money in those days. The champ gave Hammerhead such a beating that he scrambled the poor bastard's brains."

"That's terrible, Manny. Really terrible. Why does Devon do things like that?"

"Money," explained Manny. "Dan had to do it. He was broke. When Devon is desperate for money, he'll do anything."

Manny wasn't arguing. He was simply stating a fact. And he was a very worried man.

He walked to the side of the little PR man, sitting on the desk-top and bending low. "Dan is hungry again," Manny whispered. "If he's got a chance to make a bundle, he'll screw us all up. He'll wipe us out. All I'm asking, Gus, old pal, is tell me I can make one telephone call, if I have to, the day you run the Colt Stake. Just one."

146

Gus was leaning back, half-smiling, shaking his head.

"Just one call," Manny pleaded. "I know Devon. He could cut this thing so fine that the only way I can get the word to lay off in time would be to telephone from the track."

"Sorry, Manny, but I can't do it. If Buzz found out, he'd fire me on the spot."

"You damn fool," Manny said bitterly. "If Devon steals that race, it won't matter. You brought him here. Buzz will fire you anyway, and you'll never get another race track job."

EIGHTEEN

DARK, ANGRY CLOUDS were building up in the East. The skies were leaden, and there was a feeling of rain in the air. What a morning for the Fourth of July!

The weather bureau was predicting rain. We'd probably get it an hour before the first post, Gus thought, just when the bettors were starting to come, and the downpour would cut the mutuel handle by a quarter of a million.

If it was going to rain, Gus would have preferred that it start at once. That would cancel the Kiddie Tours. He would welcome any reason for canceling the Kiddie Tours on the Fourth of July.

147

He wondered what the weather was like at the Roesler Race Track, three hundred miles to the southeast. Rain there would wash out what little chance Rustling Breeze had in the Courtenay. The heavy going would take more out of the colt than out of the older horses.

Gus picked up *The Daily Racing Form*, not to review Treasure City's Firecracker Handicap, but to look over the field for the Courtenay. The handicap had only two first-rate horses, but two is one more than enough.

Block Buster, winner of half a dozen big races and beaten only a neck in the $100,000 added Promenade Purse, was the class of the field. He was top-weighted at 125 pounds. Here was a horse that could go with the best. He shouldn't have much trouble.

If he faltered, Two Daiquiris should win. Two Daiquiris had only two wins this year, but he had raced in very fast company. He would carry 121 pounds. Rustling Breeze would shoulder 111 pounds, but he was out of his class.

Bumbling Bertie was going in the third race at Roesler, a $2,000 claiming event for non-winners in the past two years. The distance, a mile, surprised Gus. Bumbling Bertie couldn't last six furlongs, but that hardly mattered. This curious animal wasn't even good for laughs any more.

Even if Rustling Breeze won the Courtenay, against all belief, Gus feared his publicity campaign was almost finished. On Monday, the professor would begin his selections. Dye's plan looked foolproof.

Dye was sure the professor could convince everyone that the Colt Stake wasn't a horse race at all, just an exhibition by the Triple Crown winner. He would drain off the drama and excitement. As far as publicity goes, he would kill the race.

In this uneasy mood, Gus jumped straight up when the call came over the track's public address system: "Ambulance to Barn Forty-Two at once. Ambulance to Barn Forty-Two! Immediately! Urgent!"

He walked to the outer corridor in time to see the big white vehicle, red light flashing and siren wailing, roll down the gap and into the backstretch. A few minutes later, he heard the siren again, dying in the distance. What now, he wondered. What now?

His premonition of doom seemed like a prophetic vision when the switchboard operator called a few minutes later.

"Mr. Scott, I have very bad news. Jay Mason was trampled by a runaway horse. They've taken him to the hospital. I think he's dying."

That was all she knew, and her information was secondhand, at that, but Gus was sure she had it straight. Good news is what turns out to be wildly exaggerated, not bad news.

A few minutes later, she called back to add: "Mr. Mason has been taken to Chatsworth General. Miss Kingsley is with him. If I hear any more, I'll let you know."

The track sent all the more serious injury cases to Chatsworth General, mostly jockeys who had taken a tumble. Gus tried to call Doc Kent at the hospital, but he was off for the weekend. After some delay, he got through to the head nurse. She had no report on Mr. Mason.

Gus had a foolish impulse to drive to the hospital, although he knew that wouldn't accomplish anything.

Without Nancy or Jay, Gus would have to take care of all the publicity chores. He would have to work in the press box and try to run the show from there. The Fourth of July is one of the busiest days of the year at any race track. Gus knew he had to stay.

Then the rains came, falling in sheets as a summer storm lashed the track. This was a day, Gus felt, when nothing would go right. Just breathing was foolhardy.

Despite the steady downpour, the horseplayers were streaming in. Gus suggested to Pierre that he get some shots of the punters operating under difficult conditions.

"Those horseplayers are nuts, going out in this rain," Pierre observed, as he buckled on his boots, pulled on his raincoat, and prepared to go out in the rain.

The rains were falling, too, at Roesler, as Gus soon found out. Dan Devon's call caught him just as he was getting ready to hike over the press box.

"You should see this race track," Dan said. "It's under water. We'll race on pontoons."

"You're not phoning from the track? How did you get a phone?"

"I looked up Kent Cambridge, as you suggested. He let me use his phone, since this is public relations business."

Kent Cambridge? Who was Kent Cambridge?

"Kent is right here, and he sends you his best. You ought to see how he runs the public relations department here, Gus. This man is a real pro, and so gracious. You were right: He's one of the best. I told him you'd be honored to have him bring a party over for the Colt Stake, and he says he may take you up on it. He's real quality, Gus."

"Kent Cambridge?" Gus yelled. "I never heard of the bum."

"Just a minute, I'll tell him," Devon was bland. Then his voice was fainter but still clear as he spoke to Cambridge: "Gus says you simply must come for the Colt Stake. He won't let you refuse. You can use the track's suite at the Fleur de Lis. Not bad, really."

"Dan, this gives you an out," Gus declared. "Scratch Rustling Breeze. That track is impossible. Get out while you can."

"No, thanks, Gus. Oakley thinks maybe the colt can go in this goo. We're going to find out, anyway."

"Listen, he can't beat Block Buster under any conditions," Gus protested, but Dan was saying goodbye. He said Kent said goodbye, too.

Gus had just hung up when Nancy's call came in. Her voice was shaky. She had been crying but she spoke clearly enough.

"Oh, Gus, this is awful, just awful," she began. "They rushed Jay right up to the emergency treatment room, and he's been up there for more than an hour. I haven't heard a word. This waiting is driving me right out of my mind, Gus."

"Hang on, Nancy. Look, every minute you wait is all to the good. It means he's alive. He'll come through. He's strong and tough. If I can do anything at all, Nancy, call me at the press box."

"I'm frightened, Gus," she started sobbing. "He looked so white, so still."

She began weeping again, almost hysterically, but she finally regained a measure of self-control. "Oh, Gus, I'm so proud of Jay. This was just the most heroic thing I ever

saw in my whole life. One of those kids set off a firecracker in the shedrow, and it scared this poor horse to
death. He bolted and he would have trampled the children, but Jay jumped in front of them and tried to shoo
the horse away.

"It all happened so fast. In a second. The poor horse
knocked Jay down, and kicked him in the head."

A pause, and then: "I'm going back to wait, Gus. I'll
call you later, if I can."

The press box is a madhouse on any Saturday, and it's
worse on the Fourth of July. The writers are struggling
against early deadlines and everybody had too much to
do. After the fourth race, Duke Jones wanted to know how
Bumbling Bertie had done at Roesler. Gus queried *The
Daily Racing Form,* and back came the reply on the teletype:

"Third—Roesler—All That Jive, Dreadful Deed, Tik-
ker Tape, Bumbling Bertie."

"Bumbling Bertie finished fourth," pondered Jones.
"He must like the mud. It's horses like that that make
handicapping a headache."

Late in the afternoon, after Kentucky Babe had come
sloshing up to win the Firecracker Handicap, Gus took a
moment to ask what had happened in the Courtenay.

"I'm getting it," bawled the *Form*'s teletyper.

"The finish in the Courtenay," he called to the working
press. "The finish—Rustling Breeze—Hangman's Noose
—Rigamarole—Tipsy Turvy."

"Find out what happened to Block Buster and Two
Daiquiris," Jones asked.

"They scratched," the teletyper answered after a moment. "Four horses scratched. It was a six-horse field."

Rustling Breeze's luck had held. Gus felt a surge of jubilation, but it didn't last long.

"I've got a message for you, Gus," the teeltyper said. "From Dan Devon. It's just coming in."

Gus leaned over the teletyper's shoulder and read the message as the keys tapped it out: "Bumbling Bertie lost on claim. Oakley taking Rustling Breeze back to farm. Won't race without Bertie. Can't talk him out of it. Situation desperate. Help. Help. Dan."

NINETEEN

WHEN THE ELEVATOR DOOR slid open, and Nancy realized they were bringing Jay back from the emergency room, she thought she was going to faint. She felt suddenly light-headed, and the hospital corridor wavered and danced in her sight.

Then she saw him, and a joyous sense of relief swept over her. The unendurable tension dissolved. The color had returned to his cheeks. He was conscious and alert. His jaunty smile mocked the menace of the bandage on his head. As they wheeled him past, he saw her, and he winked.

The young intern reassured her. "He got off easy, miss," he smiled. "No broken bones, no internal injuries, just a concussion. He'll be all right in another twenty-four hours. He just got a mean knock on the head, and he may have a little headache. We're keeping him overnight for observation, but we haven't found anything to cause serious concern. You can go in to see him in a few minutes."

After another long ten minutes, the white-haired head nurse waddled out of the room.

"You can go in to see the patient in Room 202 now, young lady," the nurse decreed. "Only for a few minutes, however. And don't get him excited. He's had a shock. He needs to rest."

He was sitting up in bed, smoking a cigarette. She took his hand in hers, and it seemed the most natural thing in the world.

"Don't take it seriously, Nance," he greeted her. "This is a publicity stunt. Gus and I cooked it up."

"Can you talk, Jay? I mean, would you rather rest?"

"I could talk to you all day, Nance. I'm all right. It's nothing, really."

"Oh, Jay, you could have been killed."

"I'm afraid I embarrassed the stallion. He tried to avoid me, and his hoof must have just brushed my head. I'm okay."

"No, you're not. You should rest. I just wanted to see how you were, and to tell you that you did a fine, brave thing, Jay."

Mason studied the filigree of smoke curling up from his cigarette. The taut lines around his mouth were softening. He never looked more handsome.

He snuffed out his cigarette with sudden savagery.

"A brave thing? A stupid thing, Nancy. Utterly senseless."

"You don't mean that. You'd do it again. I know you would."

"With all those kids? Well, maybe, but I'm not much for heroics. This is the first spontaneous, honest, foolish thing I've done in half a dozen years. Let me tell you about the last time. I want you to know."

He pulled his knees up under his sheet, clasped his hands across them and continued:

"I ran wild when I was a kid. I was a tough little hood, and a dirty street fighter. Where I lived, you had to fight to grow up. A girl like you, Nancy, can never understand how it was when I was a boy.

"As soon as I was seventeen, I enlisted in the Army. I would have done anything to break out of the prison I was in. My parents were glad to sign the enlistment papers. They were happy to be rid of me. They were sure I'd end up in jail.

"I liked the Army life, except for one thing. We had a second lieutenant that was just a miserable bastard. There's no better way of describing him. He was a bully, a sadist. He was psycho. I couldn't stand the way he kicked some of those green, scared kids around. So, one day, I slugged him. I knocked him flat.

"That kicked up some dust. I spent time in the penal stockade, scared to death. Then they threw me out of the Army. I was, they said, unable to adjust to discipline."

He searched her face.

"I made up my mind then that I was through worrying about anybody else. I look out for myself, first, last, and always. It's the law of the jungle, and it means survival.

"I worked my way through college—well, almost. I ran out of money and credit after the first half of my senior year. I have pulled myself up a little way, and I've done it by taking everything I can get. I'm hard-nosed. I don't give anything away. I don't suppose you can understand, Nancy, but I wish you would try.

"I'm going to make a lot of money before I'm very much older," he said with weary assurance. "You don't know what money means until you're friendless and alone and hungry. Then you know. Money means freedom and power and dignity. Money can get you everything you want."

He looks, thought Nancy, like a little boy who has just been cut from the baseball team. She laid her hand gently on his muscular forearm.

"You've seen so much, and you've learned so little," she said softly.

"Aw, come on, doll," he tried to laugh. "You sound like a late, late movie. I just wanted you to understand how I am. I wanted you to know."

She touched his cheek, bending close.

"You're afraid," she whispered.

"The hell I'm afraid," he said angrily.

He pulled her to him and kissed her, a hard, bitter kiss. Nancy met his defiant gaze.

"Do you call that a kiss?" she blazed. "Stop acting like a spoiled brat. If you will forget for just one moment that you're an angry young man and that all the world is against you, you can do better than that."

He could and he did and she clung to him. She could hear his heart beating wildly under the thin hospital jacket, and she could feel the strength of his virile young body. She never wanted to let him go.

They kissed again, and Nancy knew that no man had

ever kissed her like this before. His arms were her sanctuary.

Nancy had no idea how often the head nurse had to clear her throat before the signal brought her back to the little white hospital room.

"Well, I must say!" sputtered the old nurse. "Young lady, I must ask you to leave. At once! I told you not to get the patient excited."

TWENTY

DAN DEVON strode briskly from the plane, nodding coolly to Gus Scott. His old sidekick, Chalky Boyle, followed him down the ramp.

"I'm pleased you received my message, Gus," Dan said.

"I received both of them. The one at the track and the one at the hotel. Your timing was perfect. When the second telegram came, I was in danger of falling asleep."

He ignored the complaint.

"I've been booby-trapped, Gus," he said.

"Tell me, Dan. Take it from the top."

"You remember Sam Albright?" he asked.

"The Texas oil man? The fellow who tried to claim Bumbling Bertie for quarterhorse racing."

"That's Albright. His claim was thrown out here because he hadn't raced. I went to Roesler to avoid him, but he was waiting for me. I put Bertie in a claimer. Albright grabbed him. Oakley is furious."

"Dan, you look shaky. Is it that bad?"

"It's bad enough, but that is only part of my trouble. I haven't been feeling right for some time. As soon as I can get away, I'm going to fly down to New York to see Doc Reynolds. He's kept me alive for twenty years—the man has no conscience. Right now, however, I've got to keep Oakley from pulling out."

"Aw, Dan, Cal will get over it. He won't pass up the Colt Stake on account of that clown, Bertie."

"He's fallen in love with that horse. Hell, when I was managing fighters, I never fell in love with any of them. Although horses are more lovable, at that. You don't have to prowl through the saloon at two in the morning looking for your horse. Gus, I have some small talent for persuasion . . ."

"Like Demosthenes?"

"Churchill," Devon replied. "Yet I couldn't budge Oakley. He just kept saying that Rustling Breeze would be homesick without Bumbling Bertie. He gave me twenty-four hours to get the horse back. Twenty-four hours. That's all."

"What are you going to do about it, now that you've lost Bertie?"

He looked at Gus in frank disbelief. His cold eyes glinted.

"What am I going to do? I'm going to get Bertie back."

"How?"

"A detail," he shrugged. "Where do I find Albright?"

"He's had a suite in the Fleur de Lis for years. You remember, the biggest hotel in town, right across from the police station."

After they had gotten a cab and started downtown, Boyle spoke up:

"We brought twenty grand, in cash, Gus. The claiming price was only $2,000. Albright will go for the price, won't he, Gus?"

"If twenty grand won't do it, he isn't interested in money," Devon appended. "And I don't think he is."

The Fleur de Lis is a showplace hotel, with a lobby that has warmth and sweep and grandeur. Its penthouse is the highest in the city. The appointments are magnificent, so are the desk clerks. Magnificent and disdainful.

"I'm sorry, gentlemen," the clerk repeated. "We do not have a Mr. Albright registered here."

"He didn't expect us," Boyle broke in. "We're here on a big business deal, and he'll want to see us . . ."

The clerk regarded Devon with polite reserve, for Devon has no superior at conveying the impression that he doesn't care who owns the place. The red-faced Boyle was something else. The clerk had made up his mind about Boyle. "I've told you, sir, that there is no Mr. Albright registered at this hotel."

"Listen, buster, don't try to shove us around," Boyle's voice was hard and ugly. "We know he's here."

"That will be quite enough, Mr. Boyle," Devon cut him short. "We can resolve this confusion later. For the moment, we need a suite. We will regard this misunderstanding with more amusement when we have dined."

Devon had only a small overnight bag, but he decided that he needed a bellboy to carry it. "Wait for an empty elevator," he instructed the young man. "I dislike being jostled in your lifts."

The third elevator was empty, so they filed in. As soon as the elevator started up, Devon removed a hundred dollar bill from his wallet, tore it in half and handed the slightly smaller half to the bellhop.

"A man named Sam Albright is staying here, but the desk clerk says he is not registered. Should be easy to find. He's a big man, perhaps six-foot-three, and quite heavy. He wears big Texan hats and horsemen's boots and he tips foolishly. He's red of face and loud of mouth, and he owns a string of race horses. Have I told you enough?"

The bellhop said he had.

"Get me his room number and let me know when he is likely to be in, and the other half of the bill is yours. We don't want to waste time."

The bellhop was back in ten minutes.

"Mr. Albright is in Room 2265 now, sir," the youth held out his hand.

"One moment, please," Devon responded. He lifted the telephone and, in a Swedish accent that would fool the unwary, asked for Room 2265.

"Hello, Nels? I want Nels Johnson. There isn't? Isn't this Room 2165? Oh, sorry."

Devon hung up, and handed the remainder of the bill to the lad.

The bellboy matched the torn ends of the bill, smiled and threw a flippant salute. He added: "Your friend is having a few of his pals in to play poker. They usually get together about once every two weeks. They're coming in now for dinner and then they'll play until three in the morning."

"You're a good man," Devon said. He consulted his watch.

"It's five o'clock," he said. "Call room service. I want a small broiled steak, a green salad, and milk.

"Do you think there's a chance, Dan?" Gus inquired. "If he really wants Bertie, why should he sell? He doesn't need the money."

"Every man needs something," Devon yawned. "Now, I'm going to take a little nap. Wake me when they bring the food, please."

Albright answered the door in his shirtsleeves, a big cigar in his mouth and a tall, moist glass in his hand.

"Devon! What are you doing here?" he exclaimed. His leathery face crinkled into a grin as he added: "I guess I showed you something about horse racing, didn't I?"

"You're Scott, the track's tub thumper," he accused Gus. "I got a couple of pretty fair allowance horses at your place. Why can't I ever get any ink?"

"This is Mr. Boyle, an old friend," Devon murmured. "May we speak to you for a moment, Mr. Albright?"

"I told that desk clerk I didn't want to be disturbed," Albright groused. "Why can't those pretty boys ever get anything straight? I've got a few friends here, and we're busy. If you want that horse back, the answer is no. And that's flat. I won't sell him for any price. I've got a pigeon who thinks his quarterhorse can beat anything alive at three hundred yards. Wait till he sees what I've got." Albright laughed, a little too loudly. "Thought you were pretty cute, eh, Devon? Taking that horse to Roesler. I was a step ahead of you, old boy."

"You have me on the hip, sir," Devon returned amiably, "but perhaps we can find mutual interests. If we can have Bumbling Bertie for only two more weeks, until the Colt Stake is run . . ."

"I won't sell for any figure, and I won't make any deals," Albright growled, "but I will buy you a drink. Then your trip here won't be a complete wash-out." He broke into laughter again.

"Thanks," Devon smiled. "After the way you've out-maneuvered me, I need a drink."

Albright led them into a big room where four men were seated around a green-topped table littered with cards, chips, glasses, and ash trays.

"We've interrupted your game," Devon sounded regretful. "Poker? I'm sorry. Myself, I never like anything to interfere with a good game of poker."

"No harm, I guess," the Texan boomed as he poured out drinks. "Just a few old friends. We've been getting together for years to cut each other's throats. Boys, you know that horse I was telling you about? The one that can fly for three furlongs? Well, here is the late owner, kind of unhappy-like."

"Dan Devon," said the white-haired man in the striped shirt. "The fight guy! I saw Hurricane Harrison the night he flattened Denny Gilligan. What a fighter he was!"

"He could punch," Devon agreed. "He's a policeman now in a little town in Florida. He hasn't got a dime."

"Deal the cards," said the slender, hawk-nosed one.

"Poker, the most perfect game ever devised by man," Devon mused. "Deep. Inscrutably deep, as various as a woman. I love poker."

"I won't sell you the horse," Albright barked, "but I

might deal you a hand. Okay, boys? Fresh money?"

The others assented. Albright kept talking. As an after-thought, Albright added to Devon's companions: "You boys want to play?" They looked at the big bills on the table—fifties, hundreds, and thousands—and shook their heads.

"We ante fifty dollars old timer," Albright bawled. "You can bet a thousand any time. And we quit at three, no matter what. No exceptions. We quit at three."

Devon motioned absently to Boyle, who opened the overnight bag and removed two small packages of currency. "I came prepared to buy my horse back," he explained negligently. "Would you introduce me, Sam?"

The old man walked slowly around the table, offering each man a polite, formal handshake. He had already begun the contest. For this courteous gesture enabled him to appraise each man closely, measuring the man, indexing his most obvious traits. The limp handshake, the shifty eyes, the apologetic grin, the false heartiness, the slurred speech—everything had meaning to Devon. An hour from now, they might not remember how they had played a hand, but Devon would remember. And he might know why.

Gus and Boyle took seats on the big leather davenport, with the whiskey bottles on the low table in front of them. Gus poured out a couple of good belts.

With elaborate ceremony, Devon removed his jacket, undid his cufflinks and rolled up his sleeves. He took off his tie and, finally, he transferred his bifocals from his coat pocket to his shirt pocket. Curious, thought Gus. I never realized Dan wore bifocals.

From the outset, Devon concentrated on his cards. The

others drank steadily, some more, some less, but not Devon. He was all business.

The cards came his way from the start, and he won, but he did not make the most of his opportunities. Gus grew uneasy. Dan is under too much pressure, he decided. He's lost his poise.

For Devon's mannerisms were betraying him. When he had a very strong hand, he invariably reached into his shirt pocket for his bifocals and put them on. Then he leaned forward, carefully scrutinizing the others' cards. Then he would inspect the cards which he had showing. And, finally, he would steal a covert glance at his hole card.

When he had completed the ritual, he would count out another thousand and push the money to the center of the table. And when he did that, he had the cards he needed.

On other occasions, he would place his left index finger alongside his nose in an agony of uncertainty. The other players soon got the message: Devon had a weak hand. Sometimes he would become aware of the mannerism. Then he would remove his hand, a little self-consciously, but in another moment the finger would be back alongside his nose again.

He's desperate, Gus reflected. He's lost his nerve.

But Boyle saw the odd behavior; after a while he remembered, and he smiled.

Devon kept getting useful cards, however. And none of the others was as good as he should have been. They wasted chances. They made mistakes. Despite his own ineptitude, the stacks of money in front of Devon slowly grew.

He treated the others with grave courtesy, but there was a caustic sting in the way he went after Albright. At one point, Albright stayed on two fives and lost to two queens. Devon was aghast. "You stayed on that?" he exclaimed.

"I'll play my cards," Albright roared.

Later, Devon volunteered advice. "Stay off the sauce, Sam. You can't handle it and play cards, too."

Once Devon seemed to have gone too far. Albright, who liked to talk, was discoursing upon a dear friend who had entered politics. This fellow was so conservative that he still mourned the passing of the pony express.

"Old George has a heart as big as the great plains of Texas." Albright boomed.

"And a head as empty," Devon put in. Albright sat glaring at him all through the next hand.

At three, the players had had enough. They pushed back their chairs, yawning, stretching, finishing their drinks. Devon began rolling down his sleeves.

"Just a minute," Albright barked. "You're the big winner, Devon. We're all down. I'm stuck damn near twenty grand, and you ain't going to be back. I got four thousand left. I want a chance to get even."

Devon offered him a glacial smile. "Sorry, Sam. Your rule. We quit at three. No exceptions. Remember?"

The others were leaving. This was no concern of theirs. They made their brief goodbyes as Albright stood glaring at Devon, struggling for words.

"Are you going to be a sport and give me a chance to get even?" he repeated, "I said I'm down twenty grand."

"Your rule, Sam," Devon answered mildly, as the others filed out.

"Screw the rule!" bellowed Albright. "I'm asking you like a man. You going to show some class, or you going to be a prick?"

Devon gave him the half-hooded look, his whole demeanor cold and disdainful. "I have fifty grand here," the old man said. "I won't risk that to win four thousand. There's no percentage in that."

Albright was pouring a drink, his face flushed, so angry that he spilled half his whiskey. Devon spoke again: "I'll give you a shot, Sam. My way. I want the horse back. I'll give you ten thousand for him. If you win the money back tonight, I'll sell the horse back to you.

"We will play for an hour, or until one of us runs out of money. We ante five hundred, and you can bet the size of the pot. If you do not have enough money in front of you at the end of the hour, I keep the horse and you promise never to claim a horse of mine again."

"Send the money," said Albright. He took a fresh deck, broke the seal, and dumped the cards on the green table top. Devon began rolling his sleeves back up.

Twenty minutes later, Albright was four thousand ahead. Devon was giving himself away again. Why, wondered Gus, can't he keep that damn finger away from his nose? And what is this act with the bifocals? He might as well send telegrams.

Devon was beginning a deal, giving a card to Albright face down and one to himself. He looked at his hole card: The King of Hearts.

Then he dealt the King of Clubs face up to Albright and the Queen of Hearts to himself. Albright couldn't wait to bet. "A thousand," he snapped.

He's got Kings wired, Devon told himself. He hesitated,

absently brushing his nose with his index finger. "I call," he said.

He gave Albright the Eight of Hearts, and himself the Four of Spades. The Texan jumped in immediately. "I bet three thousand!"

Devon rubbed his finger across his cheek. "I call," he said, almost apologetically. Albright grinned.

Devon dealt Albright the Eight of Hearts, himself the Four of Diamonds. Albright immediately bet $3,000.

Then Devon hit Albright with the Ace of Clubs. He gave himself the Four of Spades. So he had a pair of fours, but he obviously didn't think that was good enough. He started to put his finger beside his nose, caught himself and stopped in embarrassment. "I check," he said.

"And I bet five thousand," Albright barked.

"I call," said Devon, shaking his head.

The pot had grown to $19,000. Devon had a pair of fours, plus the Queen of Hearts showing plus the King of Hearts in the hole. Albright had the King of Clubs, the Ace of Clubs, and the Eight of Hearts showing.

Devon completed the deal by tossing the Six of Clubs to Albright and the Five of Hearts to himself.

The old man stared at his pair of fours in an agony of indecision. He started to lift his hand. Then he dropped it. Albright waited, his eyes dancing. Devon's voice seemed to waver. "I bet $3,000."

Albright was gloating openly now. "Here's the three grand," he answered, "and I raise you what I have left, which happens to be $5,500."

With a triumphant grin, the Texan pushed the money to the middle of the table in an untidy pile.

"Let's see what you got, old man," he gloated. "I've got you. That little old pair ain't going to do you no good."

Devon ignored him. Gone were the old man's nervous mannerisms. He was icy and contemptuous, his face a mask.

Albright squinted, shifting his bulk in his chair, his heavy breathing now audible in the hushed room. What was the old man trying to do?

And then Devon reached into his shirt pocket and took out his bifocals.

Albright sat straight up, his eyes wide, his mouth half open. He gripped the edge of the table, his knuckles whitening. And, beneath his tan, he grew pale.

With meticulous care, Devon inspected Albright's cards as though he had never seen them before. He looked at his own cards lying face up on the table. He looked guardedly at his hole card.

Devon began quietly counting his bills, arranging them in neat stacks. Albright's eyes bulged.

Then Devon began pushing the currency to the center of the table. He was putting in everything he had. Albright swallowed, moistening his lips with his tongue.

Devon's expression was glacial. "I call your $5,500," the old man said. "And I raise you $18,000, which happens to be what I have left. That is what it is going to cost you, Sam, if you want to see me."

Devon was the man in complete command, merciless and sure of himself. "And to prove that I have a measure of class," he added softly, "I will accept your check for the call."

Albright, his forehead beaded with perspiration, stared in disbelief. He threw his cards down, cursing in anger and frustration. "I know you," he snarled. "You haven't got guts enough to bluff."

Later, as they waited for the elevator, Gus had to say it. "I suppose this will make you more insufferable than ever, Dan, but I have to give it to you; Sometimes you are almost as good as you think you are."

"An adequate effort," Devon answered, in the lordly manner of a man who sees no need to boast. "Those fellows shouldn't be allowed at a card table. They could lose their shoes playing Old Maid with the neighbor's kids. And that Albright! He brings to mind the feeding time at the zoo."

"Yeah, but you was lucky," Boyle declared. "You got all kinds of cards. They never quit coming."

Devon regarded his lieutenant sourly.

"Poker is a game," he said loftily, "where the better you play the luckier you look."

TWENTY-ONE

MISS INDEPENDENCE GREENMEADOW seemed to seethe with an inner anger.

"The cigar, Emmanuel," she said severely. "Aren't you through with that horrid old thing?"

"Yes, ma'am," Manny Goldblatt answered. The cigar

cost a buck, and it was only half-smoked, but Manny dutifully crushed it out against the sole of his shoe.

"Emmanuel!" the old woman chirped. "Not on my clean front porch. Whatever has gotten into you?"

"Sorry, ma'am, I wasn't thinking."

"I should say you weren't. I don't know where you picked up that filthy habit. You're poisoning yourself, Emmanuel. Poisoning yourself."

Since Miss Independence made such a fetish out of neatness, Manny took the broken remnant of his cigar back to the car, and deposited it in the ash tray.

"Cigars are horrid things," Miss Independence told him when he was seated in her living room. "If I ever get the smell of those things in my curtains, I'd never get it out."

Manny remembered how people used to say his mother's house was so clean you could eat off the floor. Independence Greenmeadow's home was like that, shining and orderly. He sat uneasily on the edge of the plush-covered chair. Miss Independence seated primly opposite him.

"I just stopped in for a sociable visit, ma'am," Manny explained. "You're feeling okay, I trust."

"I feel fine," she replied defiantly. "Let me make you a little tea. I'll put the kettle on. And I've just made a batch of cookies. Excuse me."

Manny began to protest, but she was already bustling out to the kitchen. That woman makes cookies that are harder than rock, he reflected. Some day I'm going to bust a tooth on those damn cookies.

I'm just an errand boy, he told himself again. An errand boy for the most impossible old biddy on earth. I got to get back to the fight game, Manny mused. Carlos Chavez could be the next lightweight champion, if I could only move him. Then I could throw this whole thing over. If I could only get Dan Devon interested. He could move Carlos right into a title shot. That man knows how to open doors.

Now I got to go along with this old broad, Manny reminded himself. She's got the only telephone within a mile of the track. Those track guys sure made it tough on an honest bookie when they bought up all those adjacent farms and turned them into a park. Sure, they were smart. The property is worth twenty times what it was. I just wish Randahl would start building the hotel and shopping center he talks about. Then there'd be plenty of telephones.

As it is, this is the only place from which a man can call to see if he is supposed to lay off any bets. I timed it, Manny recalled. Twelve minutes from this joint. Forty two minutes is the best I could do anywhere else.

Manny looked up, and perceived that Miss Independence had returned. She was watching him with bright little eyes. Like a vulture, he thought.

"I see you got the new color TV set," Manny offered. "Mr. Alfie says he hopes you like it."

"It's nice," Miss Independence conceded, "but it's a shame he didn't get the Continental model. It costs only eighty-one dollars more, and I had my heart set on a Continental model."

"But this fits in better with your furniture, don't it, ma'am? Alfie thought it would. This is a Colonial model. Very classy."

"I'm surprised that Mr. Alfie would begrudge an old

woman a few extra dollars, Emmanuel, after all I've done for him."

"Wait, now, Miss Independence . . ."

"You make a lot of phone calls, Emmanuel. Sometimes you're in and out of here all afternoon, dragging in dirt, dropping ashes on my rugs, and leaving those horrid cigar ends around."

"Now, ma'am, Mr. Alfie rents the phone, and he pays pretty good, don't he?"

"I know, Emmanuel, but this is the only phone for a mile or more in either direction. Land sakes, long before they built this racing track, those swells came in their big limousines and wanted to buy my little house. They bought all the farms, up and down the road. Then they built their racing track and they just made the land on this side of the highway into a park. Now they own everything around here, except my little home."

Manny tried to placate her.

"I think it was real nice that you didn't want to sell your dear old home."

"Fiddlesticks!" she cackled. "I put my thinking cap on. I was waiting to see how high they would go when Mr. Alfie sent you out to see me. I think you tricked me, Emmanuel. I don't think you're paying me enough."

Manny knew he had to make a stand.

"Why, Miss Independence, Mr. Alfie pays you twice as much as it would cost you to rent this place for a year, and just for the use of your telephone for a few weeks. You know we have an agreement. Why do we always have to be talking about it, ma'am?"

She eyed him shrewdly.

"I don't understand this crazy business, Emmanuel. What did you say you do, again?"

"It's like buying and selling, ma'am. Like the stock market, sort of."

"Those other people were out to see me again," she related. "They want to use the telephone, too. I don't see why it would hurt a body, as long as you aren't using it."

Manny squirmed. He didn't want to go into that again.

"You know our understanding, ma'am. And remember that loan you asked Mr. Alfie for. He wants to be your friend."

"Those other people would like to be my friend, too," she answered. "They said it sometimes takes them an hour to go out and call their office and get back to the track. They said if they could call from here, it wouldn't take fifteen minutes. Why do you men spend so much time at the track?"

"It's hard to explain," Manny stumbled.

"Good heavens, the kettle's singing," Miss Independence's voice rose. "Oh, last week that young pup from the police department was out again. He wanted to know what you do when you visit me."

Manny gulped.

"What did you tell him?"

"Just what you said. That you're an old friend of the family, and it's none of his business, anyway, and if he wants to persecute a poor, helpless old woman just because she makes a cup of tea . . . oh, the tea! Excuse me."

Manny felt better. No politician in his right mind would want to set her off.

"Here's your tea, Emmanuel. And the cookies. Help yourself. Oh, take several. They're good for you."

"I hate to make a hog of myself," Manny protested but

173

she pressed the cookies upon him. He began, with some resolution, to chew.

"I just wish Mr. Alfie had gotten a Continental model," she resumed. "The cabinet is so much nicer looking."

Manny sighed.

"How long have you had the TV, ma'am? Maybe we can still send it back and get a Continental model instead."

TWENTY-TWO

A FEW SPORTS WRITERS, in reviewing Horsepower's amazing success as a three-year-old, have said that the great colt's effort in the Continental did him little credit, but what do they know? Everybody knew that Horsepower had speed. In the Continental, he proved that he had the heart of a thoroughbred, too.

It came up mud, and he had his troubles that afternoon but who can ever forget his duel with Suburban Sam? They fought it out all the way, slipping and splashing and sliding around the turns and down the straightaways.

Horsepower had a slight lead going into the home stretch. Inside the sixteenth pole, the challenger began a furious drive and, maybe fifty yards from home, he caught the Triple Crown winner. Horsepower seemed to be fading but he somehow found a reserve of speed—or maybe it was simple courage—for he stayed right with Suburban Sam to the finish.

As they hit the wire Carl Hartley, up on Horsepower, flicked his whip under his colt's neck and the champion lifted his head. That was the difference. Those two superb thoroughbreds crossed the finish line together, but Suburban Sam's head was bobbing low and Horsepower's head was high. That gave him all the margin he needed.

In the winner's circle, J. C. Jensen announced that he was well satisfied with his colt's first race after his layoff. He was sure Horsepower would show better form in his next start—in the Colt Stake at the Treasure City Race Track.

Ned Holloway immediately disclosed that he would send Suburban Sam against Horsepower wherever he ran.

"We almost made it this time," Holloway growled. "Next time we'll do it."

Grant Thompson joined the parade with the revelation that he would enter Mean Old Man in the Colt Stake because his youngster could beat both of them. Thompson had his reasons. Mean Old Man had come charging up from sixth at the top of the stretch and he missed by only half a length for all the money.

So the Colt Stake was enriched that day by the entries of perhaps the three hottest three-year-olds on North American tracks. The Colt Stake was shaping up as one of the year's biggest three-year-old races.

Devon laid the package, gorgeously wrapped in purple and gold, on Nancy's desk. Her eyes sparkled.

175

"For you, my dear, and I'm long in your debt for so many kindnesses."

Nancy deftly removed the wrappings, and she almost shrieked.

"Earrings," she exclaimed. "They're exquisite, just exquisite!"

"My pleasure," murmured Devon.

The idyll was shattered, abruptly, as he grasped his side and gasped for breath. Gus sat him down and brought him a glass of water, but he dismissed the refreshment.

"Nothing to worry about, Gus. Just a tightness in my chest. If I don't shake this pretty soon, however, I'm going to see Doc Reynolds in New York. This thing has hung on too long."

"By the way," he went on, "did Chick Dressage call here for me? The deputy highway commissioner? It's important."

"No," the press agent answered. "If he calls, I'll have you paged."

"No! No! Just take the message. Find out where I can reach him."

"Jensen's committed," Gus remarked. "Horsepower will definitely go in the Colt Stake."

"J. C. Jensen, the fearless civic leader and captain of industry," Devon smiled. "We can learn something from that man. You don't need larceny to get to the top, if you have enough avarice."

Devon arose, a trifle pale. "Gus, I'm calling a press conference this afternoon. I want you to be present. I wouldn't think of holding a press conference without you."

176

"Maybe I don't want a press conference. You can't call one any time your name has been left out of the paper for two editions."

"I'm going to make an important announcement. Trust me, Gus."

"Trust you!" Gus roared. "Are you trying to get smart. Tell me what you want to do, and I'll tell you how we'll handle it."

Dan was in an enigmatic mood, however. He refused to say more.

"All right, Dan, I'll make a deal. Keep Rustling Breeze out of Saturday's Prelude, and I'll go along with your press conference."

"Oakley says we go in the Prelude, so we go, but I ought to tell you about Bumbling Bertie. He's bucked his shins, and we're laying him off. It's possible that he won't race again in this meeting."

"Big deal! Is that your announcement?"

"Come to the press conference, and find out for yourself," he said airly. "Here or in the press box?"

"The press box," Gus surrendered, "but you can round up the newspaper guys yourself."

Gus was worrying about what Dan Devon might be up to now when Mrs. Dolly Randahl blazed into the office. He hadn't seen her in a couple of years, and she looked at least four years younger. She greeted him like an old friend.

"Gus, how would you like to come to work for me?" she began, without preamble.

"Thank you, Mrs. Randahl," he replied. "I could

handle some extra publicity work after this meeting is over."

"Not after the meeting is over. Right now. Today. What will it cost?"

"I couldn't. Not in the middle of a busy meeting. What would Buzz think?"

"Pooh," she said. "What does it matter what he thinks? He is a very pig-headed boy, and he needs to be taught a lesson. For his own good. Well?"

"I've got a contract with your son—"

"I know all about your contract. I'll take care of that. Montgomery wouldn't sue his own mother. He just better not! You know, Gus, Montie won't be in this ridiculous business much longer, I assure you. Come with me. I'll see that you are well compensated. Agreed?"

When he told her that he couldn't, she permitted herself only a brief grimace of annoyance.

"Gus, you'll regret this. I can't endure men who stand in my way. You would have some value to me if you would come with me now. I'll give you twenty-four hours to consider. Here is my unlisted phone number."

Dolly Randahl's visit had apparently upset her son, too. When Gus stopped over to check on the prospects for the Prelude, he was curt and preoccupied.

"We should have a great field for the Prelude, Buzz."

"We have," he said, but he was scowling. "Remember Federal Agent, he's been out most of the year but he was mighty good as a two-year-old? He's coming in. So is Hinky Dinky, who hasn't raced since he won the Florida Derby. And we've got Royal Crown, fourth in the Kentucky Derby. They're all coming in. We may have to run the Prelude in two divisions."

"Will Horsepower be in?

Randahl showed his disgust. "That's a stupid question! Don't you know anything about horse racing? Jensen isn't going to run a million-dollar colt in a warm-up race, but Horsepower will be in here Wednesday with his trainer. Jensen wants him to get accustomed to the track. The Colt Stake means a lot to Jensen. If that colt doesn't get himself beaten soon, he's the Horse of the Year, and it's no contest."

Devon had assembled more than a dozen reporters for his press conference. He handed Gus a stack of mimeographed sheets that contained a summary of Rustling Breeze's victories, and Dan's own modest assessment of "the fabulous, unbeaten and unbeatable Three-Year-Old of the Year."

"Please distribute these, Gus," he said in his most lordly manner.

"Not me," Gus snapped. "How do I know what you've got here."

"Pass 'em out!" yelled Duke Jones, the *Herald-Chronicle* writer. "I can't stand around all afternoon. I've got work to do."

Gus handed out the sheets, reluctantly. As his guests began scanning the fervid prose, Devon started talking.

"Gentlemen, there's never been another colt like Rustling Breeze. This is the greatest three-year-old of the century, and probably before that. You can quote me on that any way you want, and you can make it as strong as you want . . ."

"For Pete's sakes, get on with it," grumbled Jones.

179

"Very well," Devon peered at Jones with well-bred disapproval. "We are going to win the Prelude on Saturday. That's my prediction, and I won't hedge it in any way. Then we're going to beat Horsepower."

Jones stirred belligerently. Devon hurried on.

"Cal Oakley, a great trainer, has developed some original ideas about the conditioning of race horses. Now he is ready to put these ideas into practice. I foresee that his new and imaginative methods will revolutionize the sport.

"Of course, we are unwilling to share these ideas with a rival stable. For this reason, we have accepted the offer of Mr. Dean Hewitt, who has graciously given us the facilities of his farm and private training track, which is located about four miles southeast of here. We're moving in today. Rustling Breeze will hold his remaining workouts at the farm. We have terminated our training at this track."

"You mean I have to go to Hewitt's farm if I want to watch Rustling Breeze work out?" bellowed Jones.

"Not at all," Devon smiled gently. "The workouts will be held in strictest privacy. No visitors will be allowed. This includes all newspapermen, and radio, and TV reporters. Secrecy is essential. I'm sure you understand."

"Understand, hell!" retorted Jones. "What are you trying to pull?"

"We simply feel that we owe this much to that gallant little colt, Rustling Breeze," Devon spoke piously.

"Gallant colt your father's mustache!" Jones was thoroughly incensed. "This is the oldest and stalest—and cheapest—publicity gag of them all. The secret workout! Hah. I've had enough of your juvenile stunts, Scott. You go through with this foolishness, and I'll be damned if

I'll write a line about it. You and your silly ideas, Scott."

"Me?" Gus protested. "This isn't my silly idea. This is Devon's silly idea."

The old man smiled mysteriously.

"Don't knock it," he advised. "Horsepower can be beaten, and we know how to do it. Just remember what I'm telling you now."

"Dan Devon's gone too far this time. The newspapermen are furious."

Jay Mason sounded almost regretful. He was still a trifle pale. That knock on the head may have taken something out of him, but a slightly discolored eye was the only reminder of his brush with death. He had been lucky to escape without serious injury.

On the desk lay his last day's work—a complete rundown on the records of every one of the forty-two Colt Stake nominees, additional notes on the likely Prelude starters, and the charts on the half-dozen top three-year-old races of the year. He was a worker, all right.

"Don't worry about Devon, Jay. There's no surer way of getting publicity than by running away from it. Tell the reporters they can't print something, and they say the hell they can't."

Duke Jones, however, wouldn't touch the story of the secret workouts. The silent treatment annoyed Devon.

"Jones hasn't written a line about Rustling Breeze," Dan complained. "He could at least knock the colt, couldn't he?"

Jones, however, was the lone holdout. George Hall spent his entire Tuesday column in fulminations against the scheming Devon, who dared challenge a reporter's right to see for himself. This was a cheap publicity stunt, Hall said, and he saw through it. The rest of the press corpse snatched up the story. First they announced Devon's decision to hold secret workouts. Then they denounced it. Then they began speculating upon whether Dan had actually discovered a new wrinkle in training.

"Has wily Dan Devon got still another ace up his sleeve?" inquired Derek Darlington, the dean of the Eastern turf writers. "Insiders say there isn't a chance, that it's just a grandstand play. They ought to know but, on the other hand, Devon may surprise them."

The publicity was good and it was getting better. Half a dozen nationally syndicated writers were coming in for the Colt Stake, plus an army of turf reporters, on special assignment. Gus was getting requests for credentials from newspapermen who needed a map to locate the Treasure City Race Track.

What really rocked Gus, however, was the arrival of Clint Brown of *NOW* magazine, the biggest and best news weekly in the country. With him came Giorgi Malik, the artist.

"If Rustling Breeze makes a respectable showing in the Prelude, we're going to do our cover story next week on Dan Devon, his colt, and the race," Brown explained. "The boss likes the idea of a portrait of the colt on the cover with a background of Devon and some of the great fighters he's handled."

Publicity breaks no longer excited Gus the way they once did, but this one excited him. When Dan called, Gus sounded like a small boy who had just watched the schoolhouse burn down.

"*NOW* magazine?" Devon sounded bored. "All right. I'll cooperate, if it will help you, Gus."

"Very decent of you, old chap," Gus snorted. "This magazine has the biggest circulation in the country. And they want the colt's picture on the cover."

Devon melted when he saw Clint Brown, however. That young man had the right attitude—respectful.

"Mr. Harris told me to give you his very best good wishes, Mr. Devon. He says he hopes you win the Colt Stake by a mile."

"How is Footsy?" Devon asked.

"Who in hell is Footsy?" Gus interjected.

"F. Sherman Harris, our publisher," Brown replied.

"A very sweet chap," Devon added, "but the way he plays gin, you could rent him out."

The Colt Stake made *The Congressional Record,* too. United States Senator Thum Beauregard had arisen in that sanctuary and orated for ten minutes upon the glories of Rustling Breeze, the pride of all the good people back home where this gallant youngster was reclaimed for turf immortality. He had words of praise, too, for Cal Oakley and for Dan Devon, whom he described as "the grand old man of the turf."

Gus couldn't resist mentioning *The Congressional Record* to Devon, although he knew better.

"Tom-Tom is a very wonderful person," Dan allowed.

Before Gus could ask any more rude questions, Devon explained: "Tom-Tom Beauregard, the senator. A very old and dear friend."

First Footsy, Gus thought, and now Tom-Tom!

"This is a slow day, Devon. Here it is ten o'clock, and The President hasn't called you yet."

"The President?" Devon responded. "Did I ever tell you about the time when he was a freshman Congressman, and he wanted tickets for Hurricane Harrison's . . ."

"Never mind," Gus said. "Forget it."

A publicity man doesn't need to be told when his promotion has gotten off the ground. He knows. He no longer has to scrounge around for new angles, write the stuff himself, then plead with the desk men to use a paragraph or two. The papers begin sending out their own men to dig up stories, and soon there are so many reporters they are bumping into each other. After a while, all the publicity man has to do is to direct traffic. Gus was fast approaching that felicitous situation at Treasure City.

"The coverage for the Colt Stake will be the best you've ever seen," he told Randahl.

"That so?"

"It sure is. We won't have nearly enough room in the old press box. We'll have to build an auxiliary room on top of the official's loft for the radio and TV, plus the overflow of writers. I've gotten estimates, and we can do it for $6,000."

"Six thousand dollars?" he screamed. "You're crazy."

"We'll get a million dollars worth of free advertising."

"All right," he relented, "but get it done for four thousand."

If the excitement kept building, Gus knew, the Colt Stake could achieve unparalleled publicity, including the *Herald-Chronicle* banner Buzz Randahl wanted so much. This was shaping up as the finest three-year-old race of the year.

Nevertheless, Gus was worried. He felt an increasing uneasiness about Dr. Elliott Nichols and his plan to reduce the delightful absurdities of a horse race to the chilly certainty of a mathematical equation. The professor could take all the fun out of racing with his scheme to produce nothing but winners.

On that Tuesday morning, five days before the Prelude, he was ready to start his experiment. This danger was just a tiny patch of black cloud in a bright, beautiful sky, but in another week that cloud could become big enough to blot out the sun.

That is what Gus feared.

And, as it turned out, he was right.

Doug Dye had made elaborate plans for staging the professor's forecasts. The first press conference in the series drew a disappointingly small attendance of reporters, but that didn't discourage Dye. He was so sure that he had a good thing that he was on hand to run the press conference himself.

"Dr. Nichols will not discuss his theories, nor will he explain how he reaches his conclusions," Dye said. "He will not answer any questions. He will explain his procedure later, in a scholarly paper which will be published this fall by the university. For the moment, we can only tell you that Dr. Nichols has developed an enormously complicated formula for measuring the likelihood of success of each horse. Each forecast involves thousands of mathematical equations, and only the most refined instrument of the International Computer Systems is capable of digesting all the pertinent facts and resolving the equations within the narrow time limit allowed us."

He turned and beckoned to Dr. Nichols, who had

been sitting behind him, studying the floor and nervously tapping his shoes with a long blue envelope.

"If you please, professor," Dye extended his hand for the envelope. "Thank you. I have in this envelope the professor's selections for first, second, and third in the eighth race this afternoon. He has disclosed his choices to no one. Now I am going to lock this envelope in the safe."

He did so. Then he called Duke Jones out of the audience.

"The safe is secured by a double lock," Dye continued. "So that there can be no doubt that Dr. Nichols' selection will not be touched until we open the safe tomorrow, I am inviting Mr. Jones to secure the second lock and retain the key. I cannot open it without his. We will open the safe and read the selections here at the press conference tomorrow."

That satisfied even the most cynical newspapermen. They knew they could trust Jones.

That was the start, and it scarcely created a ripple of interest. Nobody really thought the professor could do it. By Friday noon, however, the professor's forecasts had swept the track like a holocaust. The doctor had the winner Tuesday, a $42 horse, and place and show as well. He turned up a $14.20 winner Wednesday, missed on second, but had the show horse at a surprising $22.40.

The press conference Friday attracted such a crowd that the publicity department had to screen out lesser track officials, and a small army of tipsters, horsemen, and hangers-on, including Manny Goldblatt who argued strongly that he was now the official correspondent for

Old Man Mose Knows, one of the tout sheets that are hawked outside the gates each day.

The professor's Thursday selection, announced on Friday, was a blinger. Only an innocent would have announced it. He had gone for a fifty-two-to-one shot to win, and that is just what the horse did, paying $106.80 for a two-dollar ticket. He was right on place and show as well.

These unlikely achievements made Dr. Nichols the hottest conversation piece in town. He had named three winners out of three, two places horses out of three and three show horses out of three. And some of the horses had paid handsome prices.

Nancy, who never makes a bet, was catching the fever.

"Gus, do you know what you would have made if you had parlayed two dollars on the professor's three choices to win?" she asked. "You would have made over $9,000, for just two. Isn't he wonderful?"

Even Connie O'Toole, the sports editor of the *Clarion-Call,* was jolted out of his posture of amused detachment.

"How could he pick that bum Thursday?" Connie inquired, a little plaintively. "That goat got beat by eighteen lengths the last time out, and he hasn't been in the money in two years. A man would have to be out of his mind to pick him."

"The professor did," Gus pointed out. "And he was right."

"It's weird," Connie shivered. "It's unnatural."

By Saturday morning, even the professor was beginning to wonder what he had started.

"I never anticipated anything like this, never in my

life," he confided. "It's frightening. I'm a serious scientist, engaged in pure research. I'm not a race track person. Why can't they understand this? Why can't they let me alone?"

He stood with Gus in the corridor outside the publicity office, gazing down at the crowd streaming in through the grandstand gates.

"If I walked out there now, I'd be mobbed," he declared. "I never should have let the papers print my picture. Now I have no place to hide. Those people would go mad if they saw me. They would demand—yes, demand—that I tell them which animal is going to win the next race. That happened to me yesterday. They're maniacs!

"This morning at five o'clock I had a call from a lunatic in Australia," he continued. "A mad man. He told me he was flying in to see me today. He wanted to give me $200,000 in cash for what he called my system. When I explained that I am a research scientist, he assumed I was dissembling. He said he'd meet my price and give me a share of his winnings, too. When I hung up, he was babbling."

"You better get an unlisted phone number, doctor."

"I have one now. Do you know that phone has been ringing constantly for two days? Perfect strangers insisted upon talking to me. People I had never seen before came hammering on my door and shouting for me to come out. I hid, so they set up a vigil outside my home. Mousie—I mean Eleanor, my wife—was almost in hysterics. Now we have a police guard, day and night. I'm worried sick. What can I do?"

"Drop the whole thing," Gus urged. "If you want to

experiment, choose a subject that people don't take so seriously. Name the man best qualified to be our next president, or find out what Russia is going to do next, or tell people how to choose the ideal marriage partner. Anything but horse racing. Don't fool around with the sport of kings."

"I wish I'd never gotten into this," he mumbled. "I just know something terrible is going to happen."

"The way you're hitting on those forecasts, doctor," Gus said, "it's already happened."

The newspapermen were close to mutiny now over the blackout on Rustling Breeze. Gus was with them. Devon had gotten all the mileage out of the stunt that he could expect. Now he was imposing an unnecessary burden on the reporters.

So Gus called Dean Hewitt, at whose farm Devon had stabled the horses, and told him to let the reporters in to take a look at Rustling Breeze.

"This is out of my hands, Gus," Hewitt said. "Devon has paid me a good price for the use of the facilities at the farm. What he does with them is his business."

"Have you still got that old, unused equipment shed over on Houghton Road, or have you torn it down?"

"It's still there. Why?"

"Nothing. I thought it might have been torn down by now."

Gus couldn't locate Devon, so he sought out Oakley at the barn.

"I've looked everywhere for Dan. Where is he hiding, Cal?"

"Dan has been feeling right poorly," Oakley returned. "He had a bad spell yesterday morning. I reckon that scared him. He flew to New York to see a Doc Reynolds. He says this man is the only doctor he trusts. I reckon he's in worse shape than he will admit."

"When will he be back?"

"He thought for the Prelude tomorrow, but they're keeping him in the hospital for more tests. He called a little while ago. He don't know when they will let him out. I'm worried."

TWENTY-THREE

"THAT'S THE FINEST parade of three-year-olds you've ever seen at this track."

Jay Mason spoke as the horses came onto the track for the first division of the Prelude. And he was right. Suburban Sam and Mean Old Man were in the parade, together with Dubbl Trubbl, winner of the Arkansas Derby; Bubble Bath, first home in the $100,000 added Peacock Purse; and Mighty Mouse, winner of almost $150,000 in his short career.

The Prelude had brought out twenty youngsters, so the racing secretary had split the race into two divisions, the eighth and ninth events on the ten-race program. The first division was clearly the stronger.

Rustling Breeze was in the second division with Federal Agent, Hinky Dinky, and Royal Crown and an underrated little colt from the minor leagues—Hit 'Em Hard. He might be the most serious challenger Rustling Breeze had.

Hit 'Em Hard had a fantastic winning record, with eleven victories in fourteen tries as a two-year-old and a three-year-old. His money winnings were not impressive but he had campaigned exclusively in the "bull rings," the halfmile tracks where the other horses weren't quite as rich.

Ted Shirwood, called "the king of the bull rings" for his mastery of the sharper turns and shorter straightaways of the smaller ovals, would ride Hit 'Em Hard. Shirwood was getting one of the biggest chances of his career. He rarely rode on a mile track.

"I miss Devon," Gus said. "I half expected him to fire off a telegram from the hospital, protesting that the horses in the second division of the Prelude wouldn't give Rustling Breeze a good workout."

"I miss him, too," Mason said quietly.

The Prelude is a mile and an eighth, one eighth of a mile less than the distance for the Stake itself. And the first division was a horse race every foot of the way.

Suburban Sam had never looked better. He started fast, and he finished faster. He flashed to the wire in the sizzling time of 1:46.3, slicing an incredible one and one-fifth seconds off a track record that had stood for a dozen years.

He needed all his speed, too, for Dubbl Trubbl was only a short half length back at the finish. Another neck back, Mean Old Man and Bubble Bath hit the wire together for a dead heat for show. The crowd was still buzzing about that one when the horses began walking toward the starting gate for the second division of the Prelude.

"Rustling Breeze starts on the rail, and that's a break," mused Mason. "He's got the best front runner in the business up. Scotty MacTavish is great on the lead, but if anything ever catches him, he's dead."

"You sound almost as though you'd like to see Rustling Breeze win, Jay."

"If Dan's really in tough shape, winning might give him a lift," Mason said defensively.

Rustling Breeze flew out of the starting gate and took command. MacTavish was sitting first on the rail as the field went into the clubhouse turn. Federal Agent, Hinky Dinky, and Royal Crown seemed to be out of it already. They weren't showing a thing.

Shirwood held Hit 'Em Hard well in hand in sixth, perhaps five lengths off the pace, behind such undistinguished youths as Razzle Dazzle, Big Strippers, and the entry of Hi, Toots and Mr. Mercury. As the horses neared the end of the backstretch, Mason saluted an artist:

"Look at that MacTavish slow the field down. They're practically walking. He's saving Rustling Breeze, saving a lot. What's Shirwood waiting for? He better make his move."

Shirwood waited, however, until the horses had rounded the final turn and were well started down the stretch. At that point, Rustling Breeze was running easily with a lead of two lengths over Razzle Dazzle and perhaps four over Hit 'Em Hard.

"Shirwood has waited too long," Mason said. "He'll never catch Rustling Breeze now."

He tried. He brought Hit 'Em Hard up to second with a tremendous burst of speed, whipping furiously. Then the cinderella colt from the bull rings made a blazing run at Rustling Breeze but MacTavish let his colt go inside the sixteenth pole and the little bay took it all with Hit 'Em Hard, who was coming like a runaway freight train, a scant quarter of a length back at the finish.

"Wow! Rustling Breeze did it again!" Gus yipped, drawing resentful glances from the working press.

Gus lowered his voice. "That's five in a row."

"Don't let it throw you," Mason said coolly. "He won the humpty dumpty division of the Prelude. And, even then, he didn't really win it. MacTavish won it, the way he slowed the field down. Or Shirwood lost it, when he misjudged the mile track. If they had gone another furlong, Hit 'Em Hard would have won easily."

"Don't tell me Rustling Breeze hasn't got a chance in the Colt Stake," Gus challenged him.

"Are you serious?" Mason scoffed. "Five of the horses in the first division would have taken Rustling Breeze this afternoon."

"You're looney!"

"Am I? Look at the time, friend: A minute, forty-nine and one-fifth seconds. That is two and three-fifths seconds slower than the first division. I pick Rustling Breeze for no better than seventh in the Colt Stake."

Despite Mason's pessimism, Rustling Breeze was a bigger story than ever now. Why not? He had met every test.

The pressure to permit newspapermen at Rustling

193

Breeze's workouts had been mounting steadily. Now, after his win in the Prelude, there was no holding it back. A delegation of angry writers cornered Gus in the press box after the last race.

"This is pure bush," snarled Derek Darlington. "You get us cleared to watch that colt train, or you'll wish you had."

Gus checked in at the office early on Sunday, the day after the Prelude. He had made up his mind that the reporters were going to get out to cover Rustling Breeze's next workout, one way or another. He had a plan.

Gus was hard at work on the pass list for the Colt Stake when he heard a familiar voice:

"I hear you've been looking for me."

The little PR man swiveled around, and there was Dan Devon, cockier than ever.

"They sprung you from the hospital?"

"Late Saturday afternoon, Gus. Doc Reynolds couldn't find a thing wrong with me. I'm still full of bootleg whiskey from Prohibition Days. The germ that could survive in my blood stream hasn't been born."

"He couldn't find anything wrong with you? He should have asked me. Those damn secret workouts have me in a bind. You've milked that gag for all it's worth. Now, call 'em off."

Devon shook his head. "The papers have been calling the secret workouts a publicity stunt. If I call them off now, this will confirm their suspicions. Folks will begin to think I'm untrustworthy."

"You've been around a long time, Dan. Like fifty years. If they haven't tumbled to you by now, they never will."

Dan winked. "Sometimes I mean what I say, Gus. This

keeps everybody off balance. Nobody gets in to our workouts. Should we call a press conference? I'll explain my position."

"They aren't in the mood, chum. They want in. When will Rustling Breeze be on the track again?"

"Tuesday morning, at eight o'clock. You know, Gus, you could have visited the farm while I was out of town. Oakley doesn't give a damn. I'm the only one you have to worry about."

Gus studied Devon's expression, but the old man revealed nothing.

"You'll think of something, Gus," he said. "That's your hidden strength: You'd trick your own grandmother out of her shoes."

That was enough. As soon as Dan was gone, Gus called Pierre.

"I've got a job for you, early Tuesday morning, Pierre. Exciting, dangerous—you'll love it."

"Dangerous? Who needs that?"

"The key word is exciting. Rustling Breeze is going to work out Tuesday at eight o'clock at Hewitt's farm. You are going to lead a band of intrepid reporters who will sneak in and cover it."

"Won't Devon throw us off?"

"Let me worry about Devon. There's an unused shed on Houghton Road, overlooking the backstretch of the training track. Take your telescopic lens. It will be a cinch. I'm going to let *The Racing Form* clocker, a cameraman, and a couple of reporters go with you. Mason will be along, too."

"Get one thing straight, Gus. I'm not taking orders from Mason."

195

"Okay, you're on your own, but the movie cameraman is his."

Gus picked Darlington and Jones as the pool reporters. They were less than overjoyed.

"What kind of a crazy idea is this?" Jones protested.

"It's not crazy. I know the layout, Duke. You can see the workout from the old equipment shed, with your high-powered binoculars it will . . ."

"Old equipment shed! Not me, buster!"

"Okay, go back and tell George Hall that you couldn't get the story because you're too fat to climb up on a shed. He'll understand."

After the representatives of the Fourth Estate had departed, mumbling to themselves, Gus called Manny Goldblatt.

"What's Dan up to?" Manny asked. "Been out of town, hasn't he?"

"Why don't you ask him about it? Meet him at his hotel at eight o'clock Tuesday morning. Just keep him occupied for half an hour or so."

"What do I want to see Devon for? I'm taking Carlos Chavez, my classy lightweight, over to the park for his roadwork Tuesday morning . . ."

"You want an angel? Devon is in the chips. His horse has won five in a row, at some good odds, and you know how he bets. He has to be loaded."

"You think there's a chance, Gus?"

"Try it. Get to him while he's got it. If you wait until the Colt Stake is run, Devon will blow his roll on Rustling Breeze. He'll be flat broke."

"Yeah. Yeah."

"Oakley is taking his horses back to the farm after the

Colt Stake. Then what is Devon going to do? If he hands you ten grand now, he'll have a place to light when Oakley pulls out. Think what a great team you and Dan would make. You train Carlos and he lines up the fights. Why not?"

Manny was growing excited.

"Devon's a hustler, an old-line fight man. They don't come like that any more. He's a real pro. You think he'll go for it?"

"Could be. See him at eight o'clock Tuesday morning. Keep him busy for half an hour. That's my cut."

"I'll do it," exclaimed Manny. "Devon knows a fighter when he sees one. He'll be crazy for Carlos. I'll bring some movies I took in the gym. Thanks, pal."

The switchboard was closed on Sunday, so Gus had a little privacy in which to finish the pass list, the distribution of parking stickers, and the press box arrangements. He was nearly finished when Buzz Randahl came in.

"I thought I might find you in," he said. "I want to talk to you, without interruptions."

He closed the office doors, and locked them.

"I told you that you'd be the first to know if I decided to kick Dan Devon off the track," Buzz said evenly. "Well, I'm telling you now. I'm ordering him off, him and his Flowering Tree Stable."

"Why?" Gus fumbled, taken by surprise. "What's your reason?"

"I can find a reason," Randahl said, tight-lipped. "I'm putting him off. That's it."

Gus leaned back and surveyed the track president. Buzz was cold and grim. Worried, too.

"Buzz, this is the coldest, cruelest . . ."

"I'll give him an out," Buzz said. "He can say Rustling Breeze is a little lame, or he bucked his shins. Anything. Then he won't be leaving under suspicious circumstances. I don't want to hurt your friend. I am sensitive to your feelings for him."

"You're such a helluva sensitive guy," Gus responded, "that you can get yourself a new press agent."

Randahl seemed pained, but he did not raise his voice. "Yes, I do owe you an explanation," he conceded. "I'm going to tell you this in confidence, you understand. Nobody else at the track knows anything about this. It's my problem, and I keep my problems to myself, but I want you to see why I must get rid of Devon."

He walked to the other side of the room, lit his pipe slowly and then came back.

"You really started it all, Gus, with that silly build-up about how Buzz Randahl would bet on anything. I know. I know. I went along with it, and now I'm boobytrapped."

He sat on the top of Gus's desk.

"My mother is a very remarkable woman. She has amazing strength of character, and she's tough as nails. She has never liked my running this track. She thinks I'm a child playing with toys."

"When my father died, he left me an estate that is worth perhaps ten million but, by the terms of his will, mother controls my inheritance as long as she lives. I can't get a penny without her approval.

"She has tried constantly to put me to helping her with the family's business interests. Gus, it would kill me if I had to go to work for her. I'd go crazy if I got out of horse racing, and now I may have to."

He was so agitated that Gus was beginning to forget his earlier resentment. He's got problems, too, the press agent thought.

"When this track was built, it was 'way out in the country. Property here was cheap. The men who started this track looked ahead. They purchased all the land they could get on both sides of the highway. They built the track on one side, and they held the remainder of the acreage for future development. Now the city has encompassed us, and the value of this land has increased fantastically.

"I own a helluva lot of extremely valuable real estate, and all I do now is pay taxes on it. I want to build my own little city there—a motor inn, a hospital, theaters, night clubs, shopping complexes, apartment buildings, the works. In another ten years, we'll have horse racing ten months a year. My city will be a gold mine, if I can ever get it started. Gus, the possibilities are almost unlimited.

"I asked my mother for five million from my inheritance to begin the motor inn and the hospital, for starters. She refused to give me a penny. That was the first time I ever fought with my mother."

He was up and walking around. He couldn't sit still.

"She picked up the *Herald-Chronicle* sports page. With our family, the *Herald-Chronicle* is next only to the Bible, you know. My great-grandfather helped found the paper, and a member of our family has been on the board of directors ever since. Mother is on the board now. She tends to measure respectability by the degree of acceptance the *Herald-Chronicle* gives an enterprise. She thought she had an argument I couldn't answer.

"You know, baseball gets the eight-column headline on the sports page of the *Herald-Chronicle* six days out of seven, no matter what. The track never gets a headline, unless there's a suspicion of scandal. She said I couldn't get the headline for the track the best day I ever saw. I was hot. I told her the best day I'd ever see would be the Colt Stake day this year, and I'd get the headline."

He stopped pacing, and threw up his hands.

"She trapped me. My own mother! She said if I got the first-page banner, she would release the money and stop badgering me to quit the track. If I didn't, I'd get out of horse racing and take a hand with the family interests."

"You didn't bet, did you, Buzz? You didn't!"

Randahl smiled bitterly.

"I've got some pride, and I was angry," he related. "I took her up on it. Now I'm stuck with it."

"Cancel the bet. Tell her you reconsidered."

"A bet's a bet, Gus. I keep my word. And so does she."

He slumped into the chair beside Gus, a weary, dispirited man.

"Okay, but what has Dan Devon got to do with your bet?"

"Everything, Gus. Doug Dye has been on my back all through the meeting, insisting that Devon is making a hippodrome out of the Colt Stake. Old man Jensen has been screaming lately, in private. Dye got hold of me last night. He gave me an earful.

"Jensen is the *Herald-Chronicle*'s biggest advertiser. He swings a lot of weight. Dye said he'd guarantee the publicity if I would drop Devon. I asked him if that would include the *Herald-Chronicle* banner and he told me there would be nothing to it. He said he'd deliver the banner if I got rid of Devon. No ifs or buts. He'd deliver. He guaranteed it."

"So that's why Devon has to go?"

"That's why." Randahl pulled out his pipe and began to fill the bowl.

"Why do you tell me this, Buzz?"

"I'm giving you advance notice. I said I would."

"No, Buzz. You're not satisfied that Dye can deliver. You want confirmation from me, don't you?"

"I'll listen to your opinion, but, in any case, nothing can be gained by keeping Devon."

"Do you know how George Hall, the sports editor of the *Herald-Chronicle,* would react to the kind of raw power play that Dye proposes? He'd tell Dye and Twentieth Century Motors and Jensen all to go to hell. It won't wash, Buzz."

"Dye says he'll go to Si Friederich, the publisher."

"It comes to the same thing. Friederich never yields to that kind of pressure from advertisers. Believe me, Buzz. Dye's guarantee doesn't mean anything."

Randahl lit his pipe. The process claimed his attention for a long moment. "I'm not sure Dye can lock it up, Gus, but he'll cut the odds. I'd guess that I have at least an even chance for that banner right now. With Twentieth Century behind me, it's three-to-five I'll get it."

"Devon has been a windfall for publicity," Gus argued. "Rustling Breeze is the kind of Cinderella story the public loves. Don't kill my publicity campaign. If you do, you're hurting your own chances for the banner."

Randahl shook his head. "When the professor announces his picks on Tuesday, Rustling Breeze will be dead. Dye is no fool. The professor has made a dry run, and Rustling Breeze won't be in it. The professor says Rustling Breeze will be no better than eighth under any conditions. The only horses he'll beat will be the entry of Mr. Mercury and Hi, Toots. After he announces his Colt Stake selections, Rustling Breeze won't rate a line in the papers."

Gus tried not to panic. "All right, Buzz. Let Devon stay and I'll get you that banner. I guarantee it. Dye can't deliver, but I can."

Randahl gave his press agent a careful once-over. "How can *you* do it, if Dye can't?"

"I've been in this town for a long time, and I've done Hall a few real favors. He owes me something, and I've never tried to collect. I've never done anything like this before, but I'll do it now. I'll tell him if I don't get the banner, I'm out of a job. He'll do it for me."

"Are you sure?"

"I've never misled you, Buzz. I don't make many promises, and I don't make them lightly. I'm telling you plainly: Keep Devon, and you've got your banner."

Randahl sat down on the desk again, and leaned forward. "Don't play games with me, Gus. If you have any doubt whether you can deliver, back out now. Because if you don't come through, I'll fire you the minute the *Herald-Chronicle* hits the street."

He waited for this to sink in. "Well, which is it, Gus? Does Devon stay, or does he go?"

"Devon stays," Gus replied, "and you get the banner."

TWENTY-FOUR

"YOU ARE LOST, perhaps?" Gus asked. "I know your taste for low comedy. You must be looking for the ball park where the Treasure City Jewels play. It's eighteen miles from here. If you drive slow, you can miss the whole game."

George Hall, the indignant lion of the *Herald-Chronicle*, merely grunted. He nodded toward the open door of Gus's office. "I want to talk to you alone, Gus," he said. Gus closed the door.

"This is Sunday," the press agent protested. "A day which the Godly devote to rest and pious meditation and, in the fall, football on TV. How come you're working today, George?"

"I'm trying to find some thing out," the visitor muttered. "And it can't wait, not after Devon's horse won in that Prelude yesterday. I'm looking for information."

Gus wasn't really surprised that he had been subjected to so many interruptions on Sunday afternoon, which is usually a day when the track is deserted. With the Colt Stakes so close, this Sunday figured to be as busy as any race day. He waited for Hall, who was idly fingering the bowl of his pipe.

"I hear Dan Devon is going to fix your Colt Stake Saturday, Gus," he said solemnly. "I hear it all over town."

"Dan will be indignant when I tell him this, George. It's supposed to be a secret."

"Stow it," Hall growled. "I'm serious. I want to find out just what Devon has to do to make a killing here. I'm not sure that I understand how this racing betting works. Explain it to me."

Gus shrugged. "Do you mean it? You know as much about the books as I do."

"Yeah, I'm on the inside," Hall said. "And sometimes a man can be so far on the inside he can't see out. I want to hear your explanation. Maybe there are some new wrinkles I haven't found out about."

Gus was nodding. He had lost his bantering approach. "Okay, George. I'll tell you what I know. Off the record. Let's start with Devon. The average student would figure it was a good day if he put $1,000 on a twenty-five-to-one shot and won, but not Devon. That wouldn't pay his phone bill. His idea of a leading citizen is a thief who steals a million.

"Let's imagine he has somehow got a lock on the Colt Stake. In order to bring off his betting coup, he would have to make a number of very substantial bets with bookmakers all across the country. And if those bets ever get back to the track, he's had it."

Hall hadn't taken his eyes off Gus since he had sat down. His pipe had gone out. He relit it, blowing out clouds of blue smoke. "Why, Gus?" he asked.

"Every dollar bet at the track goes through the totalisator machine, which computes the odds. If Devon bet even fifty grand at the track, it would knock the odds down from thirty-to-one to about one-to-five. There are a lot of factors. For one thing, if the other patrons see a horse is getting a surprisingly heavy play, they figure somebody knows something. So they hurry to get on that horse, too. Moreover, if Devon and his cronies are pouring all that money in, they're tying up the mutuel machines and those who want to back the other horses may get shut out.

"Let's say he bets fifty grand, and that knocks the odds down to one-to-five, the minimum return allowed by our racing law. He risks fifty thousand and all he stands to make is $10,000. It's a waste of time."

Hall was so absorbed in the recitation that he did not notice the match he held was still burning. When the flame touched his finger, he noticed it. He threw it angrily to the floor, but he said nothing.

"So Devon tries to hit the books," Gus said. "The odds at the track are, say, thirty-to-one on Rustling Breeze. The book won't go that high, but he'll give you odds of fifteen-to-one. If a stranger goes to a book and wants to bet $10,000, the bookie won't handle it. But there are many men who regularly bet $100,000 in a day and think nothing of it. If the bookie is big enough, he'll handle all of those bets he can get. Even if the bookie loses this bet, he knows he'll get it back in the long run.

"Devon clearly needs a partner, a big gambler with plenty of clout in case the books don't want to pay off. The gambler can send his boys to get the bets down. Timing is important here. The books probably won't take bets, even from a good customer, less than an hour before post time for the race. They need time to move."

Hall had taken a small notebook, the kind normally used for telephone numbers. He was scribbling notes with a stubby pencil. After a moment, he looked up. Gus resumed.

"The bookies have a safety valve: the commission

houses. These are big bookmakers who will take the bets off the hands of the smaller operators for a five percent commission. There are four big commission houses, as far as I know. On the East Coast, the West Coast, New York and here. If one commission house gets overloaded, it can lay off part of the action with another house, for the five percent commission."

The old lion glared accusingly at Gus. "So Devon can do it. He gets a partner, an enforcer. The kind of guy you don't cross. They scatter $200,000 among the bookies. Why not?"

Before Hall had finished, Gus was shaking an admonitory finger in his face. "Don't you see, George, sooner or later the smaller books and the commission houses are all overloaded. And Honest Alfie, our commission house man in residence, pulls them out. Alfie is a special case. He has much in common with other successful tycoons. He's avaricious. Alfie hates to give up that five percent commission from the other books. So he sends Manny Goldblatt—remember him? A pretty fair lightweight, once—he sends Manny out to the track every day. Manny has got a deal with the little old lady who owns the house right across from the entrance to the clubhouse parking lot. He can make it to her house, call Alfie and get back in twelve minutes flat. I've timed him. Alfie cuts off bets on a race forty-five minutes before post time. So Manny has plenty of time to lay off bets. Nobody's ever proved it, but I'm convinced Manny books at the track, too."

Hall looked up from his notebook, frowning. "Why would anybody bet with Manny when they are already at the track?"

The question surprised Gus. "If Manny knows them, he will give them credit. If he takes their bets when they've tapped out, why shouldn't they bet with him when they're in the chips. They just have to be sure that no money changes hands at the track."

Hall looked up again, bobbing his head up and down in assent. "I remember. Buzz Randahl tried to bar Manny from the track three years ago, and Manny sued. The court ruled that Randahl couldn't bar Manny unless he had been convicted of a crime. Violated his civil rights, as I remember. Yeah."

Gus stretched back in his chair, linking his hands behind his head. "Well, that's it," he said. "Devon can't make a real killing because, no matter how he maneuvers, Manny can get back to the track, lay off the bets, and knock the odds down. It's an unbeatable set-up. There's no way Devon can lick it."

Hall had given up on his pipe. He knocked the ashes into the big tray on Gus' desk. He stuck the pipe in his coat pocket. He was obviously unconvinced. He shook his head in disbelief.

"What's wrong?" Gus flared. "Don't you think I'm leveling with you?"

"Oh, you're leveling, Gus," Hall said thoughtfully. "And I've heard that same drill before. But I don't believe it. I think Devon is going to fool all you wise guys. You say you can't be taken. Guys always say that just before they get taken."

TWENTY-FIVE

Douglas D. Dye faced the throng that had jammed the conference room for the professor's Monday press conference. He cleared his throat.

"We have here Dr. Nichols' choices for last Saturday's feature race, the first division of the Prelude," he began. He opened the envelope, paused for effect and then began reading.

"Dr. Nichols' forecast . . . for the first position . . . Suburban Sam . . . the second position . . . Dubbl Trubbl . . . for the third position . . . uh, one moment . . . Dr. Nichols notes that he is unable to make a firm decision for the third position . . . there are two horses . . . for all practical purposes, their measurements are equal . . . he declines to choose between them for the third position . . . Mean Old Man and Bubble Bath."

The silence that followed was absolute until the man from *NOW*, the big weekly newsmagazine, burst out:

"I'll be damned! This guy picked the dead heat for show."

The professor sat at Dye's right, oblivious of the uproar he had caused. He never lifted his head. He stared at the floor, folding and unfolding his hands, and occasionally pulling at his lower lip.

Old Man Mose, even in his brashest moments, would

never have dared predict a dead heat for show, but the professor had done it. When the reporters grasped what had happened, an excited babble arose.

"No questions, no questions," Dye rapped for order. "Dr. Nichols will not answer any questions. I've explained that. In your comments, gentlemen, I will appreciate it if you will make it clear that Dr. Nichols' forecasts are made possible through the magic of the newest electronic brain developed by International Computer Systems, Inc. Please include that Inc. because other . . ."

The reporters were crowding out of the room, but Dye remembered something. He banged the gavel down again.

"One moment! One moment, please! An announcement. Due to the unprecedented interest in Dr. Nichols experiment, we are going to hold the final press conference at noon tomorrow in the modern new auditorium of the International Computer Systems recently completed building on Fullmer Street. At that time, Dr. Nichols will forecast the finish of the Colt Stake. Ordinary press credentials will not admit anyone tomorrow. You may obtain your admission tickets from the publicity office upon presentation of your credentials."

The professor bolted for the door, with Gus in tight pursuit. The little press agent was close behind as the professor fled down the corridor toward the elevator. Two very tough-looking characters moved in and clamped Gus between them. One look, and Gus knew they were gangsters.

"Don't try anything, mister," said the shorter, bull-necked one. "Just put your hands on your head."

"Oh, no, not again! What is this, doctor? Who are these goons?"

"Police," Dr. Nichols stammered. "Lieutenant Gilhooley, Detective Wiebelhaus, this is Mr. Scott, the Treasure City publicity man. My life has been threatened, Gus. I can't move without a police guard."

"Glad to see you're on the job, gentlemen," Gus managed. "I've got to talk to the professor. In my office. Alone."

"If you want to talk to him, doc," the lieutenant declared, "I guess it's okay."

Gus took the professor into his office. He closed the door.

"I'm going out of my mind," the professor was almost crying. He sank limply into a chair. "I haven't had a moment's sleep in the last thirty-six hours. This is unbelievable."

"Why did you have to pick that dead heat for show? Any dummy could see you'll have a million more horse players looking for you when word of that gets around."

"I had no choice," he quavered. "My measurements showed only the most imperceptible difference between the two animals. One three-thousandth of an inch, as I recall."

He was a pitiful figure, pale and harassed. He was holding his head in his hands again. "Call it off, doc. Don't try to forecast the Stake. If you hit it right, the National Guard won't be able to hold off the students who will want to know how you did it. If you tout them wrong, they will want to lynch you. There are some things that our culture is too primitive to accommodate, and one of these is a surefire way to beat the races."

"You just won't believe, in the civilized twentieth century, what happened to me last night, Gus."

"I'd believe it, doc, knowing how civilized the twentieth century is."

"Somehow, somebody got my unlisted phone number. This man threatened to take me for a ride, as he put it, if I didn't show him how I forecast the race results. I didn't tell Mousie. She's near collapse, without that. I informed the police and they took us into protective custody.

"I don't like it. We're on the thirtieth floor, and I have this dreadful feeling it's a trap. It's such a busy, crowded hotel but, of course, the police are in the next room. Indeed, we're right across the street from the headquarters building."

Gus tried, desperately, to make him understand. "Don't you see, doc, the average horse player doesn't expect to win. He knows it's a good day when he breaks even. He plays because he'll be damned if he'll quit. It is this unreasonable stubbornness that made America great. Why do you think the pioneers dared to push out across the wilderness? It's my theory that somebody bet one of those pig-headed farmers he couldn't make it. Now you're making a mockery of man's noble intransigence by denying horse players their right to lose.

"You propose to take money away from the track owners, who can't live without it, and give it to the horse players, who won't know what to do with it. It's a shambles, and it accomplishes nothing. Don't try to understand the horse players. Just leave us alone. Cut and run, doc. You'll be doing us all a favor."

The professor's gaze was dull. He looked as though he hadn't slept in thirty-six hours.

"This is a perverted Alice in Wonderland story come to

life," he whispered. "I wish I had never gotten into this, but now there's no way out."

"Talk to Dye. Tell him you fear for your life. Tell him you just can't go through with it."

"I have talked to Mr. Dye. He is a very determined man. I've signed a contract. If I don't fulfill my agreement, he could accomplish my utter economic and academic ruin. There's no escape."

He was almost in tears. Gus talked to him for half an hour without getting anywhere. He and his bodyguard had hardly left the office before Gus called Dye, who had just returned to his office from the press conference.

"You win, Dye," he said. "I'm throwing in the towel. I'll go all the way for Horsepower in my publicity. I won't even mention Rustling Breeze's name. You can censor every line I write from here on in. Just call off this infernal forecast tomorrow. You must! A man's life is in danger."

Dye's sarcasm was heavy. "Listen, you need an orchestra with ninety-eight violins. If I have to listen to that sob-sister stuff, I want background music with it."

"I mean it, Dye. The professor's life has been threatened. He and his wife are near nervous collapse. This is an ugly situation. Don't make it worse. Cancel the press conference, and I'll submit every line I write for your approval. Every line!"

"Sure you will," he taunted Gus, "now that I don't give a damn whether you do or you don't. I knew you'd come whining to me. Go ahead and whine. Crawl, you bastard!"

"But, Dye, the professor is a decent human being. He's important . . ."

"Screw him!" Dye's voice rose. "And screw you, too. He's important? What do you think Twentieth Century Motors is, and International Computer Systems? They're worth big money to me, and you tell me this oddball professor is important. Nuts!"

Gus was so absorbed in the exchange that he forgot, until too late, about Dye's habit of slamming the receiver down to terminate a conversation.

Gus never knew how long he sat there, trying to think what he could do to rescue the professor. If only Sue were here, he told himself. I could always talk things out with Sue.

Finally he went in to talk to Nancy.

"I'm worried about the professor, Nancy. This foolish publicity stunt could destroy him and his wife. Actually destroy them. His life has been threatened, and the police are hiding him out. He is in terrible trouble. He wants to drop the whole thing, but Dye won't let him off the hook."

Nancy has a wonderful capacity for indignation, and she was indignant now. "Why doesn't he let the world know about the awful treatment he's received?" she asked. "Why doesn't he explain about the threats and all, and how that awful Doug Dye is just actually making him risk his life. Let the world know just what kind of a person that Doug Dye is!"

Gus patted Nancy paternally on the head. "I'm a fraud, Nancy. You're the real public relations expert. Why didn't I see it?"

"See what?"

"I've overlooked the professor's strongest weapon, an aroused public opinion. Those International Computer people won't dare go through with that press conference tomorrow if word gets out that they're putting the professor's life in jeopardy. Suppose they held the press conference, and somebody did the professor in? The publicity would ruin them. Thank you, Nancy. You've given me the answer."

Gus didn't want to move too fast. In a situation like this, if a man hasn't got timing, he hasn't got anything.

The little press agent called Hal Smith, whose late night TV sports broadcast has a top rating. He asked Smith if he could bring a mystery guest on his program. "I can't say any more now, but you'll have an interview that will stand this town on its ear," Gus promised.

"This mystery guest," Hal mused. "Will he talk freely? Whatever it is, I don't want someone who acts coy. I could have some rather blunt questions."

"I haven't contacted him yet, Hal. However, I'm sure he'll go along. If he refuses, I'll call you at once."

"No need," Smith returned. "I go on at eleven o'clock, and I'll want a chance to talk to him before. If you can deliver the guest, have him here by 10:15. Otherwise, I will conclude that you couldn't swing it."

Gus waited until nine o'clock before he set out.

The professor told Gus where he was hiding out. He was living on the thirtieth floor of a hotel across from police headquarters. That had to be the Fleur de Lis. The police often quartered witnesses there for safekeeping.

Gus became aware of the traffic jam when he was still several blocks from the hotel. The cars were hardly crawling. As he drew nearer, he saw the great throng that had spilled out of the hotel and into the street. The motorists were stopping to gawk, but the police were doing their best to keep the traffic moving.

"Keep going," the big cop said. "C'mon, let's go. Get rolling, mister, or I'll haul you in. Move that thing."

Gus had to go two blocks past the hotel before he found a parking lot that would take a car. The police had cordoned off the hotel, but this was no problem.

"Scott, Treasure City news service," Gus said, flashing his race track pass.

"Okay, okay," the officer said. "I guess you're all right, but don't try to get into the hotel. Talk to the sergeant."

The policeman at the hotel entrance was made of sterner stuff. "Nobody gets in," he said. "That's my orders. Shove off."

"I must go in, officer. This is extremely urgent. I must see Dr. Elliott Nichols."

He listened when Gus told him that.

"Did you say Dr. Nichols?"

"That's right, officer. I won't be long, if you'll just let me go up to the penthouse . . ."

"Put your hands on your head," he snapped. "On your head. Now."

"But I just . . . All right, all right. What's eating you?"

He slid his hands over the little man with practiced skill. Then he yelled: "Mike! Mike!"

"Take this guy to the inspector, Mike. If he makes a wrong move, handcuff him. He wants to see Dr. Nichols."

"Well, well," said Mike. "A live one."

Mike hustled him through the seething throng, through the lobby and into the hotel where the police had set up a command post in the manager's offices. At the desk in the inner office sat Inspector Harold Dunleavy.

"This joker wanted to know where Dr. Nichols was," Mike reported. "He's clean. We frisked him."

The inspector looked at Gus, irritation giving way to surprise. "You? You were looking for Dr. Nichols?"

For a man who had gotten so many passes to the track, the inspector looked unsuitably stern. "I know this man," he admitted. "You can leave, Mike. I'll talk to him. And now, Scott, tell me exactly what you wanted with Dr. Nichols. I'm telling you, give it to me straight or you may spend the night in the can."

"I want to go over the details of tomorrow's press conference with him. We've got a million things to straighten out. He got away from the track today before we could rehearse the press conference. He told me he was staying here, and I've got to see him."

"You won't rehearse anything with Dr. Nichols tonight. Nobody will."

He spoke with frightening finality.

"What's up? Has anything happened to the doctor?"

"What's up, he asks. Nothing much, except that some crackpot threatened to blow up this whole damn hotel if the doctor didn't tell him which horse was going to win the seventh race tomorrow at that lousy track of yours. This guy says he's planted a time bomb and, if the professor doesn't want to be responsible for the death of hundreds of innocent people, he better start talking. Do you have any idea what this means? We had to evacuate the whole hotel and check for explosives, floor by floor. Yeah, I know, it's probably a crank call, but we couldn't take that chance.

"Pardon me," he said, as the phone rang.

"Oh, yes, sir, Mr. Commissioner. No, I'm sure it was a

216

Swede. We made a tape of the call. There's some background noise, but the Swedish accent is clear enough. I think the caller tried to disguise it, but he's a Swede, I'm sure. Right, Mr. Commissioner. I'll keep you informed."

Inspector Dunleavy replaced the receiver.

"Where's the doctor now?" Gus asked.

"Run along, and just be thankful I happened to be here tonight, not some inspector who doesn't like the ponies. We've got Dr. Nichols and his wife where they'll be safe, and nobody's going to see them until we deliver him for that press conference tomorrow."

"You don't really think anyone would actually blow up this hotel, do you?"

"For a way to beat the ponies," the inspector said, "some of these guys would blow up this whole damn town."

TWENTY-SIX

THE PHONE SNARLED. Gus picked it up peevishly.

"This is Inspector Wilson," said the caller. "Traffic Safety Bureau. I have a serious problem. I need your help."

Gus listened.

"I don't know why they do these things," Wilson said

in some exasperation, "but the county road commission has torn up the freeway about a mile from the exit to your race track. They never ask me before they do these things. They just do it, and then I have to try to live with it."

"But we have our biggest day coming up Saturday? Who would do a thing like that?"

"Charlton Dressage, the deputy commissioner, is the genius who thought of this. That stretch of freeway needs some work, but it could have waited for another week or so. Two of the three lanes on the westbound freeway are closed as of right now, Scott. If we're lucky, they might possibly have one more lane open for your Colt Stake Saturday, but there's no way on earth they can have all three lanes in operation. We anticipate a substantially increased flow of traffic this year. We estimate a twenty-two percent increase over last year. That may be conservative. We could have the worst traffic foul-up this town has ever seen."

"What can I do, inspector?"

"Pass the word, any way you can. Ask your patrons to use surface roads wherever possible, and stay off the free-way. We just can't handle the traffic if they don't. Not with one lane closed down."

"I'll get on it. We'll put it on the public address system every afternoon this week. I'll send out a publicity release, and we'll add a line in our ads and our radio and TV spots. I'll ask the newspaper boys to make a special mention of the problem."

"Thanks. If everybody uses that freeway Saturday, nobody's going to get to the races."

A twenty-two percent increase in attendance for the Colt Stake? Inspector Wilson's estimate was cheerful news. He confirmed Gus's own early guess that the track could break all record for attendance and mutuel handle on the big day.

The news from the baseball front was encouraging, too. The Jewels got the banner in the *Herald-Chronicle,* almost automatically, no matter what they did. This year, however, they were a tired joke. They had lost their last sixteen games, and they were deep in last place in the league. Nobody cared any more. On Monday, only 963 had attended the Jewels' game in a ball park that seats 72,463. How could George Hall possibly give the banner to a team like that? How could he bypass the Colt Stake?

Gus knew how.

Dr. Elliott Nichols could kill the race as a sports contest. And that was just what he will do when he makes his final predictions a little more than two hours from now, Gus thought.

The publicity department was feeling the deadening effects of his wizardry already. *NOW* magazine had abandoned its plan to run its cover story on Dan Devon and Rustling Breeze.

"We just can't buck the professor," Clint Brown, the *NOW* writer, explained. "He's the hottest conversation piece in sports. If he says Horsepower will win Saturday, nobody will believe Rustling Breeze—or any other horse —has a chance. And that is just what he's going to say, you know."

Gus looked so stricken that Brown quickly added: "Don't feel badly, Gus. If the professor calls the turn on this one, we're going to have him and Doug Dye on our cover next week."

Nancy was as edgy, too, but for a different reason. The

spying expedition had departed early in the morning to breach the secret workouts of Rustling Breeze. It was almost ten o'clock now, and Gus hadn't heard from his commandos.

"You shouldn't have sent them, Gus," Nancy said. "I just know something dreadful has happened to those boys. I just know it."

Connie O'Toole's call added nothing to Gus's peace of mind.

"I want to talk to you, Gus. I've got Dan Devon cold this time. See me at the Towne Bar, across the street from the International Computer Building, at 11:30, before we go over for the professor's press conference."

"I'm not sure I can make it by 11:30," Gus answered.

"Make it as close to 11:30 as you can, Gus. I want to go over this with you personally. It's dynamite. I knew if I kept nosing around long enough, I'd find something. I've found it now, pal. This could tear your track apart."

Great, Gus pondered. Just what I needed to take my mind off my other troubles.

For the next twenty minutes, Gus tried to keep his mind on the preparations for the Colt Stake, but his attention kept wandering. What was happening at the farm?

"They're here, Gus!" Nancy called. "They're back from Mr. Hewitt's farm."

He followed her into the corridor outside the publicity office. They could see their fearless agents piling out of the cars.

"I'm going down," Nancy said.

"Take it easy, child," Gus admonished. "If they have any complaints, they'll be up here in half a minute. And the way things are going today, they will have complaints."

They made it up in less than a minute.

Duke Jones came steaming in at the head of the convoy. That was the tip-off. When Jones leads the way, it's trouble.

"You and your damned tricks, Scott. I've had enough," he bellowed. "You certainly made great arrangements. We were thrown off that farm. Me, the turf editor of the *Herald-Chronicle*, thrown off by that cheap, chiseling Devon."

The others had filed in behind—Darlington, *The Racing Form* timer, the movie cameraman, Pierre, and Mason. Mason's shirt and his light jacket were spotted with blood.

"One of our men was assaulted! Bodily assaulted!" Jones howled.

"Hold it, Duke," Gus interrupted. "Take it slow. Give it to me from the beginning."

"Everything went fine, at the start," Darlington offered. "We came in on Houghton Road and there was the old shed. We climbed up and sat there for maybe ten minutes when Rustling Breeze came out on the track, with MacTavish up. Oakley sat on a pony beside the track, holding a stop watch.

"The colt went four furlongs, and he looked very sharp. Very sharp. We saw everything we needed to see, really. Your boys got the still photographs and the movie footage. There was nothing to it."

"Then what's the complaint?"

"I'll tell you what's the complaint," Jones took over again.

"There wasn't any real trouble, Gus," Mason interposed, but Jones brushed him off.

"I'll tell it, Jay. We waited around for a few minutes, and watched them take Rustling Breeze off the track. We were getting ready to go when this jeep comes up, loaded with half a dozen goons."

"I've never seen an uglier, meaner bunch in my life," Pierre spoke up.

"They weren't pretty," Darlington agreed.

"They told us to get off the property, that we were trespassing," Jones continued. "Then one of these hoods says he wants the film in our cameras."

"He had a gun," Pierre announced.

"You're crazy, Gauthier," Mason cut in.

"This gorilla tries to grab the movie camera," Jones related. "Jay told him to forget it. Wham! This hood belts Jay in the nose, and Jay had blood all over his face. I tell you, I was scared."

"I asked for it," Jay said. "I took my eyes off him."

"And then?"

"Nothing, really . . ." Jay began. Jones overruled him.

"Like hell it was nothing! Jay knocks this guy on his can, and I thought we were in for it. But the driver of the jeep, the ugliest gorilla of the bunch, says his orders are to ask us to please leave. He says nobody told him to take any film. So we left. We could have all been killed."

"I don't see what you're crying about," Gus declared. "You got your story, and your pictures, and you're home free. Jay got a bloody nose, but he isn't complaining."

"Devon's hired thugs threatened us, and assaulted one

of our group," Jones persisted. "This time Devon has gone too far."

"For the last week, every newspaperman around here has been saying that he is unable to cover Rustling Breeze's workouts, Duke. You fellows have made it sound as though Devon had enclosed the track with rolls of barbed wire, erected machine gun towers, and mined the approach."

Gus grinned.

"How would it have been if you had discovered that all you had to do was to go out there and take a look? Dan Devon's flair for the dramatic disdains such anti-climaxes. He chose, instead, to make you look like heroes. Now you can tell your editors that you deserve a bonus for penetrating his fiendish secret at no small personal risk.

"By the way, what is the secret of the secret workouts?"

"A publicity gag," Jones snorted, "Just like I said."

"I didn't see any equipment changes, or anything that would justify such secrecy," Darlington remarked. "But he could have had a new approach, at that. A new diet, perhaps, or an experimental vitamin supplement. It's possible."

"You don't know Devon," Jones shot back. "It's pure fakery."

Gus peered across the dimly lit, hazy room. He spotted Connie O'Toole, all by himself at the end of the bar.

"Sit down, Gus, and brace yourself. I'm not guessing

223

any more. I'm sure of it. Devon is going to steal the Colt Stake right out from under your nose."

Connie isn't a man for idle speculation, but Gus had heard enough. "Oh, Lord, Connie! You on that again? You're getting monotonous."

Connie twirled a wet glass in his fingers. "Gus, do you know Louis Ponicello? He retired as chief of detectives here five years ago, and now he is in charge of security at Mammoth Motors. Remember, the cop who knows every hoodlum in the country by sight? The man with the encyclopedia memory, the man who never forgets a face?"

Gus knew him.

"Louis saw Devon and Chalky Boyle at the airport in Philly Saturday night. Dan has some rough playmates. They were with Baseball Bat Connie Ahern, maybe the ugliest hood walking around free today."

"Louis must be mistaken."

"Not Louie. He doesn't make mistakes like that. He was standing at the newsstand, his nose in a paper, when they walked past, not five feet from him. They didn't see him, but he saw them."

Connie lounged against the bar, relaxed but watchful. He gave Gus time to digest the information. Then he resumed:

"Let's presume, Gus, that Devon can rig the Colt Stake. Let's imagine he's found a way to beat the bookies. What if the bookies take a licking, and decide not to pay off? You need a man who can persuade them not to be so foolish. A strong man, like Ahern. Dan has some leverage, you can be sure. He knows where the bodies are buried.

So Ahern provides the organization and the muscle. There's no other explanation for that meeting in Philly Saturday night."

"Dan's still got to get Rustling Breeze across the finish line first, Connie, and there's no way he can do that. Rustling Breeze isn't horse enough for it. Dan can't buy off Jensen, or any of Jensen's men. Anyway, to be sure of winning, Devon would have to fix every other horse in the race. Impossible."

"Fix half a dozen horses?" O'Toole said. "I don't think he can fix a single one. I really don't."

"Okay, you said it yourself. Devon can't steal this one."

"I didn't say he couldn't cook the race, Gus. I said I didn't see how he can do it. Anybody but Devon, and I'd say there isn't a chance. I smell something, Gus. Why did Devon drop an honest jock like Parkinson? Why the secret workouts? Are you sure they're just a publicity stunt? Why was he huddling with Ahern in Philly when he was supposed to be in a hospital in New York? Why has he brought those goons out to Hewitt's farm?

"Don't write Devon off. The arts of the double cross are too simple for him. He has perfected the triple cross and the quadruple cross and you take it from there. Everything adds up. I'm not asking *will* he. I'm asking *how*. Devon sees some loophole in the rules of racing that nobody else has ever seen before. He's found a way to cheat the most carefully policed sport in the world."

"You're babbling, Connie."

"I tell you, Gus, he's going to steal that race," O'Toole was in deadly earnest. "And I have this curious feeling that nobody will ever be able to hang it on him."

TWENTY-SEVEN

CONNIE AND GUS fled from the Towne Bar at thirteen minutes before noon. They just made it to the auditorium in time for the professor's forecast of the finish of the Colt Stake.

Guards checked their credentials at the outer door of the International Computer Systems Building and at another checkpoint at the entrance to the posh theater. Connie said it was easier to get into Cape Kennedy.

The auditorium—all deep carpeting and sliding chairs, muted lighting and restful decor—seats about four hundred and fifty. Every seat was taken and the standing room crowd in the back was so thick Gus had difficulty pushing his way through to the stage.

Halfway up the aisle, he was stopped again. The usher checked his stage pass twice before waving him on. At the entrance to the backstage area, another usher was handing out the list of the starters for the Colt Stake. Except for possible late scratches, this was it:

Entries For The Colt Stake

Post position	Horse	Weight	Rider
1	Bubble Bath	126	Longstreet
2	Rustling Breeze	126	MacTavish
3	Mr. Mercury-X	126	Parkinson
4	Mean Old Man	126	DiPetto
5	Hit 'Em Hard	126	Shirwood
6	Suburban Sam	126	Perez
7	Dubbl Trubbl	126	Henson
8	Kentucky Captain	126	Buttari
9	Horsepower	126	Hartley
10	Hi, Toots-X	126	No Boy

X—A. J. Lattner Entry

As the house lights dimmed, Gus had a brief glimpse of Devon in the first row. Dead-panned, the way he always was in a tight spot.

Dye rapped for order, waited for his listeners to come to attention, and then began in a cozy, conversational style:

"Gentlemen, permit me a moment to put into perspective the experiment which reaches its climax here today. This is something much more than an attempt to foretell the winner of a horse race. This is one of the great news stories of our lifetime, a truly historic breakthrough in man's quest for knowledge."

Dye was at his best, a commanding and magnetic presence. He held his listeners, speaking with the obvious sincerity that only the totally insincere man can manage.

"What we propose to do here today is even more significant—and more terrible—than the loosing of the awesome power of the atom bomb. The splitting of the atom,

227

indeed, opened up a new world, but we seek here to penetrate an even darker, more impenetrable, more frightening continent—the kingdom of the future."

"Hurry up, will you?" somebody yelled. "We've got deadlines."

Dye pushed on. "I want to say that Dr. Nichols has done an admirable job of taking my ideas and putting them into a form that is amenable to the uses of the computer. He deserves his full share of credit, and I would not want to take it from him.

"Now, gentlemen, we come to the moment of truth. Here to open the envelopes and announce Dr. Nichols' selections is the distinguished and most able president of International Computer Systems, a youthful giant in a giant industry, Mr. Ollie Olsen."

A spattering of applause greeted Olsen. He held in his hand three envelopes, enough dynamite to blow publicity dreams apart.

"Thank you, Doug. I'll tell you, boys, Doug has come up with a great idea, but where would he have been without International Computer Systems? I'm reminded of a story . . ."

Cries of pain from the audience caused Olsen to forego the story. Then he thought of something else.

"By Jupiter, I almost forgot to introduce my distinguished colleagues at International Computer Systems . . ."

The outcries were so sharply hostile that Olsen stopped, red-faced. "Very well! Very well!" he said peevishly. "I am simply trying to give you the big picture, but if you're in such a hurry, very well. I have here three envelopes, each containing a selection—first, second, and third in the Colt Stake. I will open them in reverse order, naming the third horse first, and the first horse last."

He tore open the envelope with great deliberation and extracted a single sheet of paper.

"Here we are! The third horse in the Colt Stake Saturday—the show horse, I believe it is called—will be . . ."

He hesitated for one more nerve-tearing second, and then he bawled: "The third horse will be Dubbl Trubbl. Dr. Nichols notes that Dubbl Trubbl is preferred over Mean Old Man by only a nose. Almost a dead heat."

A low buzz swept the room. The choice was hardly surprising, but the note on Mean Old Man suggested how thoroughly the professor had researched the race. Few in that room could forget that he had called the dead heat in the Prelude.

"And now, the second horse. By three quarters of a length over Dubbl Trubbl, the second horse is Suburban Sam!"

Gus then faced up unwillingly to the harsh truth: Rustling Breeze never had a chance.

"And now, boys, we come to the final selection, the moment for which we have all been waiting . . . the horse that will win the forty-second renewal of the Colt Stake . . . the winner by a margin of a length and a quarter is . . ."

Reporters were poised in the aisleways, ready to scramble for the phones, but Olsen stopped in mid-gesture.

"The winner will be . . ." he began again. "The winner will be Hi, Toots!"

The reporters froze in their stampede. In the vacuum of sound, someone shouted:

"Did you say Hi, Toots? Will you repeat that, please?"

Olsen opened his mouth but no sound came. With an effort, he read again, but with a slight modification: "Hi, Toots? Do I have that right, Dr. Nichols? Has there been a mistake in the envelopes?"

Dr. Nichols' reply was almost inaudible.

"You have the right envelope," he breathed, never raising his eyes from the floor. "The winner will be Hi, Toots."

"Hi, Toots? That bum?" bellowed Manny Goldblatt from the back of the hall. "Them machines is just like them jocks. They'll stiff you every time."

Reporters were shouting questions from the floor, but nobody was answering. Dr. Nichols, with a police escort he no longer needed, was already leaving. Dye was in an angry huddle with the unintroduced International Computer executives. Olsen, stern-faced but in complete control, thanked the reporters, declared the meeting adjourned, and snapped off the microphone.

Gus was looking for Devon in the swirling crowd when somebody spun him around and lifted him by his necktie.

"I don't know how you did it, but you did, you cheap little conniver," Dye jerked him up so that he was standing on his toes, half-strangling. Dye is a big man, maybe six-foot-three, and he must weigh 220.

"You did it, you filthy little bastard! You sabotaged one of the great public relations concepts of the twentieth century. You made me look like a fool. I've had enough of you and your dirty . . ."

The more Gus struggled, the tighter his tie was drawn

around his neck. Panic snapped at the edges of his consciousness.

With an effort, Gus planted his feet on the floor, choking. He thrust his hand into Dye's face and pushed as hard as he could. He must have taken Dye by surprise, for the big man staggered back.

Gus tried to shift his feet, with his left foot forward so that he could get all his weight behind one right-hand punch. He suspected that one punch was all he would get.

He never made it. As he was crossing his feet, Dye hit him with a clumsy, pawing right, more a push than a blow. Gus tumbled heavily to the floor. The reporters had gained the stage, and they surged around him.

"What are you picking on the little guy for?" one of them asked Dye. Another knelt beside Gus and, in brisk tones, asked him who he was and how he spelled his name, and who Dye was and how he spelled his name.

Olsen stepped between Dye and the reporters.

"Really, Doug, this is impossible," Olsen huffed. "You seemed to have managed a catastrophic gaffe, but this is hardly a reason for assaulting this inoffensive little man."

Dye was adjusting his tie and sweeping his hair back into place.

"My apologies, Ollie," he said stiffly. "But this . . . this person . . . ruined the whole experiment. You don't know this vermin. He has a twisted intellect."

"Oh, come now, Doug, that's childish. This poor fellow didn't program the data for the computers and he didn't interpret the findings. Your own Dr. Nichols did. You gulled us into this utterly ruinous experiment, but this is no place to discuss these matters. Come to my office. We can talk there."

A mocking voice took Gus's attention. "He hit you with a right-hand lead, a sucker punch." Imps of merriment danced in Devon's eyes.

"You managers talk a good fight," Gus responded, "but I don't see you getting in the ring with us fighters when the bell sounds."

"We're the intellectual elite, my lad. We take thirty-five percent of everything, except the punches."

"You take fifty percent," Gus amended.

He offered to drive Devon back to the track. Neither spoke until they had escaped from the congestion around the International Computer Building and had gained the freeway.

"The doc dumped the experiment," Gus began. "He picked a horse that hasn't got a prayer. He chickened out."

"You moralists would never understand the professor," Devon answered. "He is a completely logical man."

Another period of silence. Then Devon spoke. "That Buzz Randahl must be a great man to work for, Gus. All he wants is a press agent who can write and move and walk on water. He tells me that you have to get the banner in the *Herald-Chronicle* on the Colt Stake or you're through."

"He told you that? I mean, he said he'd keep it quiet."

"He wanted me to realize that I must behave with the utmost circumspection, which, of course, I have no intention of doing. But he tells me you have the banner locked up."

"I haven't got anything locked up," Gus admitted, "but I couldn't tell him that."

"Can I help?"

"You can't help. Nobody can. I just take my chances."

"I have some excellent contacts at that paper. Men who would do me a favor, but they're not in sports. If it didn't have to be a sports story . . ."

"It's sports or nothing, Dan. That's obvious. They won't run a horse race story in the real estate section."

"What about George Hall, the sports editor? Will he play ball?"

"None of that!" Gus shrieked. "Don't try any payoffs, or you'll get blacklisted with every paper around here. Don't try to bribe Hall. He'll never mention the track again."

Dan dropped the notion at once. "All right, Gus, but stop worrying. I'll always have a job for you."

"Forget it. This isn't your concern, Dan."

"Of course it's my concern. You're my friend."

"I think you mean that."

"Certainly, I mean it," Devon smiled. "I have no principles, but my whims are inflexible."

Neither spoke again until they began the approach to the Treasure City Race Track exit. Gus could see what Inspector Wilson was talking about. Traffic was bumper to bumper, and hardly crawling. With two lanes closed for repairs, the freeway couldn't begin to handle the lightest traffic of the day.

Gus was glad he knew Devon so well, or he would have been ashamed of what he was thinking.

"That bomb threat was a terrible thing," he mentioned.

"The professor must have been frightened out of his wits."

"Eight-to-five there never was a bomb threat, Gus. The professor probably made it up."

"The threat was real, all right. The police had a tap on the phone. They taped the call."

Devon's face betrayed nothing.

"I suppose you can account for your whereabouts last night, Dan?"

He made a hopeless gesture. "I'm afraid I can't. Except for the time I spent at Senator Beauregard's small dinner party. He is here, you know, directing the committee that is investigating the commercial telecasting of sports events. He had a few friends to dinner at his hotel suite. I was there from about seven-thirty last night until a little after ten. Why?"

"Just stick to that story, Dan. A United States senator is a perfect alibi. By the way, did you do any dialect stories for the senator's party? You always were great with those Swedish and Irish stories."

"I haven't tried any dialect stories in years," he answered piously.

As they were pulling into the parking lot, Gus resumed the inquiry.

"You never did like Dye, did you? Not since that night at the preopening party?"

"He lacks gentlemanly restraint," Devon observed. "He called me an infamous freebooter, a dirty-minded charlatan, and a sleazy fraud. I would have preferred to keep those things secret."

Devon leaned back and contemplated the ceiling of the car. "He chose me, Gus. I didn't choose him."

234

"And you're out to get him, aren't you? You hate him."

"Not any more, Gus," Devon said quietly. "Not any more."

TWENTY-EIGHT

WHEN JAY RETURNED to the office late in the afternoon, he was a man in a hurry. He had been out in the backstretch half the day, interviewing Colt Stake owners, trainers, jockeys, even stable hands, dredging up the quotes that the writers would use in their stories tomorrow.

"You look tired, Jay, doll," Nancy told him. "Gus doesn't want you to work that hard."

"After Saturday, I can take it easy, darling," he said. "I'm taking Dan Devon down to the TV studio for an interview at 6:15. I have another appointment after that, but I want so much to see you, Nancy. May I stop by for just a minute when I'm through?"

"I'd like that," Nancy smiled, but something in his manner frightened her. His smile was cold and thin.

"Can't you cancel the other appointment, Jay? You've been going since six this morning."

"Doug Dye asked me to see him tonight at his home," Mason said in a colorless voice. "That is the other appointment."

"Doug Dye! After the way he's treated Gus! You surely aren't going, are you?"

"I'm going," he replied stubbornly.

"Jay, please don't do it. How can you have anything to do with that horrid man? How can you?"

"I told you, you'd have to take me as I am," he said in a curiously strained voice. "I'm not thinking of myself alone now."

"Don't drag me into this, Jay Mason. I won't be a part of any of it."

Jay looked stricken. "What do I owe Gus Scott?" he asked earnestly. "I told you I wouldn't do one thing to undermine him, and I haven't. But if the track is going to hire a new publicity director, it's going to be me."

She released his hands, and stood before him in her anger. "You don't understand the meaning of love, Jay. You don't understand it at all. Love is so many things. It's loyalty and sacrifice, for two."

He kicked viciously at the leg of the desk. "You sound as though you invented love," he snapped. "Tell me, what is it?"

"I don't know how to say it," she replied. "But the things that I remember most—the things that have given me the best feeling—are the things I've done for others."

He was silent after that. When he spoke, the anger had gone out of his voice. He was baffled and regretful. "I'm sorry, Nance, but you make no sense to me. I'm going to talk to Dye."

"If Doug Dye is so important to you, Jay, talk to him. By all means, talk to him. Take that old job. Sell yourself, but don't expect to find me here when you come back. I won't be here." Then the tension, the frustration, the emotional erosion swept over her, and the tears came in a hot, blinding rush. She fled weeping from the room.

Jay stood where he was. He stood there and let her run out of his life. When Nancy returned to her desk, he was gone.

She turned to her typewriter, pounding the keys with controlled fury and slapping the return carriage back with a vigor that promised to sweep the machine onto the floor.

"Hold it, baby! That typewriter can't hit back."

Nancy looked up, embarrassed, into Pierre's insouciant smile.

"Here's opportunity," he announced, "knocking twice. What am I saying? I'm knocking for the twentieth time."

Nancy tried to smile, but with small success.

"I warned you," he observed, "when a woman has too much will power, she gets out of the habit of smiling. These are the best years of your life, child, and you're wasting them."

"I've heard that song before, Pierre."

"The refrain is haunting," he countered. "How about dinner tonight?"

Nancy looked tired and joyless.

"No, thanks, Pierre."

He sat on the edge of her desk, and leaned close.

"You've been ducking me ever since that night in the parking lot. So I made a pass at you, so what? Just let me take you out to dinner. Please."

"I wouldn't be fit company for you tonight, Pierre, the way I feel."

"Even when you're poor company, baby, you're the best company there is."

She shook her head.

"I really want to talk to you, doll," he persisted. "Just to talk. Fair enough?"

"I don't feel like dinner," Nancy allowed, "but I could use a good stiff drink."

Pierre smiled.

"We'll drink our dinner. We have a lot of wasted days to make up for."

"I don't want to make up for any wasted days, friend. I just want a drink. One drink. And no lovey-dovey business."

"You drive a hard bargain, honey, but it's better than nothing. Leave your car at the track. We can come back for it later."

Jay Mason said not a word on the ride to the TV studio. After a few futile attempts at conversation, Dan Devon lapsed into silence, too. He didn't try again until they had left the studio and were riding back downtown.

"Have you eaten, Jay? How about the Knockout Bar or, if you're less foolhardy, The Steak House? We can sit around and tell each other lies."

"Sorry, Dan. Not tonight."

"Nancy?"

"No, not Nancy. Nancy and I are through."

"That's what's eating you, eh? These broads can complicate a man's life."

"She's not a broad," Mason shot back.

238

He spoke with such harshness that Devon blinked. After a moment, however, Mason relented.

"Sorry, Dan. It's not your fault. Nancy is a wonderful girl, the finest person I've ever known, but I've been kidding myself when I thought we had any future together. We're too different. We'd never think alike. In a year, we'd be hating each other. It's better this way, to quit while we still respect each other."

They drove on in silence. The spidery old man, head back against the cushion, seemed lost in thought.

"I've had a great life, Jay," he said finally. "I've made half a dozen fortunes and thrown them away and I've never regretted a minute of it. Beautiful women? Son, in my day, I've had the most beautiful women in the world. I've had it all and I've done it all, and do you know what I'm thinking right now? My life is a rotten, lousy joke.

"What happens if Rustling Breeze is up the track Saturday, and I tap out? I'll be as welcome at the Knockout Bar as if I had leprosy. Nothing will turn my friends off faster than the suspicion I want to borrow money. I go back to my lonely little hotel room at night, Jay, and I know that nobody really gives a damn if I live or die."

He closed his eyes, oblivious to his companion. "Once long ago, so long ago it hardly seems real, I knew a girl who wasn't a broad. I was like you, cocksure and on the make, and I meant to travel light. The idea of a marriage horrified me. I ran like a thief. Now I wonder, sometimes, if I didn't outsmart myself.

"I'll never know. I can't go that route again. Nobody

can, but maybe I should have tried it her way. All I know is that, after all these years, I still remember the way she smiled."

Jay looked at him in horror. He's going to start crying, Jay thought.

"Jay, let an old man tell you something: No man can go it alone. He needs someone who loves him—loves him whether he makes it or not. Those whom the gods despise never learn this soon enough."

Jay thought he had never heard such utter desolation in a human voice. Dan Devon, the hustler, the man who has done everything.

Dan decided on the Knockout Bar. He stopped with his hand on the door and offered a half-embarrassed parting remark: "I'm a very sentimental man about true love, Jay, for somebody else."

The apology made it worse. Dan Devon talks too much, Jay thought sourly. Why does he tell me his troubles?

Pierre took Nancy to an elegant, dimly lit, boudoir-with-tables kind of dining room. They had a whiskey and water. This proved so acceptable that they did it again.

"I'm beat," said Nancy. "This has been one of those days."

"You look better on your bad days than these other chicks do on their good days," Pierre smiled. "I'm serious. You stir me."

When Pierre suggested dinner after the third whiskey

and water, Nancy realized that the idea had merit. After dinner, they switched to a liqueur which Pierre had recommended, a sweet, warming drink with a delayed-action bomb built in. Two of those and Nancy was giggling.

Pierre observed her closely. "I told you you'd have to find out for yourself, didn't I, Nancy? Now you're finding out, aren't you?"

Her eyes softened, and she reached her hand across the tablecloth to his. "Can it be that you understand me, Pierre? How dreadfully unfair!"

His dark eyes glowed. His appraisal was so candid and so personal that Nancy flushed.

"You are a beautiful woman," he said evenly. "I'd love to get into your pants."

She didn't explode in angry indignation, as he thought she might. She didn't try to pretend he was amusing, as she usually did. Instead, she withdrew her hand, slowly, and she said nothing. Pierre, who was sure he could read a woman, was satisfied. If he picked the right moment, he reflected, he could take her. There would be nothing to it.

"I think we'd better go," she said, her voice flat and colorless.

Pierre nodded slowly, holding her with his dark eyes.

"Give me the keys, kitten. I'll drive you home. Then I'll come back and get your car and bring it over later tonight. I can take a cab back."

She didn't argue. She was perfectly capable of driving, of course, but why was the room whirling so? And a girl had to walk carefully, the way the floor was tilting.

Nancy put her head back as Pierre drove, with the top down. The soft breeze refreshed her, and cleared her head. The great orange moon hanging low in the sky almost hypnotized her. A great lassitude washed over her. She could scarcely keep her eyes open.

As he pulled into the parking lot, Pierre doused the lights. He leaned over her.

"Nancy, darling, don't you understand how I feel? This isn't just for kicks, you and me. This is for real."

He brushed the dark hair back from her face with solemn tenderness and his strong hands caressed her. A strange rebellion began welling up within her.

"Please, Pierre, don't," she said shakily, as she sought to disengage his hands.

"Please, don't! Please don't!" he bit off. "The trouble with you is, you don't know what you do want. I wish I liked you less, or loved your more!"

He unlocked the door to her motel room without another word. She paused with her hand on the knob.

"Thank you, Pierre," she said. "I enjoyed being with you. Pierre, I'm all mixed up. Please try to understand."

He towered over her, vibrantly alive. When he kissed her, she made no pretense of resisting.

"You could be a helluva woman," he said. "I might come back tonight and get in bed with you. Think about that."

She stood in the doorway watching him until the car's lights disappeared in the traffic.

The air in her little room was stale and sticky, and that is the way Nancy felt. She opened the windows and turned on the fan. Then she undressed slowly, trying to sort out the events of the last few hours. After a shower, she felt a little better, but the summer heat lingered like a stifling blanket. She lay down, naked, on the bed.

Jay drove aimlessly for almost an hour before he headed for his appointment with Doug Dye. He felt a moment of searing envy when he pulled in to Dye's estate. The stately stone mansion in the distance was magnificent. At least twenty rooms, Jay decided. The green rolling lawn, which extended to the lakeshore drive, was big enough for two football fields.

This is it, Jay thought. Dye has got it made. This is what I want.

The white jacketed houseboy led him down a long corridor to the library. Dye rose to meet him, smiling warmly. He took Jay's hand in both of his, and held it for a long moment.

"Jay, my boy, delighted you're here. Sit down. A drink?"

"A beer, please."

"Scotch for me, Joe," Dye told the houseboy, settling down on the dark leather davenport beside his visitor.

"Jay, I want you on my team. I've got big plans for you. You're tough and smart and you get the job done. I need you. I need a man I can groom to take my place some day."

The young man sat up straight, suspicious. Distrust and irritation were evident as he said: "Doug, why don't you tell me exactly what you have in mind."

"Of course, I'll get to it," Dye responded, with hearty geniality. "You know how your boss pretends that he took Devon in just because he likes that old faker? Crap.

243

He works with Devon to rig races. They're cleaning up on their bets."

Dye was watching Mason closely. The young man, he observed, seemed to be staring in fascination at the enormous diamond ring on Dye's finger.

"I have the sworn statement of a former employee of the Flowering Tree Stable, Jay. On the night before the Colt Stake Trial, this man took a bottle of whiskey and got the groom for Hit 'Em Hard drunk. With groom out of the way, he injected the colt with phenylbutazone, which is identified as a forbidden drug by our racing commission. This man has confessed the whole thing to me. He's sick about what he has done. Dan Devon paid him $1,000 in cash to dope Hit 'Em Hard."

Jay stared, incredulous. "You don't really believe that, do you? For one thing, how would the guy know which horse to dope? Did you ever go into a barn, at night and try to pick out a strange horse? Impossible."

"It's the Gospel truth," Dye said piously. "See how Scott's twisted mind works? He calls the shots for Devon. That old coot never has an idea of his own. Scott figured that Hit 'Em Hard was the only colt that might beat Rustling Breeze, so he had this poor groom dope the horse. He figured he had it both ways.

"The state racing commission tests every winner to see if he has been doped. If Rustling Breeze wins, he's okay. If Hit 'Em Hard wins, however, he would be disqualified. Scott loves to get cute."

Jay laughed nervously. "I know the groom you're talking about. He's a helluva witness. He's a pill head. He doesn't even know what he is doing, most of the time. Nobody would believe anything he said."

Dye thrust out his right hand, his palm toward Mason.

244

"Yes, they will. I have a witness who saw the payoff. A man that everybody will believe."

"Who?"

Dye moved closer to his visitor. He put his hand on Mason's forearm, squeezing slightly. "You," he said. "This is what you can do for me. For yourself, too, because this will finish Scott."

Mason couldn't conceal his surprise. He sat, mouth agape, as though he were trying to digest this proposal.

"I pay for what I get, Jay. I pay damn well. You will be the new publicity director at Treasure City, and I'll give you the damndest contract you ever saw. This will make you."

Mason appeared to be thinking out loud, trying to collect his thoughts. "It won't wash," he finally observed.

"Of course it will," Dye burst out. "The papers love a race track scandal. It will be all over the front pages. You know O'Sullivan, the racing commissioner. He isn't going to get the right people sore at him. He'll throw Devon out before you can bat an eyelash."

Jay sat contemplating the lace of foam around his empty glass. "Yes," he said at length, "I guess you're right. Devon wouldn't have a chance."

This was it, Jay knew. This was what he had come for. This was the break that could start a whole new career for him. What had Devon ever done for him? Or Scott, either, for that matter.

"Scott is no good," Dye growled. "That son of a bitch crossed me for the last time. I'm going to get Scott's head."

Jay Mason knew what he had to do. He had known it, he realized, for some time.

"I'm going to get Scott's head," Dye repeated.

Mason measured Dye. Their glances met and held. Now they understood each other. Mason spoke in a low voice.

"Not from me," he said. "You're not going to get Scott's head from me."

Dye flung his glass to the floor. The shattered slivers of light danced across the inlaid flooring.

"If you're so pure and holy, why in the almighty hell did you come out here to see me tonight?" Dye roared. "When I called this morning, you knew what I wanted."

"I knew what you wanted," Mason agreed, "but I didn't know what I wanted."

Later, as he turned the key in the ignition switch, Mason felt no satisfaction, only a terrible emptiness.

The low, insistent whistle cut through the thick fog of sleep. Nancy sat up, bewildered, frightened. She needed a minute to orient herself, to remember where she was and when it was. She felt as though she had been drugged.

She heard a voice. A whisper too faint to be understood, but it shocked her into full consciousness. She struggled to her feet, hurriedly slipping into her dressing gown.

What was it Pierre had said? "I'm going to make love to you. I might come back tonight."

She felt so alone, close to panic. She was fighting to control her fear. The safety chain was in place, but how strong was it?

With trembling fingers she turned the knob and pulled the door open to the limit of the chain, an inch or so.

"Jay!"

Now he filled the doorway and, like the slash of a knife, Nancy knew how much she wanted him. How much she would always want him, no matter what he did.

"I had to see you, Nancy," he was saying. "I came here as soon as I could. I realized tonight that if I lose you, I don't have anything. I don't have a thing."

She placed her small hands on his big fist, and drew him in. "Don't stand there," she murmured. "When I welcome gentlemen callers in the middle of the night, I like to keep it a secret."

He stepped in, and she pushed the door shut.

"I had to see you, Nancy. I had to tell you . . ."

"Don't talk, darling," she whispered. "Not now. Just hold me. Hold me close. Don't ever let me out of your arms again."

TWENTY-NINE

JOCKEYS HAVE SOMETHING girls can't resist: money. That is why, at any horsemen's dance, there are these gnome-like little men with these goddesses clinging to their arms. And that's the way it was at the Fearless Fore-casters' Frolic at the Duck Corners Golf and Country Club on the eve of the Colt Stake.

Hartley, Perez, Shirwood, DiPetto, MacTavish—all the Colt Stake riders were there. The beauty of their partners could make a man wish he had never grown up.

Except Parkinson.

He refused to depart from the austere celibate regimen that had lifted him back into the saddle and made him the leading rider at the Treasure City Race Track in the comeback of the year. Gus found him standing by himself in the Men's Grill, sipping orange juice.

"It's a shame you don't have a better Colt Stake mount," Gus consoled him. "You've got the jockey championship wrapped up. What a climax if you finished off with a win in the Stake. I hear you could have had Hit 'Em Hard or Bubble Bath. You should have grabbed one of them."

Wade Hampton Parkinson leaned easily against the bar, a man at peace with the world. "I'm satisfied to ride Mr. Mercury," he allowed. "He's an honest kind."

"Yeah, but you're just taking that ride out of friendship for Jamie Lattner. You haven't got a chance."

The great, rough-beamed central hall of the club was a dazzle of color, aglow with the silks of all the Colt Stake entries. Horsemen in their Western shirts and string ties mingled easily with the tuxedoed guests. Only two of the owners came in white tie and tails—J. C. Jensen and Dan Devon.

Gus had set up temporary press headquarters in the club's private v. i. p. bar room, with four teletype machines, half a dozen phones, tables, and typewriters. The Fearless Forecasters' Frolic usually provided some last-minute news, for the custom of the occasion dictated that each owner should arise after dinner and offer his appraisal of the race. Then the reporters fired questions. These exchanges rarely produced any fireworks, but they did offer a fresh sidelight on a greatly overworked subject.

Gus found Devon with a dozen writers in a far corner of the dining room.

"Horsepower is overrated," Devon was saying. "You saw what he did in the Continental. He just lasted, and that's all. The Colt Stake is another three-sixteenths of a mile. He won't be up to it. He's lost his edge. You can scratch Horsepower. It's among Suburban Sam, Mean Old Man, Dubbl Trubbl, and my colt. And my colt is going to hit the wire first. You can quote me on that any way you want."

"Shrinking Dan Devon, he fears no man," called Derek Darlington, the Eastern turf writer.

"You better believe him," Gus smiled. "There's a man who speaks the truth."

Gus had just left Devon's table when Pierre collared him. He had been shooting publicity pictures of Helene, the gorgeous Colt Stake queen.

"I want a gag shot, Gus, a picture of Mr. Jensen placing the queen's crown on Helene's head. The king of the Colt Stake crowns the queen. Get it?"

"I don't think Jensen will go for it."

"Of course he will," Helene told Gus. "He'll love it. Where does Pierre get all these cute ideas?"

Gus had difficulty keeping his mind on the conversation, for Helene is a creature who can bring cerebral processes grinding to a halt. She is a stunningly beautiful woman.

"Okay, Pierre. If Jensen doesn't want his picture taken with Helene, we should give him a saliva test."

As Gus approached, Dye glowered at him, but the press agent gave it a try.

"Mr. Jensen? I'm Gus Scott, Treasure City publicity. May I take a moment?"

The old tycoon turned slowly, surveyed the publicity man with evident distaste. He stood up. He was shorter than the newspaper pictures would suggest, but he was every inch the icy aristocrat. His thick white hair, his carefully trimmed mustache, his ruddy countenance and his ramrod-stiff carriage were just right.

"You're Scott? Hah, sir, I resent the circus atmosphere you have created at Monty Randahl's delightful little track. The Stake is a keen sporting event, but you have done your miserable worst to turn it into a hippodrome.

"All the witless speculation on the heart and fitness of my colt. In vile taste. Vile taste. No track in the world should be burdened with a huckster like you. You rob a great sport of its inherent dignity. Good day."

Gus pressed the matter.

"I regret that I may have provoked your displeasure, Mr. Jensen, but I would like to have you pose for a picture with our Colt Stake Queen. This will take only a moment."

Jensen was a model of cold outrage as he looked Gus up and down, unable to find words for such effrontery.

"You see, sir, we want a picture of you adjusting this beautiful crown"—Gus held up the glittering bauble—"on Helene's head. The idea is . . ."

"Never!" he roared. "I will not play the fool!" He

sputtered into silence as a stricken Doug Dye seized Gus's arm and pulled him away, not gently.

"Aw, forget it," Pierre said. "Come on, Helene, child, we'll get Devon. He'll stand on his head if we ask him to. Devon's got class."

Dan had never been more courtly.

"You honor an old man with this attention, my dear," he bowed. "You have only to command."

Nancy and Jay waved when Gus went by their table, and he smiled in return. Gus had told Jay to have a good time, and forget about publicity work for the night. What he had done that morning hadn't been easy, Gus recalled.

Jay had been waiting for Gus when he had arrived for work some twelve hours earlier. The younger man got right to it.

"I have something to tell you, Gus," he said, with cold formality. "If you want to throw me out when I finish, I have it coming to me. Here it is: When I came here, I had the shiv out for you. I wanted your job. You knew it. Doug Dye wanted me to grease the skids for you. He didn't have to ask twice."

He stopped to allow a rebuttal. Gus said nothing.

"When Dye latched onto Dr. Nichols, he probably felt he didn't need me. He left me alone. When that blew up, he put the arm on me again. Last night. I went out to his home and he propositioned me. He wanted me to help him frame you. He guaranteed me your job if I would say that I knew you and Dan Devon had doped Hit 'Em Hard so he couldn't beat Rustling Breeze in the Prelude. Dye was desperate."

Jay stopped again. His gaze was level and frank. For the first time since Gus had met him, he was sure his assistant was giving it to him straight.

"I considered it. Seriously. I turned it down, but I was tempted. I think you ought to know."

"So?" Gus smiled. "So what else is new?"

Jay almost smiled. "Thanks, Gus," he said.

That's why Gus had told him to take the night off.

As the diners were finishing their desserts, the owners of the Colt Stake entries assembled in the rear of the room for the traditional group picture. Fifty-eight of these pictures, the first from before World War I, now hang in the lobby of the Treasure City Race Track.

After the ritual, Randahl stepped to the bandstand and took his stance before the microphone. The lights blinked out, except for the spot that bathed him in its white light. The Fearless Forecasters' Frolic was nearing its high point: the moment when the owners arose and told the throng what they thought their colts might do on Saturday afternoon.

Randahl cleared his throat and made a start. "We are most honored to have here tonight a renowned captain of industry, a matchless civic leader, and a really grand sportsman—the owner of the most brilliant three-year-old in my memory—a philanthropist and a man who invests a wonderful sport with new dignity and stature. Ladies and gentlemen, Mr. J. C. Jensen, owner of the unbeaten Colt Stake favorite, the magnificent Horsepower. We will be privileged, Mr. Jensen, if you will say a few words."

Randahl gestured toward the renowned captain of industry's table, right in front of him, but there was some delay before Jensen stood blinking in the spotlight's glare. He looked at the microphone the way a mongoose looks at a cobra. Then he seized the thing by the throat and began belaboring it with staccato bursts of sound. "I was, hah, unaware that this inquisition was a part of this little dinner tonight, or, hah, I should not have attended."

The matchless civic leader allowed his listeners to digest this intelligence. The applause which had greeted him was stilled. Even the murmur of conversation stopped. J. C. Jensen glared into the silence.

"I have it in my mind that too many of us believe we have come here for a debate, not a horse race. Too many of us have already said too much about this race. Much of it, I am candid to say, simple rudeness. I will have no part of this caterwauling. I will not add to the bloody din. My colt will be in the paddock before the eighth race tomorrow, ready to run. I do not think that any owner can, in good conscience or good grace, say more. Good evening!"

Gus began circling around toward the bandstand.

Randahl, aware that his cherished stint as master of ceremonies was likely to be considerably shortened, tried to regain his aplomb.

"Thank you, Mr. Jensen. Of course, I am sure that we all see the merit of your observations. We respect the judgment of the first citizen of our state. Indeed, we are inclined to talk too much, and this disease may infect horsemen more than others. We are indebted to Mr. Jensen for reminding us of this tendency. I presume that the other owners of Colt Stake entries may wish to show their deference for our guest of honor by waiving their right to speak. Well?"

253

Cal Holloway, Suburban Sam's owner, arose to shout his assent. Jamie Lattner, who had the far-out entry of Mr. Mercury and Hi, Toots, was next to fall in line. Gus had advanced to within thirty feet of Randahl when, coming from the other side of the room with the nimbleness of a broken-field runner, Dan Devon made his dash for the microphone.

"Mr. Randahl! Mr. Randahl!" he called in a high, quavering voice.

Randahl acted fast. "Ah, Mr. Devon waives his right to speak," he said. "Thank you, Mr. Devon."

This was too much for Gus.

"Aren't you going to talk, Dan?" he yelled. "Please say something! Speech! Speech!"

Buzz surrendered, after skewering Gus with a glance. "Any comments, Mr. Devon?" he inquired.

Dan climbed to the bandstand with feather lightness, bowed politely to Buzz and peered scornfully at Jensen's table. "I came here tonight, in keeping with the agreeable custom of this dinner, to talk about the Colt Stake," he said. "I suggest that any attempt to deny me the pleasure of an exchange with the press would be—your phrase, Mr. Jensen—simple rudeness."

Devon was cold now. "Rustling Breeze has responded better than we had hoped to our new training methods. He never looked better. I believe he will win tomorrow afternoon, but I acknowledge the stature of Suburban Sam, Mean Old Man, Dubbl Trubbl and several other superb colts. My friends, this is going to be a horse race."

"What about Horsepower?" a reporter shouted.

"Horsepower is a sacred cow," Devon responded. "And two weeks ago, in the Continental, he ran like one."

J. C. Jensen and his horrified entourage moved within ten feet of the bandstand as they strode out of the hall. Doug Dye shook his fist at Gus, black fury in his glance.

Devon threw up his hands to check the sudden babble. He watched the procession file in front of him with roguish glee.

"I was happy to visit here tonight to talk about my little bay, but the first citizen of your state came to sit in Olympian silence. This is the difference, friends, between a visit and a visitation."

Jensen was almost out of the room now, but Devon's taunts pursued him. "Your captain of industry, your matchless civic leader, sportsman, and philanthropist has come here tonight for the first time," Devon's voice cut with scorn. "Now he goes, and we can only wait prayerfully for his second coming."

Devon's clash with Jensen had given the reporters something they had hardly expected—a spate of real last-minute news. They came piling into the improvised press room as soon as Devon had stopped speaking. The crowded little v. i. p. bar room of the Duck Corners Golf and Country Club took on something of the frantic hubbub of a city room with a big story breaking.

The four teletype machines weren't enough to handle the flow of copy. Gus was glad when Jay came in and insisted upon helping out. They were both on the phones, calling in stories, for almost an hour.

Nancy came to work, too. She kicked off her shoes and carried copy from the writers to the teletype operators.

And Devon was there, moving quietly among the newspapermen, always happy to answer questions or to expand upon his earlier remarks. When the work began to ease off, Nancy found a moment to take Dan aside for a brief exchange. Gus thought she was going to kiss him. Finally, she did.

When only a couple of reporters for the afternoon papers were still toiling over their stories, Devon bid the press corps adieu.

"I appreciate your kindness, boys," he proclaimed. "You've been very good to me."

"I've been watching you act out these little dramas for a long, long time, and I'm growing weary of them," Derek Darlington groused. "They're getting monotonous. The way you tell these stories, the hero is always Dan Devon."

"Of course," Devon replied. "Nobody celebrates the Fifth of July."

THIRTY

DAN DEVON was bone-tired. The Fearless Forecasters' Frolic had gone well, but he was glad it was over.

He hoped the newspapermen would quote him exactly in tomorrow's papers. His jibes at Jensen could lose something in translation but he had resisted the temptation to try to check their quotes. He had learned long ago that the line between a cooperative subject and a publicity hound is shadow thin.

He switched on the lights in the Presidential Suite. His weary spirit was soothed by the soft beauty of the expansive living room with its great window walls, by the costly draperies, the deep carpeting, the elegant furniture. If you can't go first class, he thought, why make the trip?

No alien sound penetrated his domain. He was aloof in his sanctuary, shielded from the clangor in the streets far below. Dan Devon liked it this way.

In front of the full-length mirror he jauntily removed his tall hat, coat, jacket, collar, tie, and vest and threw them negligently on the brocade davenport. Then he pulled the recording of "Iolanthe" from the cabinet and put it on the turntable, lowering the volume to a whisper. The hotel people, he noted with approval, had understood his taste in record players.

"If you can save any money on this purchase," he had told them, "don't."

The well-loved words and music flowed over him. This was the sweet companionship he cherished. Show me a woman, he thought, who knows the uses of tranquillity. Most of them can't ever stop yammering, even in bed.

He stood for a long time on the balcony, watching the sleeping city spread out before him. The city tonight was a docile cat, purring contentedly at his feet. He loved the cities when they held nothing that could make him afraid.

He managed a frosty smile as he recalled how little Nancy, so beautiful and so sure of her victory, had taken him aside in that thrown-together press room at the golf club hardly more than an hour ago. He remembered her hushed voice, and her soft warm smile. He remembered her words: "Thank you, Dan, for giving Jay back to me. You try to act so cynical, but underneath everything you're a generous, wonderful human being. Oh, Dan, I wish so much that you had married that girl. I wish you had."

Dan smiled. That girl from the long ago, the one who wasn't a broad, was quite good. A little overdone, perhaps, but he had an uncritical audience.

I did the boy a favor, he repeated. He's too soft for this life. I thought once he might cut it, but that was before he found himself a girl. She will blunt his edge. He's like a jockey who has taken a bad spill and can't forget it. A man like that is always looking back, to see what's coming up on his flank.

Jay is like Gus Scott. Gus can move, and he's a cutie, but he hasn't got the guts to finish a man off. I've seen fighters like that. They had the weapons and the brains but they had no stomach for a dirty fight. In this racket, you've got to have a little hood in you. You let a man off the hook, and he will come back to destroy you. That's what separates the men from the boys—the readiness to use a shiv.

Dan removed his shoes, sat down and put his feet up on the hassock. In calm detachment, he reviewed his preparations for the next afternoon's sport. He hadn't overlooked a thing:

Ahern knew the necessity for the most delicate timing. If the boys didn't understand that, The Bat would get the message across.

Manny Goldblatt would give him no trouble. The poor bum will never know what hit him.

Charlton Dressage, the deputy road commissioner, had been perfect. Of course I can move the highway repairs on that stretch of road ahead of schedule, Dressage had told him. What are friends for? Devon liked Dressage. The man was so obtuse that he still doesn't realize what he has done.

Gus's headline in the *Herald-Chronicle* is safe enough. That deal should stand up. Gus wouldn't believe the agreement I've made. "All I need is an excuse," the man had said.

Cal Oakley has made the most of those secret workouts. Devon chuckled aloud as he recalled the skepticism of the newspapermen. A publicity gimmick, was it? They would find out how much of a publicity gimmick it was.

The tap on the door disturbed these pleasant ruminations. Dan turned off the record player and answered the summons.

"Here's the ice water, sir," the bell hop said.

For a man who didn't want ice water, Devon greeted the visitor with warm cordiality.

"I'm glad you remembered," he said, standing aside to let the young man enter.

"Your phone is bugged," the boy whispered. "They put a bug on it tonight."

Dan gave a barely perceptible nod, but he pressed a bill into the boy's hand.

Did this kid have the audacity to try to outslicker Dan Devon? The idea appealed to the iconoclast in Devon, but the boy should have come with a better story. How could anybody, even a kid, think I wouldn't have taken precautions against a tap, he wondered?

He sat down to await the call. I'm glad I instructed

Ahern not to make the long-distance call directly to me. Calls like that can be traced too easily. This is no time to trip up.

Promptly at midnight, the phone rang.

"This is Sylvester, Mr. Devon. I guess maybe you don't remember me, but you'd know me if you saw me. I used to work the fights at the old arena on Twenty-Ninth Street. I carried the water buckets. Remember? The little red head? You always called me Carrot Top."

"Mmmm? Sylvester, eh? Well, Sylvester, isn't this an odd time to be calling?"

"Sorry, Mr. Devon, but I had to find out. Do you really think Rustling Breeze can win tomorrow? I like those odds, but has he got any kind of a chance? Honest?"

"We'll win, my friend. We'll win big. This is a helluva colt. He's going to run those other horses right off the track."

"You think so, Mr. Devon?"

"Certainly. Get aboard, but don't spread it around. All conditions are go."

Softly and distinctly, he repeated: "All conditions are go." Then he hung up.

I've done everything I can do, he realized. Now I can only wait. He had attended to the last preliminary detail, and suddenly he felt sick with helplessness.

This thing isn't air-tight. These things never are, he pondered. The horse could fall down or break a leg or get stuck in the starting gate or throw his jockey. A man has to take his chances.

What if the horse isn't up to it? What if he simply can't run fast enough to get to the wire first. Oakley is sure he can, but Oakley could be wrong. In a horse race, there are no sure things. The secret workouts will do it, Oakley had said, but was it enough?

Can I go back to hustling for peanuts again, back to scrounging and digging and hoping?

He thought of the past few years, the most painful of his life. How the money had slowly run out of the fight game, how desperately he had tried to find something else. The swimming show was just the last in a series of disasters: the wrestling promotions, the rodeo, the selling jobs, the biography that nobody would print, the stint as advance man for that sad little circus. He knew that the wounds still bled.

And, worst of all, the brutal hammering fear that maybe this was the end of the line, that perhaps the fabled Devon luck had finally run out.

For years, everything had gone sour, Devon told himself. Now, in the last couple of months, everything has gone right. I've had all the breaks, but will my luck hold? If I lose tomorrow, I lose everything.

Fear slashed at him. A cold shudder ran through his thin body, and his hands trembled uncontrollably.

I'm too old to pick up the pieces again, he admitted. I'm too old and too tired. If I don't make it tomorrow, I'll never make it again.

With an effort of will, he tore his thoughts away from these intimations of doom. The moment of weakness passed. Devon was in command again.

"Hell," he said aloud, "if I worried about things I can't control, I'd have been dead long ago."

He wasted no time in preparing for bed. He turned the lights out, climbed between the sheets, and pulled the blankets up over his frail body. Almost as soon as his head touched the pillow, the old tiger had fallen into a deep slumber that could scarcely have been distinguished from the sleep of the just and righteous man.

THIRTY-ONE

THE DAY OF THE forty-second renewal of the Colt Stake broke sunny and clear. The Treasure City Race Track's biggest day was at hand, and conditions couldn't have been better.

Gus had scarcely arrived at his desk when Inspector Watkins called.

"We've got two lanes of the freeway open, but that won't be enough," he said. "Drivers who live in the city simply must use the surface arteries. If they don't, we'll have the granddaddy of all traffic foul-ups. It scares me. Can you get the word around?"

"We've done about all we can, inspector, but we'll fire off a bulletin saying that the situation looks worse than we had anticipated. It's too late to do much more."

"Everything helps, Gus. This is going to be a rough one. Our forecast is for the heaviest traffic the freeway has ever had."

The atmosphere was electric with the anticipation of big events. Post time for the first race was two hours away but already the publicity offices were thronged with reporters who had dropped in to pick up Jay Mason's carefully researched fact sheets on the Colt Stake, to check credentials and accommodations, and to bug Gus for more passes.

And there was Devon, cocksure and voluble, willing to be interviewed. "We're running Bumbling Bertie in the tenth race," he announced. "Maybe you could use a sidebar on that, boys. You know, Cal Oakley is a very sentimental man. Even in his preparations for the Stake, the biggest race of his life, he hasn't forgotten his other child, Bumbling Bertie. He's going to give old Bertie a chance to run, too. It's a mile, but the racing secretary was having trouble filling the race so Cal put the five-year-old in. He's a very thoughtful man, Cal Oakley."

"A mile?" scoffed Duke Jones, the *Herald-Chronicle* writer. "He's never run more than three furlongs. You can forget that freak today. Who needs him?"

"Amen," Connie O'Toole said.

Gus had a chance to take Jones aside for a moment, and make a pitch for the *Herald-Chronicle* banner.

"Getting that banner means more to me than you may ever know," Gus pleaded. "I'm not asking for anything unreasonable. I just want a fair shake. The Stake is the big story, isn't it?"

"George Hall himself is on the desk tonight," Jones answered. "Nobody tells him what to do. You should get the banner. This is a once-in-a-lifetime day. The track is a cinch to break all records. The Colt Stake has a better field than the Kentucky Derby. By rights, you ought to make it."

"Hall can't banner anything else, can he?"

Jones grimaced. "You know Hall. He loves baseball and he despises horse racing, but he's a great editor. I don't see how he can go with the Jewels today. Those bums have lost their last eighteen games. Honest, they're the sorriest team I've ever seen, and their attendance is nothing. They're dead. What else is there?"

Gus wanted to get away from the constant phone calls for tickets he didn't have, so he walked over to Pierre's dark room.

"What a day this is going to be," Pierre laughed. "What a wonderful day!"

"We'll have a few people, and they may bet a dollar or two," Gus assented.

"Who cares?" Pierre shot back. "Helene was just in for some color shots. Brother, you should see her in that new gown. She's gorgeous."

"Look at the students come in," Jay Mason remarked as he and Gus stood on the catwalk, next to the film patrol camera, in the officials' loft high above the grandstand. All the roads to the track were clogged with cars in an unbroken, vari-colored column stretching in every direction out of sight. Randahl put the post time for the first race back half-an-hour, but the roads to the parking lot were still jammed when the second race went off.

After that, Gus went back to his office. He had enough to do. Pierre brought the crowd shots over. Gus wrote the cut lines and dispatched them by cab to the papers and the wire services. Then he checked a multitude of last-minute details. The floral horseshoe had finally arrived, new cars were ready for the parade of the queen and her court, the governor had just checked in and had been escorted to his box on the finish line. Everything seemed to be in order.

He took a minute to bring in the ball game on his transistor radio. The news was welcome. The Rebels had knocked three Jewels pitchers out of the box in the first six innings and the hometown heroes were losing, 15–0. They had made just one infield hit. The paid attendance was a pitiful 1,012. Even Hall couldn't give them the banner this time, Gus told himself.

After the seventh race, Gus started back for the press box to watch the Colt Stake. He was walking through the betting area under the grandstand when Manny Goldblatt overtook him. Gus scarcely recognized him.

Manny is a fellow of fastidious habits. He is always nicely dressed. He wears a subdued sports jacket even on the hottest days. He is a man of quiet deportment and calm demeanor.

But not today.

He had a wildly agitated look. His hair was awry and his pale blue sports shirt was black with perspiration. He was carrying his wrinkled jacket. Little rivulets of sweat coursed down his round face, but he did not seem to notice.

He seized Gus urgently by the arm. "I got to talk to you, Gus. Where can we talk, alone? Please, Gus, I got to talk to you."

"We can talk here, Manny."

He hesitated, his gaze sweeping the crowd that churned around them. He half-pushed Gus to the rear of the cigarette stand, and he spoke in a voice so low he was scarcely audible.

"Gus, I got to use your phone. I got to! This is a terrible emergency. Just give me the key to your office. You can say you dropped it. I won't take two minutes, Gus. One minute, that's all I need."

"Impossible, Manny. Go use that nice little old lady's phone."

"She's gone! There's a sign on the front lawn. The joint has been sold. How do you like that? She cleared out overnight, and you should see the nice colored TV Alfie sent her. She took that, too, the double-crossing old hag."

"The phone's still there, isn't it?"

"I got a key to the house. When I went over after the second race, I let myself in and called Alfie. He didn't like it, the house being sold and all. Devon has him worried sick. Nothing he could put his finger on, but he knows Devon. He told me to call forty-five minutes before the eighth race—the Colt Stake."

"Well?"

"I hustled over there after the sixth race. I tried the phone. It's dead. I looked around, and somebody had cut the wire outside. Now I *got* to use your phone. It's my only chance."

"Try somewhere else. There's half a dozen public phones down at the next traffic light."

"You kidding? That's a mile down the road, and the traffic is backed up solid all the way. The Stake will go off in another twenty minutes. There's no way I could make it. Please, Gus, just this once."

Gus shook him off, and started to walk away.

"No dice, Manny. I can't do it."

He took after Gus at a dog-trot. "Alfie thinks Devon is

going to pour it in on the Stake. I've got ten men here to lay off bets. If Devon is laying off money, Alfie will be getting calls from bookies all over the country by this time. Gus, this is big money. Please. I'll give you a grand. Right now. In cash. Just gimme the keys."

He didn't give up until Gus entered the elevator marked "Officials Only." As the door closed, he was still pleading. He was close to tears.

"Your friend must have tapped out," remarked the elevator operator. "You did the right thing. Never loan money to a broke horse player."

The parade of the queen and her court was the kind of a spectacle a press agent always dreams about and rarely sees. The slick new convertibles with their beguiling cargoes moving slowly past the grandstand provided a moment of innocent beauty. The governor and his party rode in the first car, and behind them came the four ladies in waiting, each sitting in the back of an open car. They were lovely, but Helene made the show.

She was perched regally on the back of a glossily re-furbished vintage sports car. She was enough to make the punters forget the tote board. She wore the silver tiara and the gold cape that half hid the scarlet ribbon which proclaimed her the Treasure City Queen. She was thoroughly enjoying the moment, bowing and waving and throwing kisses. She invested a tired charade with youth and freshness and beauty.

After the queen and her court and the dignitaries had retired to their boxes, the equine beauties came out for the Colt Stake. For a few minutes, the finest assembly of three-year-olds Treasure City patrons have ever seen warmed up. Then the jocks began walking their haughty mounts down to the starting gate, which was positioned at the head of the stretch.

The Colt Stake distance is a mile-and-a-quarter, and the Treasure City Race Track is a mile oval. The horses would go past the finish line twice in their run for the Colt Stake crown.

Horsepower was one-to-five, the minimum payoff the law allows. Suburban Sam, the second choice, was three-to-a-half-to-one. Rustling Breeze got in at nineteen-to-one. The entry of Mr. Mercury and Hi, Toots was fifty-to-one.

The starter's assistants were shoving and pulling in their efforts to get the animals into their narrow compartments at the gate. Most of the youngsters were tractable enough. Rustling Breeze walked into his little cell as though he were going to dinner. Then he stood there. He did not make a move.

Horsepower, however, resisted the invitation to get into position. He pulled nervously away from the assistant starters, delaying the start of the race for fully two minutes. It took three attendants, two shoving and one pulling, to get him into his slot. He was skittish, banging against the sides of the enclosure as Hartley fought to control him. Mason saw it first.

"Horsepower's giving Hartley a bad time! Look at him! He almost threw the jock!"

Gus fixed his fieldglasses on the one-to-five favorite as he bumped against one side of his prison, and then against the other. Hartley, almost unseated by the recalcitrant thoroughbred, jerked back angrily on the rein and Horsepower seemed to go straight up. He was pawing the air, all four feet off the ground, when the bell rang, the gates swung open, and Gary Mills called: "They're off!"

Rustling Breeze's only chance was to go on the lead and Scotty MacTavish, his rider, knew it. He took the little colt out of the number two post position fast, breaking well in front of Bubble Bath on the inside, and streaked out in front on the rail.

Horsepower almost lost the race before it was well begun. He came away tenth in the ten-horse field, his intransigence in the gate costing him perhaps six lengths.

Rustling Breeze ran away from the field as the horses came up to the finish line for the first time. He blazed into the clubhouse turn a full six lengths in front, and he turned the first quarter in a shade over twenty-two seconds, which is impossible on that track.

"He's trying to break the race wide open," murmured Mason. "He's flying now, but he has a long way to go. And look at that Horsepower come."

Jensen's colt could run. He came pounding up on the outside, picking off his rivals one by one—Mr. Mercury, Bubble Bath, Bad Hangover, Hit 'Em Hard, Kentucky Captain, Hi, Toots, and Dubbl Trubbl. Near the midway point in the backstretch, Horsepower overhauled Suburban Sam and Mean Old Man. Then he took off after Rustling Breeze, still four lengths in front.

"They went the second quarter in 43.2," Jay Mason said. "They're still flying."

Horsepower steadily closed the gap. Now three lengths,

now two, now only one, and Jensen's big colt was still full of run. That was when Gus admitted the truth that he had never been quite willing to accept: No three-year-old alive could stand against Horsepower.

Well into the far turn, Horsepower caught Rustling Breeze. Jensen's great colt was just too fast, Gus realized. Slowly but inexorably, Horsepower asserted his authority, pushed a nose in front, then a neck, and then a good half length.

"It's all over," Gus said aloud, surprised at how disappointed he felt.

But it wasn't all over. Rustling Breeze fought back somehow, he was a scant head in front of Horsepower.

Now they were running neck and neck as they burst out of the far turn and headed for home, still at a furious pace. Rustling Breeze was taking command again, driving away by a neck, and then by an unbelievable half length. Devon's colt held the advantage of a clear length.

At that moment Gus knew, against all belief, that Rustling Breeze could do it. He could! He could do what no other three-year-old had ever achieved. He could beat Horsepower.

And he did.

Unfortunately, Horsepower was the only colt he did beat. Those two magnificent thoroughbreds had spent their speed with heedless prodigality in their battle for the lead. They had nothing left for the run to the wire.

They faded pitably in the stretch. The whole field came at them, and rushed past them as though they were standing still.

Suburban Sam had seized the lead at the eighth pole,

with Dubbl Trubbl and Hit 'Em Hard close behind when a familiar figure, whipping and kicking like a wild man, came rallying up to bid for the Colt Stake crown.

Wade Hampton Parkinson is a master of the subtle and intricate arts of the pace, and he had never timed one better than he did that sunny Colt Stake afternoon. He was coming up fast on Mr. Mercury. The leaders were tiring and his colt was moving but could Wade get him through the traffic in time?

Gus thought Parkinson was going to get shut off as he charged up behind Hit 'Em Hard and Dubbl Trubbl inside the sixteenth pole, but he came busting up between horses, breaking clear in the last fifty yards, and catching Suburban Sam at the wire with a feat of horsemanship that brought a thunderous roar from the throng of humans packed in the stands.

When Wade rode back to the grandstand and snapped his whip in the traditional salute, even the punters who had lost their bankroll stood and cheered. They knew that they had seen a great race rider on his greatest afternoon.

THIRTY-TWO

"How sweet it is!" Mason sang out. "You bet two bucks, and that nice man at the cashier's window gives you back one hundred and four smackeroos. And on an entry, at that, the two biggest bums in the race. My, didn't that Parkinson show the folks something?"

"I'm glad Wade won," Gus said, "but I hate to see Devon blow the last chance he'll ever have."

"Don't take it so hard," Mason counseled. "Dan is a pro. He rolls with the punches."

Gus spoke bitterly. "Dan isn't the big operator he used to be. Right now he is just a beaten little old man who has seen his poor chance slip through his fingers. He never stood to cut it. Never!"

Typewriters were clicking in strident chorus as the reporters sent off their first bulletins on the finish of the Colt Stake. The press box was crowded and clamorous, and Gus wished he were somewhere else. Somewhere by himself, just for a moment.

Then Mason did a curious thing. He put his arm around the little man and gave him a tight, hard hug.

"You really love that old guy, don't you?" he said, not really asking.

"He fights," Gus explained. "He fights for the things he doesn't believe in."

There was work to do, however. Newspaper deadlines don't wait.

"Parkinson isn't riding again today," Gus bawled. "As soon as he's showered and dressed, a guard will bring him to the press box. In the meantime, Jay and I are going down to the presentation ceremony in the infield. We'll talk to Parkinson. Jay will get back as fast as he can with a few quotes."

On the way out of the press box, Gus stopped beside Duke Jones. "You got yourself a terrific story," Duke. "Parkinson's comeback—it's perfect."

"It's better than that," he offered. "Don't you realize that the professor had the winner? He picked Hi, Toots, which ran as an entry with Mr. Mercury. For one ticket, you got both of them. Anybody who bet on the professor's pick can cash their tickets now."

"Hall will have to banner this one, won't he, Duke?"

Jones was fighting a deadline, and he fights his deadline hard, but he looked up and smiled sympathetically.

"This is a tremendous yarn, Gus, I'm writing it for all it's worth. I hope you get the banner. I mean that. I really do."

"Anyway, the Jewels are out. They lost again, didn't they?"

"The final score was 16–3. That makes nineteen in a row they've lost. A miserable game, too."

"At least," Gus said, "this is one time I don't have to worry about the Jewels."

At the presentation ceremony in the infield, beside the tote board, Helene presented the silverware to a smiling Jamie Lattner, draped the floral horseshoe over Mr. Mercury's neck, and gave Wade a big, juicy kiss.

Pierre took pictures of the battery of movie and still photographers who were taking pictures of the queen. Gus reasoned there might never again be that many photographers at a Colt Stake. He wanted proof that they had been there once.

As they walked back across the track, Wade told how it was. "I knew the pace was suicide. I couldn't go with Rustling Breeze, and I didn't try. I just rode my own race. If that wasn't good enough, too bad, but I didn't think any colt could stay with that pace.

"When we came to the far turn, I was lying ninth but the other horses were starting to come back to me. When

I asked my horse for it, he gave it to me. We got through on the rail and when we came out of the turn, I moved up fast. I saw that I couldn't go all the way on the inside, so I came up between horses. Then, just as we came up on Hit 'Em Hard and Dubbl Trubbl, my colt seemed to hang.

"I switched the stick from my right hand to my left, and I hit him a good whack. That surprised him and it woke him up. He started running again. I knew then that the colt could do it if we didn't get shut off."

Before Jay left for the press box, Gus had one last suggestion. "Would you bring your notes over as soon as you can, after the interview with Parkinson? He may have some new stuff. I've got a few pet announcers I'd like to call with the latest inside word."

Gus tried to sprint through the crowded clubhouse, but he hadn't gone far before someone took his arm.

J. C. Jensen was still ramrod straight, meticulously barbered, and ruddy of countenance, but his eyes had lost their frosty glint. They were warm with pride.

"One moment, please, sir," he said. "I want to apologize for my bad manners last night, sir. And would you please convey to Mr. Devon my sincere regards, and compliment him upon a splendid race."

"That is generous, Mr. Jensen. Horsepower would have won if he hadn't been left at the post."

He scorned the excuse. "Rustling Breeze made an excellent start, sir. Admirable. I underestimated Mr. Devon, and I underestimated his colt. I regret it."

"Mr. Mercury didn't deserve to win, Mr. Jensen. And he didn't really. Wade Parkinson did."

"Parkinson was splendid. There are not more than two or three race riders on North American tracks who could have made the move he did at the finish. Simply astounding. But he didn't beat my colt. Mr. Devon's little bay did that. I am an arrogant, vindictive man, Mr. Scott. I knew Mr. Devon's little bay liked to go on the lead so I told Hartley, no matter what, to finish him off as fast as he could. I never anticipated what magnificent heart that little bay has. He just wouldn't quit. Magnificent, sir. My compliments to Mr. Devon, and please tell him that I hope he enters his bay in the Grandeur Stakes. I would be honored, sir, to send my colt out again to contest with him."

After Gus got back to the office, he closed the doors and began dialing. He called a few helpful radio and TV announcers and gave them a few fresh, inside observations on the race.

Pierre sent a runner up with a pile of Colt Stake pictures, which Gus identified and sent off by cab. The newspapers and wires had taken their own, but these were insurance.

When Gus had completed these chores he couldn't restrain his curiosity any longer. The *Herald-Chronicle* strives to have its papers at the Treasure City gate when the crowd pours out. The newspapers would be here in a few minutes but, after waiting so long, he couldn't wait another five minutes to find out whether he had suddenly become unemployed. He called George Hall, the sports editor.

Nobody answered. So he called Jack Longley, the press room superintendent. "Jack," he asked, "how did Hall play the Colt Stake story?"

"Wait, Gus, I'll get you a proof of the first sports page. Hall gave you great position. Hang on for a second."

He was back quickly, happy to report good news.

275

"You'll love it! Hall used six columns of pictures, a two-column head shot of Parkinson and a four-column drop-off on Jones' story. Want me to read Jonsey's stuff?

"Hello? Hello, Gus, you still there?"

"I'm here," I answered weakly. "No banner, huh? What happened? What in the world got the banner?"

"The banner? I'll read it to you, Gus, Ready? Here goes:

JEWELS DROP NO. 19, SET NEW WORLD RECORD
          Hit All-Time
          Low, Bowing to
          Rebel Bats, 16–3

          Losing Streak Shatters
          69-Year Mark; Manager's
          Job Safe, Owner Insists

Gus stopped the recitation.

"Thanks. That's enough, Jack. I appreciate your doing this for me."

"Glad to, Gus. Hall is a tough guy, sometimes, but he sure takes care of his friends, doesn't he?"

"If he took any better care of me," Gus said, "I'd be dead."

THIRTY-THREE

"DEVON'S GOT CLASS," Mason observed. "Think he's running out, his tail between his legs, because he just blew the Colt Stake? No way. Look at him. You'd think he'd won it by ten lengths."

Gus put his field glasses on the old man in his box at the finish line. Devon looked cocky as ever, cool and relaxed, nodding negligently to the passersby. He scarcely looked like a man whose world had just fallen apart.

"He blows one sometimes," Gus remarked, "but he does it with style."

The horses were approaching the starting gate for the tenth race of the afternoon and the final race of the meeting. Gary Mills, a sentimental man, was already beginning to blubber as he dusted off the recording of Auld Lang Syne. Another season was almost over. The press box was curiously hushed.

Gus looked at the box again. Cal Oakley had joined Devon, shaking the old man's hand and patting his back. Poor Dan, Gus thought.

The horses were in the starting gate when Gus put the glasses back on them. He was surprised to realize how much, just one more time, he wanted to see Bumbling Bertie come flying out of that gate and go to the top.

A mile, Gus thought. Why did they put Bertie in a mile race? He will come in so far behind the rest that it will be dark before he finishes. They'll have to put the track lights on.

"They're off!" Gary Mills cried for the last time that year. Bumbling Bertie showed how undependable he could be. He came away seventh in the ten-horse field. Scotty MacTavish tucked him in on the rail.

"It's Cheyenne Cross by two lengths . . . Springtime Idyll on the outside . . . heads apart for the lead . . . Happy Day third . . . Montha Sundays . . . Forest Ranger . . ."

Gus felt a curious emptiness. They were going into the clubhouse turn and Bumbling Bertie wasn't on the lead. It was unnatural. He felt a bitter kinship with the strange animal.

Bumbling Bertie is just like the rest of us, Gus thought. All losers.

Like Rustling Breeze, who hadn't been accepted as a great colt until he was beaten and through.

Like Buzz Randahl, banished now from the only life he ever wanted.

Like Dan Devon, naked against the world in his old age, his last preposterous defenses overrun.

Like Gus himself, booted out of the best job he ever had.

Bumbling Bertie is one of us, Gus thought. He hasn't got a call.

On an impulse, Gus put the glasses on Devon again. Surprising, really. The old swindler had lost something of his icy reserve. He was standing at the rail of his box, his hat crushed in his hand, every line of his body betraying his tension. Gus had never seen the old man so excited.

Oakley was gripping Devon's arm, leaning over his shoulder, the glasses fixed on the race.

Gus switched back to the race. The horses were out of the clubhouse turn and into the backstretch. Bumbling Bertie was moving up steadily on the inside but MacTavish had him under a taut rein. And he hadn't gone for the whip. He's saving that bum, Gus realized.

These were cheap $2,000 claimers, Gus reflected. A soft spot if a man had a horse that could run any. And now Bumbling Bertie was running sixth on the inside and MacTavish was starting to wave his whip as the horses thundered down the backstretch.

Devon was almost falling out of the box, leaning so far over the rail, shaking a skinny fist. Oakley was jumping up and down, whacking Devon on the back, waving a ten-gallon hat and cutting the air with a high piercing rebel yell.

And then Gus saw it, and wondered why he hadn't divined the plot long ago. So this was it: So logical, so unexpected, so beautifully simple. Rustling Breeze was the decoy. They were going with Bumbling Bertie, now forty-to-one on the tote board. As Oakley had once told him, this isn't a show horse, it's a race horse.

Devon, however, had often observed that horse races are hard to cook. He was right. They are so devilishly complicated. So many improvident things can happen.

And one was happening now.

Ron Grayson, up on Cheyenne Cross, laid a trap for MacTavish and Bumbling Bertie—and MacTavish fell into it: Grayson was on the lead, a little out from the rail, leaving just enough of a hole so that MacTavish thought he could get by on the inside. As MacTavish started to shoot for the opening, Grayson moved

Cheyenne Cross in toward the rail, ever so slightly just enough to close the hole. Bumbling Bertie was locked in on the rail.

They were in the final turn now, and Bumbling Bertie was in a box. Cheyenne Cross was in front of him and two horses were racing beside him. The only way Mac-Tavish could break free was to drop back again to sixth and then go three horses wide to the outside as they came out of the turn and hit the home stretch. The maneuver cost him something.

They were inside the eighth pole, with Bumbling Bertie sixth on the outside, when MacTavish went for his whip, slashing left and right. Bumbling Bertie laid back his ears and started to pour out that one furious burst of speed. He went past those cheap players like a freight train going past a bum.

He was fading at the finish, but he lasted. It wasn't even a photo finish. He reported home first by a clear half length over Forest Ranger with Montha Sundays third, another half length back.

It's unreal, Gus thought. How much has Dan made? A million? Two million? Gus was sure the old bandit had laid off every nickel he could. Dan always was a big shooter.

THIRTY-FOUR

Manny Goldblatt was waiting in ambush when Gus stepped off the elevator from the press loft. His face was dark with the terrible pain that only the loss of money can bring.

He seized Gus roughly by the arm and pulled him violently to the side. "You ruined me, you crumbum," he squawked. "Alfie took a terrible bath, just because you wouldn't let me make one lousy phone call. He wanted to lay off everything we had on Bumbling Bertie. He had bookies calling him from all over, like you wouldn't believe it, but I couldn't get through to him in time. One lousy phone call was all I wanted, but you shut me off, you bastard!"

As Manny spoke, his indignation grew. His face was scarlet. A big vein stood out on his forehead. Gus thought he would have a stroke.

"They took Alfie for over a hundred grand. He's just one. Devon must of cleaned up a couple of million. That old goat must of took the bookies like they never been took before. And you was in with him, don't tell me different. God, Alfie says if I ever show my face around the joint again, he'll kill me. And he might."

"Alfie has a great competitive spirit, Manny. He hates to lose."

"Of course. He hates to lose money. He starts getting the calls from all these other bookies. They want he should lay off their bets on Bumbling Bertie. He waits, and he waits. He finally sends Boats Brannigan out by cab, but the traffic is piled up so Boats will be lucky to make it by midnight. I finally took a cab to the nearest drug store, must be a mile away, but it's the same thing. Traffic is so bad, I can't move. That freeway traffic was awful. Screwed everything up."

Manny released the little press agent's arm. His shoulders sagged. "What am I to do? I got no job. Alfie won't let me train my classy fighter, Carlos Chavez, at his joint. I got a good green heavyweight, too, big kid, name of Boris Soskowicz, but what can I do? Thanks to you, I'm done for."

"You will be, if you hang around here much longer, but you could hit it big if you'd start moving."

Manny scowled. "Now hot shot is telling me what to do. He fouls me up, and then he tells me what to do. You always were a two-bit comedian, Scott."

"You're not thinking, Manny. The loss of money makes you emotional. Who's the softest touch in the world when he's in the bucks? Dan Devon, of course. That guy makes money for one reason—to throw it away. If you get to him before the parade of moochers starts, he just might buy a piece of the greatest lightweight in the world."

"Yeah," Manny brightened. "I'll throw my new heavyweight in for nothing. Great idea, Gus."

Gus watched him barge through the crowd, as fast as

282

his stubby legs would carry him. I might as well catch Devon, too, he decided, before I go back to the office and start cleaning out my desk.

Devon, Oakley, and Manny were sitting in the tack room, engaged in earnest conversation, when Gus got there.

"You've been good to us, Gus," Oakley said solemnly. "I sure do thank you."

"I thank you, Cal. And, Dan, Mr. J. C. Jensen sends you his compliments and he says he hopes to send his colt against Rustling Breeze again. He says he would be proud to do it."

A stablehand stuck his head in the doorway and asked if he could see Dan in private for a moment. "In a few minutes, Pancho," Dan said.

"Rustling Breeze is through," Oakley was saying. "He broke that little bone in his foot again. I'm taking him back to the farm. He'll stand there."

"And Bumbling Bertie?"

"We're selling him to Sam Albright," Devon spoke up. "You remember. The poker player?"

"So the Flowering Tree Stable is out of business, eh? Where does that leave you, Dan?"

Manny Goldblatt supplied the answer: "Gus, old pal, meet my new partner. Dan is back in the fight game, where he belongs."

Gus had expected Dan to give Manny a grand or two, but not this. "You're going to manage the next lightweight champion, Dan?"

Devon made a delicate gesture of disdain. "I've told Manny, there's no money in the little fellow but I like this big kid, Soskowicz. He's big and dumb and mean.

He can hit and the way the heavyweight division is today, that's all we need. We'll move him up fast . . ." He stopped abruptly. "Forgive me, Gus. I meant to ask: You did get the *Herald-Chronicle* banner, didn't you?"

"A near miss, Dan. Close, but no cigar."

For a moment, he betrayed his cold anger. "I've been had," he murmured. "And I thought I had a sure thing."

"What do you mean, *you've* been had? *I've* been had, pal."

"I made a small wager you'd get that banner," he was smiling now. "It's unimportant. Nobody can bet smart all the time. Don't worry, Gus. You've got a job with me. The best job any press agent ever had."

"I'll pass, Dan. Look, I hope you keep hitting, friend, but don't be foolish. Save something. Put it in the bank. You may get old some day, pal."

His cold eyes glinted. "Never," he said. "That's not in my plans. I'm going to have a small party at the Fleur de Lis tonight, Gus. Plan on attending. Please do."

"The Fleur de Lis? I'm surprised you're talking to Mike Stern, their catering manager. He had it in for you."

"He's a wrong guy, Gus."

"Yeah. Stuffy. He doesn't like to be swindled. When you ran out without paying the tab the last time, Mike spoke of you in highly unflattering terms."

"He's greedy, Gus. It's his most endearing characteristic. Anyhow, I paid him. We're square.

"But why give him the party? I know you. That will cost some money. Why not hold it somewhere else?"

Devon was wearing a veiled smile. His eyes were half-hooded, inscrutable. Buy a used car from a man like that? Gus thought. I wouldn't borrow a match from him.

"He says he is really very fond of me," Devon declared. "He insisted I hold the party at his joint. He was quite aggressive about it."

"You know what you're doing," Gus shrugged, "but does he?"

Gus shook hands all around, waved to his friends and walked away. When he came to the end of the shedrow, he looked back. He saw Dan Devon in the gathering gloom. The old man had his wallet out, and he was handing something to Pancho. From the groom's expression of pop-eyed delight, Gus knew this was Devon's day for regal largesse.

The party in the Paddock Room was starting to swing when Gus got off the elevator. I might as well go in and see Buzz, he thought, and get it over with. He can fire me, but I'm not going to sneak out.

Standing at the bar just inside the door were Nancy and Jay. Randahl was at the far side of the room with a little knot of horsemen and their ladies.

"Oh, Gus, I have the most wonderful news," Nancy gushed, holding up her left hand. The diamond ring, gleaming on her third finger, must have put Jay in hock to the track credit union for six months. He was unmindful of sordid economics, however. He was in love.

Gus embraced her, and kissed her. He shook Jay's hand warmly, suddenly too choked to talk. He remembered the day he put a ring on Sue's finger.

"We're going to be married next week, Gus, between race track jobs," Nancy said. "Jay is working in publicity at Gordon Park. I couldn't let him go alone."

After a moment, Gus left them. Even in the crowd, he felt like an intruder. He sought Randahl out. "Hi, Buzz," he moved in. "This has been a great meeting, hasn't it?"

Randahl raised an eyebrow. "I saw the story in the *Herald-Chronicle*," he said softly. "I don't know what happened, and I don't care. Spare me the details. I saw the story, and that is enough for me." He turned to his circle of friends.

"Did you see the story in the *Herald-Chronicle*, folks? This is very interesting. For me, anyway. It shows what kind of a publicity man Gus is. I told him I wanted the banner in the *Herald-Chronicle* tonight, and I wanted the words 'Colt Stake' in big, black type in the headline. You'll never know how much I wanted it.

"Well, would you like to see what my clever press agent got me in the *Herald-Chronicle?*"

He's mocking me, Gus realized. This wasn't Buzz's style. I thought he had more grace. Yet he's losing his job, too, and he likes his as well as I like mine.

"Did you see the story?" he repeated. "Let me show you."

He picked the bulky Sunday edition of the *Herald-Chronicle* off the bar, and shook out a section. Gus gawked. There, across the top of the news section of the *Herald-Chronicle*, he saw two big black headlines:

BIGGEST COLT STAKE THRONG
CAUSES RECORD TRAFFIC JAM

116-CAR CRACKUP
STALLS FREEWAY
FOR 20 MILES

WILD DISORDER AS MOTORISTS
ABANDON CARS, CLIMB FENCES TO
GET TO TREASURE CITY TRACK

HIGHWAY REPAIR WORK BLAMED FOR
UNPRECEDENTED CONFUSION: NO
SERIOUS INJURIES REPORTED

Gus recovered quickly. A man should always be ready to accommodate a felicitous conjunction of events.

"That's better than a single line on the sports page, Buzz. We couldn't get both, you know. And I figure everybody reads the news section."

"I'm with you, Gus," he put his arm around the little man's shoulder. "This is the greatest job I've ever seen. The greatest. I don't know how you did it, and I don't care. You're a smart aleck, at times, and a clown, but you're the greatest PR man in the business. I wish I was home right now," he added. "I'd love to see mother's face when she reads this. I couldn't do it, eh? The hell I couldn't." He continued to gaze at the headline, a man enchanted.

"By the way," he remarked absently. "What do I owe you for this? What do you want?"

He took Gus off balance. "Give me an extra ten percent," Gus said. He regretted it at once. Gus gets twenty grand a year. He knew Buzz would have gone for more than two grand. He spoke too soon.

"Right," Buzz said, still in a fog. He stared at the paper like a man transfixed, but he finally came out of it.

"What did you say?" he seemed embarrassed to ask. "Ten percent or ten grand?"

"Ten grand," Gus answered instantly.

Gus never made it to Devon's festivities at the Fleur de Lis. For the first time in months, he got smashed at the party in the Paddock Room.

He resented the insistent summons of the telephone that awakened him the next morning. He tried to bury his head in his pillow, but that didn't work. With considerable reluctance, he struggled out of bed and picked up the receiver.

"Mike Stern here," an angry voice boomed. Gus feared the noise would split his aching head, but he tried to be polite.

"Sorry I missed Dan's party at your place. I'll bet that was something."

"Oh, it was elegant," the caterer sounded unhappy. "The best of everything. Spare no expense. You know Devon."

"Yeah. Nice of Dan to throw the business your way."

"Yeah, it was," Stern's voice was rising. "That old crock skipped out at six this morning without paying the tab."

Stern was screaming now. The noise made Gus ill.

"Don't get excited," he pleaded. "Dan will be back in town again one of these days."

"Yeah, he will!" Stern roared. "And he'll stiff me again."

"Dan Devon?" Gus protested. "That poor, sweet, helpless little old man?"

288